C.L.O.U.D.S.
Part one

BY ARTEM K. PRATT

TO MY GREAT GRANDMOTHER
ANASTASIA PAVLOVNA
WHO WILL
ALWAYS
BE
IN MY HEART

To David.

From my heart.

Enjoy the reading.

Artem K. Pratt

CONTENTS

PROLOGUE

"Breslin, bring me some coffee please". The staccato request came from the head of the world's largest computer corporation, Migren, Inc. The voice sounded weary and in definite need of some serious caffeine.

"I'll have it for you in five, Madame Litsiona", assured the secretary.

"No rush, my dear; I've got enough time"

"Yes, madame"

Migren Litsiona was a short woman of 45 years with raven black hair that was woven neatly in place at all times. She was incredibly successful with a life about which she could not complain. At the same time, she was incredibly lonely. She had no children, her parents lived too far to be an active part of her life, and as for her "friends" – well, most of them held a one-way entry ticket to the benefits of her wealth. A long time ago, she had chosen her work over any semblance of a personal life. More often than not, she felt she had chosen correctly. Her work had brought her untold wealth and power. Her company was so successful that it nearly overran the world; every second citizen owned at least one Migren product.

It was growing late in the day and the twilight was descending across the city. Migren Litsiona stood up from her throne-like chair and drifted smoothly over to a span of floor-to-ceiling windows in her office that framed New York City. It looked particularly beautiful in that moment, gleaming with light and sparkling with money and success. She could feel the heartbeat of all below her, most of which sat atop the palm of her hand. But the power and majesty she knew no longer brought her any real joy. A great gnawing of loneliness inside her made all the tears she held so tightly within hard to contain. The truth was simple; while having everything, in

1

actuality she had nothing. This small woman felt a cold sensation pass through her body from head to toe as she placed her dainty hand on the cold, wet window. She really wanted nothing more than to touch the magnificent city. Her reverie was suddenly interrupted by a discomforting noise that was rising from the dark corner of her office space.

Breslin poured some of the freshly-brewed coffee in to a wide cup emblazoned with the Migren logo. She placed the cup on its matching saucer and introduced to it a small silver teaspoon. She looked toward her boss's office and smiled. It was nearly the end of her work day so all her thoughts were beginning to drift over to her evening plans of a romantic dinner with her boyfriend. On the way to deliver the coffee, her cell phone rang.

"Hi Nick", her voice was suddenly easy. "I am almost done... can I call you back in a few minutes?

In one hand, she was balancing the coffee while trying to manage the phone in the other. Gripping the phone with the fingers she had left, she managed just enough to turn down the handle to open her boss's office door. Suddenly a strong unexpected stream of air blew into her face like something born of a half-opened window. It was extremely cold and dark as she entered the room. She thought it was very odd, but proceeded onward.

"Madame, your coffee's ready", announced Breslin. At the conclusion of the last syllable, she lost track of her phone as it fell from her hands to the floor. She naturally bent down to pick it up but with an overwhelming sense of unease. In that exact moment, she saw Migren Litsiona lying on the floor in a pool of blood; her mouth was held in a motionless scream and her lifeless, open eyes stared out to nowhere.

The cup danced on its saucer as her left hand began to shake. Breslin's eyes glanced upward from the floor to see a tall, faceless silhouette with nightmarish claws. The secretary lost her power to utter a sound, let alone to scream or to speak. She was staring at the place where the shadow appeared when its long, sharp claws impaled her neck. The cup in her hand fell to the floor, shattering into many shards. The logo on the cup disappeared under the streams of blood. Breslin was still alive when her eyes finally met the entity who was taking shape and form. From the dark visage were two glowing holes of white light that served as eyes. She would never learn what they saw. The specter opened its mouth into a gaping, macabre smile, bearing rows of sharp, shark-like teeth.

"I don't think you have what I need, do you?", seethed the shadow and then violently dug into what would no longer be her face.

Her body convulsed for a minute and then became numb and lifeless. A small glowing ball of energy rose from the cadaver and floated momentarily in the dead air. The shadow retracted its life-draining claws, tossed aside the flotsam of the body, and devoured the shining ball of light. Suddenly the shadow began to shudder and vibrate as one would look in a distorted, fun-house mirror. In a post-apocalyptic moment, the shadow moved to the windows to look out over the city. Its mouth closed to a thin, nefarious smile. Through the glass, it knew that it was looking at immeasurable opportunities.

CHAPTER 1: DARK SIGNS

A storm was approaching the small town of Blackwood, Pennsylvania. The night was noticeably darker than usual; such natural phenomena were quite rare in this part of the state. That day it was as if a curse had fallen over the quiet enclave. Sarah Brown, daughter of local Baptist minister, Thomas Brown, lay aside her Bible and looked wistfully out the window. She was wondering how her father was doing in such terrible weather and if he was awake because of the storm like she was. "Unlikely" she heard herself say; the answer came right after the question. These last days were hard for the Brown family. Sarah's father had to spend his fourth night in a row with his elder brother, Abraham, who was quite ill, in Newtown, about seven miles away. It was certainly not easy for a man of his age to rush about between the two homes. Maybe it was not that far, but it was mentally tiring. Sarah could understand and supported her father as much as she could, but even she, at some point, started feeling lonely because she was all alone in a big house. Sarah knew that everything always turned out as God wanted, and she knew that everything lay in His hands. It was only He who would decide what was better for all of them. She also believed that He would never leave them suffering in pain without a solution.

While in a reverie, the girl's forefinger gently touched the cold window. She could see little else but endless streaks of rain running down the glass and flashes of lightning preceding muffled echoes of thunder. The local winds howled like a furious beast. Sarah was thoroughly frightened, particularly given that she was alone in the house. She knew that coyotes were commonly seen in the area, causing folks to always be on guard whenever they were outdoors. Over time, the coyotes had learned to evade the traps set for them, even boldly attacking some of the livestock birds on the property. Sarah decided she would double check the barn to be sure it was secure from night hunters in light of the inevitable, impending storm. She located the hunting rifle that always stood at attention in the corner of the entryway of the house, always at the ready. It gleamed with desire to be discharged into something threatening. She donned a raincoat, armed herself with the rifle, and ventured out into the dark direction of the barn. It was as dark as a rabbit hole, lit only by distant lightning and uttered sounds of muttered thunder. The force of the wind gusts, and occasional sleet, made it hard to traverse the grounds while keeping a steady hold on her firearm. A small flashlight in her hand meagerly lighted her pathway just to be sure she was on track. Sarah trudged along to the big red barn located just behind the chapel.

She arrived to find that the door was locked, but there was a noticeable gap in its side which meant someone or something had decided to pay a little visit. Slightly opening one of the doors, the girl walked toward the circuit breaker box. She opened it and pushed down the activation lever. In a moment, a bright, white light filled the former darkness. A crackling sound as the energy enlivened the lights startled the fowl into worrisome clucking. Sarah was worried too. She felt as though she was held in someone's gaze; a sickening, terrifying feeling defied description. Her inner feelings never failed her, and she knew that something was wrong. Slowly, as to confirm her assumptions, Sarah cast her glance at the door gap where two fire-yellow eyes were staring back at her. It was a snarling coyote seeking shelter in the inviting barn. Overcome by fear, Sarah dropped her flashlight, blithely aimed at the gap, and fired. The predator was hit and quickly retreated, whining as it disappeared into the night. The girl was not terrified, but those beasts could sometimes be very dangerous, and this fact have well rattled her nerves. Once she regained her composure, Sarah picked up her flashlight and again stared at the gap to make sure the coyote was gone. Once confirmed, she continued across the barn hoping the coyote would not return and that it was not part of a pack.

All else was calm now. Sarah exited the barn, locked the door behind her and was heading back to the house, when she was startled by a bolt of lightning that struck very closely to the ground near the chapel. In the flash of light, she noticed that the doors were opened and a human-like figure slipped inside. She decided to walk over to investigate what was going on. Once Sarah entered, a warm candle glow lit the figure she saw in the distance. It was a golden-haired, feminine creature who knelt in front of the altar, oddly beautiful and completely nude.

"Excuse me Miss, but it's very late and you shouldn't be here" Sarah said as she lay down her rifle on a pew. She closely approached the girl who, to this point, had remained silent.

"Miss…", Sarah repeated, "Did you hear me?"

She came very close to the strange visitor and was about to touch her shoulder, in hopes of at least getting her attention, when the figure screamed wildly. It screamed with such force that everything in the chapel started to shake. Sarah jumped back in fright and wanted to run for the rifle when the golden-haired girl abruptly turned to face Sarah and grabbed her by the wrists. What Sarah felt was best described as unending fear. The strange female looking back at her was clearly not a human, but some kind of supernatural creature – a demon or an angel of some sort. It had no mouth and the correctly-situated eyes appeared as white holes of light. The skin resembled the material of which a dressmaker's mannequin is covered.

"You must help me!" A voice arose from nowhere as if it had a life of its own.

A moment later, Sarah felt a wild, burning sensation on her wrists and her arms felt hot as if they were on fire. She slipped into a trance. It was like a dream in which time stands still and everything around changes shape and alters its being. Everything started to glitter as if bathed in reflected sunlight from atop the surface of a calm morning lake. Sarah's mind abruptly filled with flashing images and words that were all jumbled together and indecipherable. Her head was reeling. She wanted to run -- anywhere -- but her body remained in the sculptured rigidity of a marble statue.

"When I am seen no more", the odd voice warned, "Run as fast as you can far away from this place. They are already close; they will come for you. You must hide among others. Become part of a crowd of many. That is your strength. If evil appears to you in any form, be brave and touch it. It will be instantly blinded so you will have time to escape".

Sarah was confused and had many questions, but her lips would not move and her hands would not obey, and her legs felt rooted into the floor.

All she could do was listen. Listen carefully and try to remember every subtle detail.

"One more thing" said the voice, "Soon you will see a string of multi-colored beads on the floor. Put them on and leave this place. I will protect you as much as possible. This body is dying from the vicious pummeling I have had, so very soon you will be completely on your own. Protect the beads at all cost; the safety of the whole world depends upon them, and now, upon you.

"But why me?!?" shrieked Sarah, "Why me???"

Suddenly, everything stopped. All the sounds and all the visions. The creature was gone. The burning of Sarah's arms came to a peak. Like hot steam they burned and Sarah cried out and then fell to the floor. She looked at her forearms and saw scalded remnants of fingerprints. She also saw the string of beads just next to her left arm.

"Take them", the familiar voice gave an order from somewhere in Sarah's head.

With an unsteady hand, Sarah quickly and firmly grasped the beads in her hand. She heard the wind rustling outside the chapel. By the sound of the thunder she knew the storm was still all around her. Still, for a while, Sarah could not move. Her eyes were spellbound and riveted on the altar. She heard the familiar voice again:

"Run… I can feel them… they are so close now. Save your soul… Save your soul!"

Something released her and she was free. She donned the beads which felt warm against her skin. She flew to the back door and ran home. She completely forgot about the rifle. Heavy raindrops were pummeling her face, but she was unstoppable, running with all her strength and giving no attention to anything else. She grabbed her car keys from the table as she dashed into the entryway of the house, and ran upstairs in a panic to pack her bag. As she madly gathered what she needed, she heard a loud crash downstairs. The sound was so strong, like an explosion, that surely the front door had been reduced to splinters. Sarah ran out of the room to see what had happened. Downstairs in the entryway were two men. Each man was under six feet in height and were aggressively focused in their search.

"My God…" she heard herself whisper aloud and noticed two pair of red eyes staring at her. These were evil eyes. Sarah ran back into the room, shut the door, and propped a bureau in front of it to protect herself. She could hear the approach of a heavy footfall. Suddenly, a fist struck through the door. It struck so hard that it toppled the bureau and Sarah found herself in a mix of paralysis from fear and a dictum to escape. She grabbed her packed bag and bolted out of the second story window on to the sloped roof. At the edge of the roofline, she turned around to see the two figures following her.

"You can still escape… GO!" boomed a voice in her head.

Sarah could see her car parked next to the tree to her right. Time was of the essence. She tossed her bag to the ground below and shimmied down the tree and headed to the car. The two men were right behind her. She had only a minute or two to quickly get into the car and speed off, slipping and sliding in a cloud of rain and mud. The rain was so strong that even the windshield wipers at full speed could not clear the glass. Sarah sped along until she was sure she was no longer being pursued. Slowly, the speed of the car returned to normal. What followed was a long, deep sigh, and wondering what was next. Sarah put in an autodialed call to her father, praying that he would pick up the ringing line. Each attempt to reach him ended in failure. No answer. It seemed that misfortune continued to fall on her head, one after the other.

"Dad… God, come on… pick up the phone" Sarah was almost crying.

She had great difficulty concentrating on the country road because it was so poorly lit, but she somehow managed to redial his number again and then again. Her head was ready to burst at any moment because of the flood of thoughts that gripped her. She was afraid - terribly afraid - that those two thugs might again appear out of nowhere as they had at her home. That thought filled her with unimaginable fears of what would happen then. The ominous, black sky flashed another lightning strike, this time it was so strong and so bright that for a moment Sarah became confused and disoriented. She had never been so scared by the forces of nature in her whole life. She found herself in a deserted field where there was not a single living soul. The storm raged with unprecedented strength with the dark night as her only companion. Sarah prayed to herself that this nightmare would soon stop. She nearly decided to turn around and to go back to her cousin Peter's home, when suddenly and quite unexpectedly, her phone flashed the incoming number of her longtime friend, John Wishep. Was this just a coincidence? Hardly. Sarah didn't believe in coincidences. She was quite certain that this God-sent call did not arrive by happenstance. The line connected.

"John?" She breathed out and felt tears form in her eyes.

"Are you okay"? Was the anxious inquiry heard from the other end. The call was interrupted, on again, off again, by interference because of the storm.

"I... I need help. I think someone is trying to kill me. I'm afraid John.", Sarah began to cry, not able to restrain her emotions any longer.

"Gosh...". John was completely lost. It took a couple of seconds for him to realize what his friend had just said. "Where are you Sarah? What happened"? his voice was full of worry. "Tell me... tell me everything".

"I... I don't know where I am" the girl said sobbing. "Some horrible men broke into the house and somehow I miraculously escaped. Thank God dad was not there. I don't know where to go, John, I just know that I can't go back there... I can't".

In the middle of her words, the interference started again making it incredibly difficult to distinguish John's words. She could only hear the guy desperately asking where she was.

"John", Sarah repeated. "Can you hear me?"

"Yes, yes" A voice emerged from the noise. "Just tell me where you are?"

"I was able to escape", Sarah said. "Yes... able to escape" her voice was overcome by emotion causing tears to fall from her eyes. Her words had boldly reminded her just how lucky she'd truly been to have escaped a

9

terrible fate.

"How far from home are you?"

"Forty miles or so, maybe a little more…"

"Please don't stop and get as far away as you can. I am waiting for you".

"Do you want me to come over?" Sarah was not sure if she heard what she heard.

"Of course. Just be safe, promise me".

"Oh John", Sarah was doing her best to compose herself, "Thank you… I didn't want to bother you..."

"Are you serious? You're not bothering me at all Sarah. Not at all. You understand me?"

"Thank you…." repeated Sarah. "I think there is another 2 hours of road ahead of me".

"Please be careful, Sarah. You can stay on the line with me all the way down if you like. That would be no problem at all".

"I'll be all right. You better get some rest now", Sarah said. "I will let you know when I'm getting closer to you.

At that very moment, she was disconnected. She tried to reach John again several times but was unsuccessful. She was on her own. The road had led the car and Sarah deep into the woods where the signal was very weak. The girl's only option was to muster the courage and continue through this craziness. The miles were flying by but the signal did not appear to gain any strength and that, in fact, scared Sarah. She forced herself to ignore what *could* happen without a signal along the dark, forested miles. She felt physical tension all through her body, but could do nothing but continue forward. A few minutes later there was a breakthrough. She heard the notification sound of several incoming text messages. She quickly scooped up the phone and eagerly read the screen. Some of the messages were sent earlier from her father, but most were more recently sent from

John. They all had the same request: to call him back as soon as she got a signal again. She grabbed the phone with one hand while guiding the car with the other. She began typing a reply to John when a new torrent of rain fell and a bolt of lightning struck nearby. A frightened, disoriented buck jumped directly onto the road in front of her. Sarah used all her strength and hit the brakes. So hard in fact, the wheels locked up and a skid screamed from the tires. The screech was bone-chilling. Her eyes momentarily snapped shut, anticipating the collision; it seemed like an eternity. If she were able to avoid the buck, she could only thank her lucky stars. If a crash occurred, then her only hope of survival rested in the good will of the Lord. At the end of that eternal moment, she momentarily lost control of the vehicle and spun out. The car lurched to the left, veered off onto the gravel shoulder, and came to an abrupt stop. Dazed, she looked straight ahead into the sheets of rain hitting the windshield with only the rhythmic sound of the wipers to jar her back into the here and now. No buck. No crash. No tragedy. After such shock Sarah tried to calm herself down which seemed almost impossible to do. Intuitively she put her left palm on her forehead and only closed her eyes just for a second when suddenly, her phone rang, startling her. She wasn't yet ready to hear any noise, especially right next to her. This time it was her father.

"Sarah... what happened?", he asked with a sleepy voice. Sarah knew her father used to sleep deeply and could not hear the phone ring even if it was next to his bed, especially after the last couple of sleepless nights in his brother's house. Only God could know exactly what woke him up this night and made him check his phone. It could be just a coincidence or perhaps it was a miracle. No matter what it was, for Sarah it was a sign.

"D..D...ad" she stammered, unable to add anything else.

"Sarah, are you crying?" her father became confused.

"It's crazy... it's all crazy..." she replied, not able to find any other words.

"What happened?" Her father asked anxiously.

"Some people broke into our house." Sarah's voice faltered, almost making her cry.

"What?!? My girl, are you all right?" Her father's voice broke as soon as he heard her words. The hair on the back of his neck stood on end. He did not know what he had expected when she answered, but he certainly did not expect to hear anything like this.

"I just ran away. That was the first thing I could think of to do..." She paused, pressing the phone closer to her lips. "Dad... I'm scared..." she whispered.

"Sarah, where are you... *where are you?*" Fear flooded her father's words.

"I have no idea dad, I just drove away from the house as fast and as far as I could", Sarah exclaimed.

"Just tell me that you're safe", her father pleaded with great pain in his voice. He just hoped that his daughter really was okay.

"I am safe", she blurted and started the engine, realizing that she could not continue onto civilization while she remained motionless on the gravel shoulder. "I just spoke with my old friend John. I'm going to his place..." Sarah fell silent, anticipating how her father would react.

"*To John's...* John who?" Her father became more confused.

"John Wishep", she explained, as she looked through the windshield into the endless night. She finally managed to go navigate the car back onto the pavement, continuing the journey this time with greater care. She knew now, all too painfully well, that the wilds of the night could bring anything.

"Oh yes. I remember John Wishep. Doesn't he live in New York?!?"

"Yes. Yes Dad, he does..." Sarah gently paused. "I just don't think it is safe to return home right now and I don't want to bring any further danger to you". Just the thought of going back made her body shudder.

"What about going to Peter's"? Her father began looking for options, trying to stop his daughter from the crazy notion of going so far away.

"I'm afraid those thugs might also know where he lives...".

"You think you're being pursued?!?" Her father was horrified at this thought.

"They wanted something from me; I just know it".

"Sarah, my daughter," He desperately exclaimed. "What are you being dragged into?"

"I don't know Dad", Sarah uttered. "It all scares me. Those men... what I saw in the chapel..."

"What do you mean you saw something in the chapel?" His confusion was now complete.

"I think it was an angel" she said with great hesitation.

"An angel? But how? Why?" It all seemed to be something so far beyond the limits of the ordinary.

"It appeared to me when I went in to check the chapel. It warned that I'm in great danger and said that some people would come after me".

"Wait a minute, Sarah", her father interrupted. "You mean that an angel appeared to warn you of a confrontation?"

"Yes. I believe it did", She said with a shudder. "It was standing right in front of me. I saw it, heard it, and talked to it. Well, not with words... It's so hard to explain."

"But how do you fit into all of this my daughter?? I would think an angel would be sent to protect you, not to put you in danger".

"I don't understand all of this either, Dad." Then Sarah revealed the most unbelievable part of her story. "The angel gave me a string of beads and asked me to protect them from evil. It said the whole world depended on it. I'm sure that was what those thugs were looking for."

"Are you sure this is about ...these... these beads", her father finally asked. He still believed that there was a big untold part of the whole story. For him it all sounded like the ramblings of a very scared person who convinced herself that an angelic presence had put all this responsibility on her.

"Oh Dad, I just told you!" Sarah was very disappointed that her father didn't understand.

"Sarah, I completely trust your words, there is no doubt. I am just trying to put things together because I worry about you a lot. Things like that don't happen just randomly. There must be a reason…"

"If I only knew why this happened me!" The girl sounded desperate.

"Listen, I am calling the police now and…" Sarah cut him off.

"Dad, after hearing this whole story, you really believe that the police could protect me from evil forces? I really doubt they would even listen -- or could do anything even if they did."

"I understand…but we must do everything we can. Someone's tried to bring you harm and possibly even kill you. This is very serious Sarah. I hope the authorities will catch those men quickly."

"Only God can protect me right now, Dad." There was a long, silent, reverent pause before Sarah went on. "The angel was sent by God and it was only by His grace that I managed to escape. If this is indeed a sacred mission to protect something dear to Him, then with His help, I will do it without hesitation!"

"I know, daughter… I know. Of course, God will protect you. I just keep thinking of what might happen if the thugs find you before the police find them."

"Dad, this is why I am heading to John's. It's somewhere far away enough where they will never find me. I'll be all right", Sarah promised. "Please don't worry."

"Let's pray to God to protect your soul and to keep you safe." He breathed a deep sigh of relief.

Once again, interference interrupted the phone line as Sarah left the open space and entered the next forested area.

"Dad, the phone signal is dropping out, so please listen." Sarah started to panic. "Please, whatever you do, do *not* go back to the house alone".

"Yes... sure... I, I understand", he replied. "I won't do that."

"I'll call you as soon as I get to John's. I think I'm just outside the City now," That was not true, but she wanted to spare her father more worry.

"I love you Sarah. Please be careful," her father said with great affection and fatherly concern.

"I love you too, Dad".

Nothing. Again the signal was lost. Sarah just hoped that her father heard her last, heartfelt comment. She was alone again. Just her and a very dark night. A night dark in so many ways. She was less and less comfortable being in a wild and solitary place. All she wanted was to get back to civilization. In a short time, her thoughts and wishes were heard; Sarah had finally turned onto the highway, out of the forest, and just that much closer to The Big Apple.

***

Autumn in New York City has always been something amazing, soothing and extremely beautiful. Streets flooded with crazy brown colors, the air filled by the smell of fallen leaves, fragrant flowers, wet plaster, and diesel fumes. It was a simultaneous, strange mixture of so many things that the average bystander would reluctantly inhale as if taking in a deadly gas. Subtle, unique details always lent an odd twist of cozy charm to the seasons of The Big Apple and autumn was no different.

Sarah stretched lazily in bed, burying herself among goose-down pillows and wrapped in a comfy blanket. Not yet fully awake, she noticed how her body ached with fatigue from the night before. She needed a few more minutes at rest before she could commit to fully opening her eyes and starting a new day. This was quite unusual for someone who used to get up every day at dawn for morning prayer, to feed the animals, and to bake for the family café. Sarah had steadily grown into being in charge of both her family and the café that had been around for the past 60 years. In her short time as "the boss" she had kept everything running smoothly. At work, she built a solid foundation of steady routine and excellent service. Only on holidays and special occasions when there were too many orders for one powerhouse to handle, Sarah sought help from her cousin Peter.

Peter enjoyed the occasional café work opportunities when they came along. It was a chance for him to interact with his cousin with whom he had limited contact despite the fact they did not live far apart. They were so unalike in character that no one would have imagined that these two could even be related. Peter was an ordinary village boy who along with his family lived on a local farm. His meaning in life was inextricably tied to continuity of the family business. He enjoyed the business so much that he never dreamed about anything else; the life he had created was comfortable just as it was. He was perfectly cast in his role.

Sarah was raised in the small town of Blackwood, PA in a small-town family guided by strong, small-town religious principles. Faith had always played an important role in her life, beginning in an early and formative childhood that culminated in an early and responsible adulthood. It took on an even more dedicated and decisive role just after her mother's death. She, just as Peter, had become inextricably tied to her role. Nevertheless, Sarah was full of ambition to move from a small town and open her own café in someplace grand, like the place of her mother's birth, New York City. For years she had lived with this idea in her head and heart. But birthright alone was not enough. One would have to be both physically and mentally prepared for The Big Apple. New York City was known as a place of unlimited possibilities that could magically realize the most daring of dreams. It was also a place that never forgave mistakes. Some people would lose everything they had there, including their lives. The Big Apple, although inviting and glittering, was often harsh and competitive. People routinely moved into the city with high hopes and ambitions, blithely thinking that everything would fall into place - and too often their dreams were quickly undone before they knew what hit them.

Sarah could not decisively commit to such a drastic change as moving from her hometown to New York City. It was important to patiently wait for the right time to arrive. However, life often presents odd surprises that are impossible to foresee. Some events push timelines, plans, and better judgment into reckless, unprepared actions. Actions that could have life-changing consequences. In a blink of an eye, Sarah found herself surrendering to the circumstances at hand and deciding to get away from Blackwood. Fleeing from something eerie at home that scared her to death; New York City seemed to be a perfect place in which to lose herself.

The girl believed in the existence of God. She always had. She believed that He had heard her requests and was always out there... somewhere. She believed that her guardian angels had always been nearby as well, guarding and helping her walk through every step of her life. During her short 26 years, she had managed to cheat death twice; that surely happened only by the Grace of God. The first time was ten years ago when she and her younger sister Julia were visiting their grandfather in England. The second time was just a few short, terrifying hours ago. She was confident that God and the guardian angels had been hard at work, indeed. She was also confident that those two thugs didn't burst into her home so late at night just to scare her or to hold a conversation.

The long night drive to New York City was a tremendous challenge. She was nearing the point of absolute exhaustion, digging deep to find the strength to continue. Sarah had spent a lot of anxious time behind the wheel this night and it had worn her down with its dangerous mix of fear, worry, desperation, and a need to escape. She knew up ahead there would soon be morning traffic jams at the entrance to The Big Apple; a challenge she had to be ready to face. She could not and would not give in nor give up. She had to push on. Thankfully, John had patiently spoken with Sarah several times during the last leg of her journey into New York City. She arrived safely, but dead tired and in desperate need of rest.

There was little wonder why it had been so hard to wake up this morning. She had to get her story together to share what happened last night with her dear friend John Wishep, who had so kindly welcomed her into his house in the middle of the night.

They grew up together in Blackwood. John and Sarah's childhood friendship had grown and bloomed into an adult friendship. Throughout the years they had always stayed in touch, even after John was sent by his family to the City to further his studies. He eventually graduated as an IT specialist and quickly found a very well-paying job with the renowned conglomerate, Migren Inc. John was even able to buy a beautiful house in Brooklyn. Sarah knew that this purchase was possible only because of the financial support of his wealthy parents. They knew things like that about each other.

Nearing the end of her morning reverie, Sarah yawned and instinctively turned her head to the side facing the nightstand. There she could see a lovely framed photo of John and his parents from a trip to Florida. Sarah was smiling sleepily, about to drift off again, when suddenly it seemed like cold water washed over her entire body. She had unconsciously noticed that the alarm clock, stationed just behind the photo, showed the time as a minute or two shy of 11:00 pm.

"How could that be???", she wondered if she had said it aloud.

She immediately awoke in an adrenaline rush and fumbled for the phone. The screen showed many missed text and voice messages from her father, her sister Julia, and another unknown number which might belong to the Blackwood sheriff. She knew that her father would be very worried, so she called him first. Last night was not easy and had frayed everyone's nerves. Her father's voice was calmer this time. She knew that she made the right decision to call him as soon as possible; it was important to him just to hear his daughter's voice. His calm spread directly back into her heart and mind. She breathed more easily and peacefully. All night she had been completely unnerved and now she felt better. The most important thing for Sarah was to hear that her father was all right. It was also important to hear that the police were already involved in the search for the criminals. And she was right; the Blackwood sheriff had tried to contact her. She also learned that wisely and dependably, as Peter always was, he had come to stay with her father because of what happened.

Sarah touched the "end" button and the phone went silent. She gently put the phone on the table next to the bed as if it were her father that she was placing there. She looked up and shot a long, blank stare at the ceiling. The ponderous decision to stay in New York City wasn't easy, but she believed with all her heart and soul that what she did was right to keep everyone safe. She knew all too well that sometimes decisions made to be made in life that were not in line with one's deepest wishes but were in fact for the highest good. She had been to New York City many times but this time it was going to be different. She had a premonition that she would stay there for quite a long time. It wasn't easy to accept the fact that she would have to live for a time away from the only home she had ever known. It also meant that her only source of inner strength would come through her faith. She would have to rely heavily on the unseen and the unknown. She began to whisper a silent prayer when suddenly her peace was interrupted by a strong knock at the door.

"Come in", Sarah said.

A tall, brown-haired man entered the room. He wore an old Migren Corporation t-shirt emblazoned with a brief tag line below the company name that reminded everyone: *Advanced Technologies.* John looked exhausted for good reason. Sarah would certainly say that he worked too much and didn't take enough time for enough sleep. Despite his weary state he was still smiling. There was indeed a reason as there are reasons for everything. For this young man of 28 years it was the simple happiness of seeing a friend who represented one of the best parts of his childhood. She was someone about whom he cared deeply. John walked over to the bed and leaned back on his haunches. He crossed his arms on top of the sheet, his piercing gaze met the girl wrapped in a blanket.

"How are you?" he whispered his inquiry. His voice was very soft and, at the same time, brought a presence of energy that both fascinated and comforted. Sarah sat up and leaned heavily against the headboard and took in John, still not believing that she was in his home safely away from danger. She drew a deep breath to respond, but no words seemed to follow. It felt like she had swallowed her tongue. The question was where to start because there was so much to tell.

"It's just unbelievable that I am here. I feel so embarrassed about sleeping so long" Sarah said tenderly.

"You needed to sleep, especially after all that happened. ...Lord...," John shook his head imagining the horror that Sarah had experienced the night before. "I just hope my sleeping pill helped you".

"It did. It worked perfectly" The girl stretched her neck and felt how heavily her head rested upon it. Her eyes became empty as her mind momentarily drifted to an earlier time and place. Unrevealed, her eyes abruptly shifted back and she went on.

"I just don't know how to thank you, John".

"You don't have to thank me. This is what real friends do. I'm glad you're safe and that's the most important thing".

"Oh, thank you" Sarah heard herself repeat several times.

"Have you spoken with your father since you are arrived? I think I heard you on the phone a while ago"

"I just talked to him".

"I hope he is all right".

"He is…" Her words were brief. "It was a tough day for all of us".

"Certainly. So… what are the police saying?"

"Nothing for the moment" Sarah sounded disappointed. "I wish they'd have already found those creeps".

"They will. You'll see" John said convincingly. He crafted his words carefully to assure his friend that there was no reason to feel fear and that everything would be all right.

"It's still hard to process everything".

"I understand it very well", John said. "Right now, you need to relax and regain your strength. That needs to be *priority one*. Why don't you take a bath, put on comfortable clothes, and we'll have some dinner and talk about whatever you want".

"Yes" Sarah nodded. She was just amazed by the attention and caring her friend had for her. It was something she always knew but now it was crystal clear because she was living it. In her mind, she thanked John for not asking her to immediately recount the events of the previous night. She was not yet ready.

"You do know don't you, that you are more than welcomed to be here", John said awkwardly. "There is no question. You can stay as long as you want, for as long as you need".

Sarah just smiled broadly. She was deeply touched, like never before. She always believed that real friends would be there - particularly through hard times. In any event, she was sure that John's kindness was an authentic, brilliant light that enveloped her.

Throughout her life, Sarah had always taken care of everyone but herself. As a child, she took care of her sweet dog, Ronnie, then it was her younger sister Julia. When her mother fell ill she focused all her attention on caregiving, which unfortunately lasted only a short time. After that, she turned to her father who needed monumental moral support. It was easy to understand why, over the course of her brief 26 years, she had remained single. Every time she embarked on the journey of her own life, family problems would sabotage the voyage. Now for the very first time in many years someone else was taking care of her - such an amazing yet foreign feeling.

"You are a real friend" Sarah said. She felt it was important for her to say the words aloud. "I don't even know what else to add".

"You don't have to say anything. Just know you are in a safe place and that I am here for you. Any time. No matter what".

"I know" Sarah smiled reassuringly as she hugged her friend.

"I hope you are hungry. I am making some delicious pasta" John said joyfully.

"If you made it, then you know I am" Sarah nodded her head and wiped away the tears of joy that had followed her smile.

"Take your time. I will be downstairs. There's no rush; when you're ready just come down to the kitchen".

"All right".

When John left the room, Sarah paused for a while thinking about recent events, about her father, her sister, and what might happen next. The unknown brought her feelings of anxiety - normal for most, but not for her. Sarah was courageous. So much so that she spontaneously moved from a small town to a big city with a very different life, different people, and different principles. She believed that it was a very serious, but clearly the right, decision.

She looked at the chair beside the bed and saw her neatly folded clothes crowned by a string of colorful beads. It still felt unbelievable to be chosen as the keeper of this unusual artifact. What purpose could these shimmering, multi-colored beads have? Sarah carefully took them with closed eyes and began to recite a silent, private prayer.

She knew there was a God and His guardian angels. As she had already seen a real angel, there was no question that something existed on the spiritual level. Sarah prayed hard to get at least some kind of sign, but nothing... disappointment... just disappointment. She looked down to see the string of beads clutched in her hands with no idea what to do with this decorative object. To her, that's all it was. A gleaming, decorative object. She sighed and placed it back on top of the clothes. As she labored to exhale, she decided that the steam from a hot bath might help to clear her mind, even if only for a little while.

What an unprecedented pleasure it was to immerse herself in a relaxing, hot tub. All her anxiety seemed to disappear with the help of the gently massaging bubbles. It was exactly what Sarah needed. She did not want to leave this blessed place despite the fact that John was downstairs patiently waiting for dinner. No, she was not selfish but it felt so good just to be surrounded by swirling hot water as she lowered herself into the luxurious tub.

Many joyful thoughts raced through her head from the past to the future. The best were the ones that made her wonder what would happen if she were living in a happy family, if her mother were still alive, and Julia hadn't gone to live with her aunt. What could be more joyful and happier? With all her heart, Sarah knew that if these things were possible she would not need anything else. But, life had worked things out differently. The girl tried her best to think positively, helping herself to build strength. She knew for sure that even though her mother was gone, her spirit was there all the time. Julia was only in Europe temporarily and would be coming back to New York one day. Even her father was not all that far away.

Time passed slowly - even reluctantly - but eventually she had to leave the warm, fragrant water. Sarah dried herself, walked to the mirror and put on some makeup. She caught her reflection just for a second, but it was enough to say that she needed more rest.

"Everything will turn out okay," she said, rubbing both her hands from the corners of her eyes to her temples, hoping to wipe away the fatigue on her face.

Sarah felt relief and realized that much more time had been spent bathing than planned. Feeling uncomfortable about keeping John waiting any longer she hurried herself along. Opening the door, she turned on the hair dryer pretending to be almost finished but realized it was a useless ploy. The blaring downstairs TV would have prevented John from hearing anything anyway. Sarah was in a rush. She quickly started putting the final touches to her appearance when she heard something alarming. It was a TV news story about a series of ongoing murders across New York City. Immediately, she stopped and moved into the hallway to listen further. Something in her head said everything was somehow connected. And if things were, Sarah couldn't ignore it.

The newscaster was warning the residents of the great metropolis to be vigilant and to refrain from visiting deserted or empty places, like parks or abandoned buildings, especially at night. From the breaking-news ticker it was revealed that at least 19 people had become victims of an unknown maniac dressed as a clown. The City had declared an emergency threat level. Sarah stood motionless for quite some time. It was not at all what she expected to hear on her first day in a new place where she thought she would be safe. Every place seemed to be dangerous now, except perhaps for an uninhabited island. The breaking news concluded and the station returned to its regularly scheduled programming.

Sarah slowly made her way down the stairs to join John in the living room and soon saw him leaning against the frame of the doorway with his arms crossed. Staring squarely at the large-screen TV, her attention was captured by what looked like a modified logo of Migren Inc. It was a large black star with the company name changed to *"MAGiC"*. Sarah moved forward to get a better look. What she saw was a huge crowd of reporters and photographers gathered around the head of the company, Migren Litsiona. She was skillfully assuring everyone that the name change did not mean she was leaving the former post as CEO of Migren, Inc. She pitched the name change as part of a marketing strategy aimed at developing a new branch of the corporation. Migren calmly and carefully explained that the new venture dealt with space exploration and research and that it would create thousands of new jobs. She further tantalized the journalists by revealing that the silent partner was none other than the US space agency, NASA. Together they started a big project named the "DX Superstar" a silent, supersonic spaceship powered by a quantum drive. The purpose was surprisingly new: exploration of other solar systems and searching for so called "time collapses" created by black holes. The work was scheduled to be completed in two years, but that was the extent of the public details. At the end of the interview, answering a last question about the new company name, Migren explained that ironically there was really nothing mysterious: *MAGiC* represented not a supernatural power, but her family's Catalan origins. That's all.

"First Blackwood, now all this…" Sarah heard John exhort, "I don't think we need to watch this stuff now, especially late at night". He pressed the power button on the remote and the room fell silent.

"I don't understand what's going on with this world" Sarah's voice had an edge of palpable fear. The words hardly had time to leave her lips before she recognized that it could have very well been her name that appeared on that list of last night's victims had she not made her daring escape to New York City. Her thoughts brought a wave of nausea up from deep in her gut. She just wanted to stay hidden somewhere for a little while to feel safe again. Really safe.

"Sarah, are you okay?" John asked. He could see that something was wrong. The girl was disturbed when the front door creaked under the pressure of the wind that rose sharply.

"I … I think so …" her words fought to escape from behind her most contrary, inner thoughts. She was still staring at the door as if hypnotized. John did not understand, but it gave him great worry.

He replaced the dismal drone of the TV with some soothing instrumental music that created an easy and natural atmosphere, and invited Sarah to the table. She felt a little awkward jumping directly into fully recounting the events of the previous night, understanding that it was something John was waiting to hear from her. When John looked at her with a serious, probing face, she couldn't say anything except to ask how he was doing. He just smiled and realized the true nature of this mental dilemma. He understood everything, and relaxing, spoke about the beginnings of his life in New York City. The narrative shifted to his professional life, the difficulties he had faced, and how he had to overcome them. John also talked some about his new friends, traveling around the world, and unexpectedly, street racing - which occupied some of his meager free time. Several more minutes were devoted to discussing his family. Sarah knew them very well - or at least that's what she thought. What she learned from John's story completely shocked her. He shared all the disagreements endured with his parents who had insisted on selling his late grandfather's mansion. She had no idea of any of this. The problems focused on the fact that the John's maternal grandfather had died and bequeathed his home in Los Angeles not to his daughter Kate, with whom he had a strained relationship, but to his grandson John. It was a shocking surprise to everyone -- especially to John. It happened just about two years after he received financial support from his parents that he needed to purchase his current home in Brooklyn. Had this tragedy happened earlier, it would be unlikely that John would be living in Brooklyn now. He basically refused to sell his grandfather's house because he had so many memories there. He could not do so for the sake of someone he loved so much and with whom he had so often visited. John loved his grandfather and that house. He flatly refused to sell it despite the threats from his parents.

Sarah listened intently to the situation and circumstances that caused the impasse. When all had been told, she still felt only support for her friend in his difficult, stoic choices. In her heart, she hoped John could find some common ground with his parents. She believed there was a solution regardless of misunderstandings between them. Sarah also firmly believed that parents were something sacred since they were given only once in a lifetime. She was particularly aware of this since having lost her mother. She knew first-hand the feelings of regret John would have for many things that he had done and about the words he had said. Now was not the time to try to influence his opinion but the day would come when he would have to take her words seriously, hopefully sooner than later.

Once the door to conversation was opened, Sarah cautiously recounted what had happened worrying that John would think she were crazy. Much to her surprise and relief he listened with great understanding. He didn't comment on the paranormal component of the story. Instead, he hoped that those who had threatened the life of his friend would get what they deserved and be apprehended as soon as possible. Sarah had been through a series of difficulties spanning her entire lifetime. Actually, it was as though her whole life was a big test. If it were not for her faith and stubbornness, she would surely not have been able to cope with everything she'd experienced. What happened last night had strongly shaken her, and she instinctively knew that life could not stop because of it. Her only choice was to continue forward, otherwise nothing good would lie ahead. She had to be patient and to pray constantly that everything would turn out well so the sacrifices she endured would not be in vain. New York City seemed to be a good start of a new life; the only question was how easy it would be to pull off.

Somehow the conversation turned to more deeply addressing a relationship between John and Julia. John was not sure if anything serious was building between them. Time and distance had brought a lot of pain. Although they were still in touch, there was no outward evidence he'd won Julia's heart. He assured himself that he must continue fighting for the one he loved to get the right result. He believed in this and so did Sarah. She hoped for a happy, fairy tale ending because she just truly loved the two of them.

Fueled by the hopes of convincing herself that John and Julia really could make it as a couple, Sarah's feelings for John still stubbornly floated to the top. Yes, it was all a long time ago and life had indeed moved on, but the buried sentiments were still there. She believed that her feelings were well guarded and that John would have never guessed otherwise. However, it was still hard to be a part of this love story.

At first Sarah was listening to John without making commentary.

Soon she decided to redirect their conversation to more basic topics since the subject of this discussion seemed too emotional for their first evening's chat. In just the right moment, Sarah smoothly shifted to sharing a little about Blackwood thinking it would interest John - and it did! It was such a pleasure to see his happy face while he was listening about a place that was particularly special. The town of their childhood was full of incredible, warm memories and dear to both of them. They were jumping from one memory to another and thoroughly enjoying each other's company. At some point, Sarah understood that there was not much more to tell, besides Blackwood, but that was wrong. She didn't realize that in fact even in her small-town life she had such big interests and responsibilities: God, church, her father, and even though it sounded funny, a "family café" about which she could speak all day. Yes, Sarah was a coffee lover and as soon as John learned this, he mentioned a good spot down the street that was open 24 hours a day.

"We'll have to go there sometime", he managed through a yawn. He started dropping hints that it was time to put the conversation to bed. Sarah was oblivious. She did not even notice that two hours had passed like two minutes.

It was suddenly a quarter past three in the morning. By this time, John had completely lost track of what his friend was saying. With a full mind and heavy-lidded eyes, his yawning had become more regular and his face showed fatigue. Sarah felt badly that she had made him listen to her stories for so long into the night. She was ready to suggest that they finally call it a night, but John said it first.

"I think I'm about ready to fall right out of my chair" he said with languid voice and laughter. "I'm sorry Sarah; I've got to get to bed".

"Oh of course, John". Sarah felt terribly guilty. "I completely forgot that you have to get up in just a few hours".

"We can pick up our conversation tomorrow", John promised. He glanced over to the kitchen table. "I will leave you a spare key for the front door just in case you need it".

"Thank you, John" Sarah smiled, and gave him a hug before she even thought to do it. It was nearly automatic.

"I just don't want you to worry about anything" John said. "You are not alone. I am here for you anytime". His words, as always, were carefully chosen and deliberate. "I know it's not easy making a big decision, as you have, to move to a new place. Especially to such a big city as New York".

Sarah was again reminded of John's kindness. He felt to her as comforting as a hand-knit scarf. Time and the many years had not changed John from whom she knew all along. Sarah watched him head up the stairs with very heavy steps until he disappeared from her sight. She loaded the dirty dishes in the dishwasher, and in absolute silence, sat a bit longer at the table alone with herself. Even though it was still a dark outside the kitchen window, soon the sun would be rising on her second day in The Big Apple. Sarah smiled through a reverie that felt nearly too good to be true. It was indeed short-lived as the unwelcomed chill of reality began to creep into her mind. She found herself immersed in the swirling thoughts of last night's fright when she was face-to-face with a creature that might have been an oddly angelic presence. In her mind, she could hear the haunting, lilting voice and its warnings and pleas. She clearly remembered its flat, bright, and translucent body with two luminous holes in place of eyes and thin hands that were hotter than fire. Sarah rubbed her wrists, feeling as though they were burning after the angel's touch, but it was just her imagination. Her heavy thoughts drifted to her father and the fact that she felt guilty having left him all alone with everything that happened. What followed were the memories of her mother, and how she might have handled what had come to pass and how she would feel about her daughter's sudden decision. Sarah felt the jarring mix of the pull of the past and the thrust of the present. What she knew best was that her moment had arrived and it was necessary to move forward. If she had wanted to continue her old life it certainly wouldn't be in an exciting and vibrant place like New York City.

The girl hadn't even noticed that she was in a rushing river of a million simultaneous thoughts. She began experiencing strange dreams which became incomprehensible stories without any logical ligament to connect them. It would have continued, but a loud noise startled her into consciousness. She had fallen asleep at the silent table with her head on her hands. The kitchen was eerily dark with only dim light seeping in from distant streetlights and strange noises emanated as if there were someone, or something, making its way toward her.

"John?" Sarah called as she rose from the table with a suspicious glance into the darkness. There was no answer. She again called her friend's name. Nothing. The noise abruptly stopped and there was deafening, dead silence. Sarah could feel her heart start to pound. She did not have a clue as to who or what might be in the room. The fear of a nocturnal animal making its way in search of food completely chilled her blood. "This is Brooklyn. There aren't any wild animals here", she tried convincing herself with logic. If so, then what was it? Timidly, she walked to the corner and glanced outward. She strongly hoped all that was going on was no more than her fears provoked by the previous night. But she soon learned she was wrong. At first, Sarah didn't see anything but then she distinguished something that was neither an animal nor a human. There stood a black shadow, blacker yet more visible than the darkness from which it appeared. It was about two meters tall - a height that Sarah all too fearfully remembered. It had the shape of a big foot with a hairy body, knee-length arms, and eerie, glowing green orbs for eyes. As in all her nightmares, Sarah wanted to scream but she couldn't. She was frozen with fright, unable to believe what was appearing in front of her. All she could manage was to quickly run through a flood of escape plans should the monster give chase. The most terrifying thing was that the big foot stood motionless, just staring at her. Sarah's horror increased as she felt the eerie creature literally drilling into her with its eyes and slowly draining her life energy. Its demonic face grotesquely twisted into a snow-white, wide smile of sharp shark-like teeth.

"Give it to me" barked an outraged, angry voice that could not and was not at all human. It was something unimaginably terrifying.

In a burst of speed, Sarah made a break for the stairs and ran up into her room on the second floor. She slammed the door and firmly leaned against it.

"No... No... this can't be happening again!" she pled aloud in disbelief.

Soon she heard footsteps from outside and the first thought this was it.

"No God, please, not now". Sarah began to pray in earnest out loud and asked God to not let the evil harm her.

The terror of the present and the terror of Blackwood merged into one event. It seemed like the damnation continued and would never stop. There was no place to hide. Sarah was about to die from fear when she noticed that the ominous footsteps were heard no longer. There followed more silence in which Sarah could feel the pulse in her neck. After waiting an eternity, she believed that the threat was gone. She exhaled her long-contained breath when the door handle shook violently. The monster was still there. Trying to enter the room, it started pummeling the door with even greater, unceasing fury, thirsty for blood. It screamed like a demon-baby whose evil life grew more powerful with each scream and each strike at the door. Sarah's eyes were sealed shut while still praying that the frantic sound would stop, but it did not. Instead it became stronger. Her body could bear no more strain as she felt herself collapsing to the floor.

Sarah startled again and opened her eyes realizing that what had happened was just a bad dream. She was still sitting at the dining table when from outside came a rumble of thunder like the one that had surely caused her to waken. The nightmare that she had experienced felt so real and so vivid that she needed some time to recover. She looked around, but was still unsure if the worst was truly over. Involuntarily, her eyes continued to surveil the dark, silent kitchen. No one was there and nothing was happening. Sarah's heart slowed and her breathing finally relaxed as her body returned to normal. She wanted to check through the dark kitchen but her fear still controlled her senses.

It was now five o'clock in the morning and still dark outside. Sarah had no wish to sleep any longer. She needed to busy herself with some distraction. What would be better than a good cup of coffee? She put on a coat and quietly slipped out of the house, remembering a 24-hour café or coffee bar, located just a few minutes away. The street was empty at that hour which was not a surprise because this was Brooklyn, not Manhattan. She stepped up her stride as the cold and the wind passed through her. The only sound was the constant rustling of leaves on the trees. At the end of the street and across the road shone a blue-light neon sign of the café named *Jack's Bean*. Looking around every few steps, Sarah continued down the sidewalk that was covered with wet leaves, for a half a block.

"Morning" droned the flat-line voice of a skinny blond barista girl when Sarah entered. The name tag that hung from her right lapel was inscribed with the moniker, "Lily". Sarah thought she didn't look much like a "Lily" - more like an Olivia, Amelia, Foley, or some other refurbished millennial name. In any event, it was certain that she was a poster child for anorexia. She stared at Sarah with an empty glance with all the customer service of someone who had smoked all night instead of sleeping. No amount of caffeine could force her into reality.

"Good morning Lily" mirrored Sarah as she looked up to the order board where all kinds of coffee concoctions were listed. She decided that this was quite a decent-looking place where it might be nice to have breakfast with John. Her eyes tracked straight to the flat white and came to a halt. That was what she wanted and that was what Lily would be making.

There were some acoustic, coffee-house tunes playing in the background that invited the listener into an early morning calm. The music competed for attention with a cranky overhead fan that buzzed loudly, begging urgently to be replaced. Sarah's gaze shifted from the barista to the vintage photos of New York City that lined the walls. There was only one other patron sitting in the café at a small corner table. It was a petite woman with poison red lips and big round glasses. She wore a black coat that was two sizes too big and her head was covered with the hood as if it were windy inside the cafe. Unaware of other humans and buried in the disconnected, digital world of her almighty cell phone, she was more furniture than customer. In this moment at the *Bean,* females prevailed: just Sarah, Lily, and the furniture.

"How's it going tonight - or should I say this morning?" Sarah asked.

"As usual, nothing special" Lily replied, as she shook her head and yawned deeply. "We've had busier days".

Between Sarah's arrival and the delivery of her flat white, she noticed that no other customers had appeared to claim their morning caffeine. Lily would have flatly greeted them but instead she mindlessly placed Sarah's almost-full paper cup on the counter.

"Sugar is next to the door" Lily said as she motioned her head to the left.

"Thank you" replied Sarah.

She never drank coffee with sugar believing that it would spoil the taste. She took a sip. Mmmm… delicious… just as John had promised. At first, Sarah considered staying at the café for a while, but with the rain falling outside it seemed a better idea to head home before it got any worse. There was genuine worry of getting stuck there for a long time since Sarah had neither an umbrella nor a raincoat.

"It's coming… it's very close" announced the sharp, odd voice of a café visitor that made Sarah wince.

"What's coming?" Sarah asked without understanding what was going on.

"Apocalypse… what else?" the woman excitedly waved her hands and inadvertently overturned her cup of recently poured coffee.

"My God Rosa, not at five in the morning!" Lily scolded as she dashed out from behind the counter with a rag in her hand to clean up the calamity. "It's been a couple of years and your apocalypse hasn't showed up yet", Lily added. Sarah was surprised to hear Lily string that many coherent words together.

"It's near. I feel it" the woman repeated, directing her wild, bulging eyes at Sarah. "I know he's here", she croaked.

"I think you should stop watching so much TV" Lily managed a dull chortle while Sarah's attention grew more intense.

"If you want to know the truth, speak to Antoine. He knows the future." Rosa continued, "You'll find him in the heart of Manhattan, and you'll see. He's a psychic medium *extraordinaire* - he knows more than you could even dream about. But one warning: you must be ready to hear what he says. It's the truth, I tell you - It's the truth you'll hear!" Her crazed sermon abruptly concluded.

"Thanks" Sarah helped to finish the moment. "I think I better go now", she mentioned as she looked out the all-glass, double front door.

"Don't mind her… she's nuts" Lily winked.

Sarah was surprised. An understanding soul resided in the blonde barista. Lily continued wiping the table while resting her hand on the wall to reach the table's distant corners.

"Be careful out there", she warned, "I bet there's a pretty good storm coming"

"Yes, I will. Thanks" Sarah nodded and walked out of the café. "See you next time Lily".

The weather had turned sharply cold in a very short time while the wind blew with increasing strength. Sarah shivered and kept her head down as she started to cross the road, continuing to sip her delicious coffee. She felt alone at first since it was so quiet, but then an odd feeling overtook her. She stopped halfway across the road because of an irresistible urge to look left. One more block down the street, right under a red traffic signal, loitered a tall figure wearing a grotesque clown mask. His creepy, snarling smile and yellow eyes like a wild animal were visible to Sarah even from where she stood. She knew that it was not Halloween, but she remembered the news about the maniacal clown rampaging through the City. The blood in her veins nearly froze with horror at the sight of him prompting her to not know how to react. What she knew for sure was not to panic, at least not visibly. The same way that you never let a mad dog know that he is scaring you. Sarah understood that in this situation it would be better to not give him any reason to attack.

Keeping her eyes sharply tracking the stranger, Sarah quickly walked up the street toward the house. As soon as he was out of sight, her walking pace became a run. She was doubtful of what she saw but was too terrified to look back. Was it the maniacal clown or was it just her imagination? And as if she needed one more thing to think about, the skies opened and torrents of rain began to fall. The girl tossed the coffee cup and ran up the porch stairs while frantically fumbling the key into the lock and quickly entered the house. Just as she latched the front door deadbolt, peering through one of the sidelights, inches away appeared the clown's head. His terrible, grimacing face was draped in rain-blurred makeup as if his skin was starting to peel. Sarah was literally numbed by fear and began to back away from the door but it all turned into a nightmare. The girl backed up one more step when found herself unexpectedly gripped by a pair of strong male hands. This was the limit; Sarah could no longer contain her fear and released a primal scream at the physical attack. She gyrated wildly to break free of the grip.

"Sarah, what's wrong?" The tone of John's voice was firm and frightening.

"John you scared me to death!" Sarah was shaken up and was about to start crying. Her glance immediately flew back to the door but the clown had now mysteriously disappeared.

"I am so sorry". John took Sarah's hands in his. "I didn't mean at all to scare you.

"It's ok, John… It's ok", Sarah repeated nodding her head. She stopped and closed her eyes, having a hard time feeling her own body.

"I startled myself awake and then I heard the noise…" John continued.

"John, that maniacal clown we heard about on the news last night - he's outside", interrupted Sarah, choking back tears, "I *swear* it. I just saw him!". Sarah was inconsolable. "Please check the doors - check all the doors, John".

"You saw a *clown?* John asked incredulously. "I don't understand". He was not sure if he heard everything correctly, or if he had, what it meant.

"Yes, it was just a minute ago. I mean it John, he was right outside the door. I saw him right there through the sidelight" Sarah's hand trembled with fear as she pointed to the right of the front door.

John put his arm around her shoulder and held on tightly. Time stopped for a moment as he tried to take in all he had heard. The whole situation seemed crazy, but clearly terrifying. It was not that John didn't believe all of it, but perhaps after what happened in Blackwood, Sarah's mind was not processing clearly. It was certain she'd been through a real trauma which would explain so much.

All John knew instinctively was to attend to Sarah's current state of mind. He had to do whatever it took to help calm her down and to make her feel safe. Everyone knew that New York City in the past few days had become quite a dangerous place. At the same time, John found it rather unlikely that a "maniacal clown" would appear in Brooklyn at five in the morning - let alone at his front door. He looked out the sidelights, but saw no one. There was not a single soul in any direction. None of it added up to make sense, but at least his ideas and actions were setting the stage with logical actions.

"Stay here, Sarah. I'll check outside", John said. He picked up his father's trusty baseball bat that always stood at the front door entrance and looked through the peephole. All clear. He cracked open the door and stepped out onto the porch now bombarded by heavy rain. Again, not a soul in sight anywhere.

The view further down the street was filled with mist that kept visibility to a minimum. John now noticed how quickly his heart was beating. It all seemed ridiculous but at the same time so close to being real that it made his pulse go higher. Making sure there was no one else present John cautiously returned to the house and proceeded directly to the backyard where everything was quiet. It was so cold that he didn't want to spend any extra time outside. He made an about face to enter the inviting warmth and safety of his house when heard a rustle near the gazebo in the corner of the garden. It immediately captured his attention. He would not move until he was certain it was not a scampering squirrel or tumbling leaves. His eyes were unblinking while carefully approaching the source of the noise.

"Who's there?", he asked loudly.

No one answered, but the noise abruptly stopped. John clenched the baseball bat tightly and peering forward continued walking to the source of noise when saw a small, shivering kitten cowering against the wall. A big smile appeared on John's face and he held out his hand to the poor, frightened animal who shouldn't have been there on such a cold night. But instead of accepting his outstretched hand, it hissed in fear and immediately ran into the darkness. John just shrugged his shoulders and turned back toward the house when a strange cracking sound caught his attention. Before there was time to even turn around, he was suddenly and violently forced to the ground by a pair of very strong hands that felt unhuman.

"J-o-o-h-h-n!!!", Sarah screamed out his name.

John looked up into the rain. What he saw was a creepy silhouette above him with something in his hand prepared to strike. Instincts kicked in and prompted John to roll to the right just as a long-handled ax hit the ground with a sickening thud. It was now buried deeply where he had been lying only a moment earlier. John saw sinister yellow eyes staring down from the tall shadowy figure in a long leather coat with blurred makeup all over its face. He could also make out a red clown's wig, a sharp nose and full, red lips stained with blood. The maniac's mouth distorted into a twisted and excited grin; there was no doubt of the gleeful satisfaction of his actions. Pulling the ax from the ground, the only thought it had was to split John in half. The rage boiled up inside him like a geyser. John knew his life depended solely his actions. Not on luck, not on Sarah, only on him. Mustering great strength and adrenaline-filled legs, he managed to push the clown away and to jump up. There was no time to think, so John grabbed the bat from the ground and delivered a crushing blow directly into clown's face. The *monster* -- no other name existed for it -- was only momentarily dazed and then laughed wildly as if being struck was what he wanted. In an instant, his entire face had been transformed into a bloody mess. John did not waste another precious moment and ran as fast as he could into the house. Sarah immediately slammed the door behind him.

"Quick. Call the police and get out of the house. I'll stop this bastard", John shouted orders to Sarah as he ran into his office where he kept a loaded gun in a desk drawer.

"John please...", Sarah begged, "You can't stay here...". It was too late; he'd already disappeared into the other room.

Sarah ran toward the exit when the back door literally flew off its hinges, disintegrating into a million wooden splinters. By the Grace of God, Sarah was spared harm from the shards which had flown through the air. In the doorway appeared the sinister clown: threatening, panting, streams of blood on his face, clutching a giant ax in his right hand and showing a euphoric smile. There was no time to run. Sarah screamed in horror as she heard a booming gunshot and she was immediately dazed by the concussion. Everything in front of her eyes blurred like rain down a painted canvas. Stunned, she fell forward onto the stairs. Her only focus was to get to the second-floor room where the beads lay waiting. With strength that was surely inspired, she climbed as quickly as she could to reach it all the while hearing sounds of struggle from below. Setting foot on the last stair, she thrust herself forward into the room, slammed the door and grabbed the beads. After a second, unnerving gunshot, Sarah pinpointed the phone and dove under the bed. Her hands were trembling so severely it took two attempts to successfully dial 911; it seemed like an eternity for the dispatcher to answer.

"911...what's your emergency?" Finally, a voice came on the line.

She squeezed the beads now with such force that they made an impression in her palms.

"Please" Sarah whispered and was about to sob. "He wants to kill us, he is in the house, the maniacal clown that the whole city is talking about".

"I need your exact address and where you actually are right now".

"1145 Seventh Avenue, Brooklyn. I am in a second-floor bedroom of the house. Please help us!! I think he is inside!!" Wild fear overtook Sarah when she heard heavy, gruesome footsteps followed by the sound of the ax dragging along on the floor. She stopped talking, hung up the phone, and lay in silence.

She wished she could turn back time. She knew though that she could not escape her destiny or what it would contain. Sarah deeply regretted ever having come here and exposing John to such terrible danger. Now she felt helpless because there was nowhere to go and all she wanted was to know that John was alive. Sarah was under the bed, lying on the thickly-carpeted floor, one hand muffling her whimpers. Her eyes flowed steady streams of tears that were impossible to control; her human side won out. Suddenly the sound of heavy steps disappeared and for a moment there was an eerie, complete silence. The uneasy calm was cut short by the scratchy turn of the door knob. Sarah's heart was about leap out of her chest. From under the bed skirt, she saw the ragged, mud-caked boots, the hem of the black cloak, and the hideous ax blade. The clown's breathing was so loud that it could be heard throughout the room like the ticking of a grandfather clock. Sarah could not feel her own body and felt as if she turned into stone. Even though the clown stopped next to the bed for just a few seconds, it was enough for the monster to find her. What did it mean? The end? Fortunately, instead the clown lumbered over to the walk-in closet on the other side of the room. This was the only chance to escape the room unnoticed and she couldn't miss it.

Sarah placed the beads around her neck and began to crawl out from under the bed when suddenly the ax swiped down past her head. Its heavy blade dug into the floor just a few inches away. Sarah lay stunned for only a moment, and then she saw that the space around her began twisting and oddly bathed in a terrible red light. In horror, she escaped from underneath the bed and instead of a sinister clown she saw a faceless, vibrating shadow. The beads immediately lit up as if somehow connected to a source of energy. The demon's eyes flashed like two yellow lights, as if matches had been struck. This terrible situation was completely out of the ordinary; it was something alien. Sarah found herself in a parallel reality in which everything seemed different: time slowed, objects lost their former sharpness, and the air was filled with a distant roar reminiscent of buzzing bees. Sarah became part of a slow-motion movie, moving like an astronaut on the moon. The eyes of the demon were seeking something and at some point sighted the beads, the actual target. Her hand touched the cross on her chest and she whispered a prayer. Sarah was asking God to take away the darkness and its ways and point the way to the light, but it only made the demon laugh loudly. It was a blood-curdling sound that could stop a heart from beating at any moment.

Sarah tried to rush to the exit, but it was easy to say and not so easy to do. Instead, she stumbled out into the corridor and encountered heavy, black-smoke hands appearing on either side of her shoulders. Something started to squeeze her body and she believed she was face to face with death. There she remained, on the brink of a horrifying reality and an abyss of nightmares. Intuitively grasping the beads, which she was entrusted to keep safe, Sarah closed her eyes, mentally apologizing for failing to protect them from evil. What happened then was completely different from what Sarah expected. There was a deafening scream delivered with such force that the girl nearly fainted. She opened her eyes and saw the shadow folding in on itself becoming a miniature version of a black hole. Realizing that the colorful beads caused this to happen, Sarah plucked them from her neck and held them out toward the spinning, swirling mass. An invisible force immediately pushed Sarah to the edge of the stairs and she lost hold of the beads. The howling ceased as suddenly as it had begun, and out of the black clouds that continued to spin, stretched two long, gnarled hands made of no more than smoke. One hand lunged forward and grabbed the coveted beads. At this point, Sarah felt only one thing - the fierce desire to preserve this piece of God, something sacred and something very important. She still did not realize the importance of this artifact, but she understood that it had to be saved at all cost. There was a voice imploring not to let the demon possess the beads. The voice did not come from her, but from somewhere or something else - a completely different form of life that coexisted in the body from the time when Sarah first saw the angel at her father's parish.

"N-o-o-o" the girl screamed and jerked forward toward to the mass, grasping the beads with one hand.

Powerful, unnatural forces stopped her in her tracks, and then again two lights flashed in the dark. Sarah shivered as she felt something alien penetrated into her body and started to tear at her internal organs. She couldn't stand such pain and screamed wildly, ready to release her fingers, but then a strange thing happened: each of the beads began to glow with light, causing the spinning mass to explode which triggered a blast wave. The house shook with convulsion that it seemed it would collapse. Paintings fell from the walls, objects that stood precariously toppled to the floor with a crash, and the windows shattered, showering half the room with shards. Sarah experienced a strange, alien feeling as if she dove into depths of the ocean. When all the sounds finally dissipated, the room was left with only the distant sound of a steady downpour. Sarah turned and saw that the ominous red light had vanished, and time had returned to normal. The clown was nowhere to be seen. The only reminder of him was the giant ax with its gleaming blade still buried deeply into the floor.

The wail of police sirens rose up from the streets. Disappointingly, as in the movies, the help came a little too late. There was a loud, booming sound that came from downstairs as the door smashed open. Sarah immediately ran to the stairs. For her it was important to make sure that John was all right, it was the only thing she could think about right now. She was fearful that something would bring an even bigger regret. All Sarah's past anxieties and concerns became painfully palpable. More overwhelming than when as a vulnerable child, she lost a pet. More devastating than the image in her adult mind when doctors delivered her mother's death sentence, smashing Sarah's heart into small pieces. She had always tried to be stronger than all the others, regardless of her age or circumstances; it was still a weight sitting on her shoulders. The tragedy that had happened to Sarah's mother had come so suddenly; she could not withstand anything else. Endless prayers to God pleading for a miracle were not heard. Sarah had lost the most precious thing in life after which the existence of God became just a big question. What was happening now was about the same; she was terrified thinking about what might have happened to the one whom she cared about so much. She could not hear John and it was both alarming and frightening.

"Sarah" suddenly there was a loud voice.

"I'm here, I'm here!" She shouted and rushed down the stairs and the first thing she saw were five policemen's guns aimed directly into her face.

Sarah was stunned. As soon as John, appeared, still covered with blood, she forgot about everything and ran to him. From above, they heard the rumble of feet quickly moving about. The New York City police were already searching the upper floor while the girl and the guy were in each other's arms. The worst was behind them and Sarah could finally breathe freely. In this moment she did notice how surprisingly heavy the beads felt now.

"Sir, we did not find anyone" barked one of the policemen who had just descended the stairs. "The window is broken and he is likely hiding somewhere in the area".

"Cordon off the perimeter", ordered someone who was clearly in command. He looked to be about 35 years old - probably the youngest police commissioner Sarah could ever remember. "Don't let him escape!"

John had some minor injuries which required minimal medical attention. The EMTs arrived promptly along with additional police units and backup. Despite the early morning's heavy rainfall, the street filled with cars and people. The urgent howl of sirens literally alarmed the whole neighborhood. Everyone came out to see what was the matter; even journalists showed up. Most of all Sarah did not want to see herself plastered on the front pages of newspapers or TV screens, surely her father could not survive that and it was why she hardily tried to avoid everyone.

Sarah typically cared about others before herself; her needs came last. This old habit didn't play well in her favor; many times before it became the root of her suffering. Looking at all the madness going on around her, she squeezed the beads with all her strength and found herself in a different reality of eternal silence. Her mind was so presently occupied with other things that she didn't have space for the present.

Convinced that her dear friend John was now safe, Sarah had a sense of relief and could step back from everything for a moment. Vague "YES" and "NO" responses occasionally slipped through her lips while in her mind she was somewhere far away. The incident mixed the past with the present and she was left to try to piece together what was truly happening. The way the darkness had stared at her with those terrible eyes, stuck in Sarah's head. There was no getting rid of it. In the depths of her soul she really wanted to see the angel again, to ask questions and get answers.

Sarah was completely exhausted from the police interrogations that lasted until noon. It was not what she expected for her first night in New York City. The feeling that the ground was slipping from under her feet did not leave her. She knew that no one would have believed what she'd experienced, that the clown was not really a clown, or that she had actually met an angel. It all seemed too absurd to be true, but it was. The quaint Blackwood and bustling New York City had a mystical connection at which Sarah could only guess. Coming out of the police station in Brooklyn, she wanted nothing more than to clear her mind. The most reliable way to do this would be to take a walk through the city. This is what she always used to do when she felt lost – long distracting walks. She took the nearest subway and headed straight into Midtown. She didn't want to go back to the house where so much happened. Even thinking of it sent chills all over her body.

Station after station swiftly flew by in front of her eyes, finally reaching Fiftieth Street. Sarah had now arrived in the heart of the City. *Hell's Kitchen* had become somewhat of a gentrified, gay-artist colony, like an updated version of the original East Village. Everything "New York City" was here: restaurants, bars, shops, theaters, and masses of people. Like a magnet, this area drew thousands to all its events. It was also the location of some of the major hotels. Sarah walked slowly north a couple of blocks to Sixth Avenue. In front of her were huge, glitzy posters advertising one of Broadway's biggest and most recent hits, "Wicked", which had enjoyed longstanding success with every audience. There were two nearby hotels, the *W* and *CitizenM*. Initially Sarah had planned to the rooftop "Cloud Bar" at *CitizenM* when suddenly her eyes were drawn to an intriguing door on the opposite side of the street. Above the door hung a sign: "Psychic Medium" which in itself instantly captured her attention. Sarah never really believed in such things, but today was different. A voice in her head whispered to go there and seek the answers to the many questions that plagued her. Before she could take five steps, she heard blaring horns and screeching tires that pulled her back to reality. Sarah realized that she'd almost been run down by a rushing, erratic yellow taxi. She darted across the street and tried to yank open the cherished door, but it was locked. In its small window there was a handwritten sign telling all comers that "Medium Antoine" would return to the storefront at eight o'clock. Sarah put two and two together and remembered the crazy woman Rosa from Jack's Bean who mentioned this very medium. It was a shocking surprise, which now made the girl think that things happened for a reason. So many events and people were connected to each other in mysterious ways.

The noise of the metropolis did not stop even for a second; constant movement was everywhere sending the energy that supplied the city, splashing out in endless waves. People busily scurried back and forth like ants, creating an hypnotic momentum. Present was a group of Chinese tourists, photographing almost every corner while on the other side of the street, the ongoing works of various building reconstruction projects kept the same frenetic pace. Such a full tableau: very close to another building stood countless employees talking on their cell phones, city workers demolishing the old asphalt on the road preparing to pave a new one, and worker bees hailing taxis to deliver them all over the City. The autumn air held unprecedented heat so everyone was exhausted and only dreamed to be somewhere cool. Sarah started thinking about a fantasy of relief which appeared for her as salted caramel ice cream which she loved so much.

Weather in New York City was often a surprise. If early in the morning there was a very bad rain it might feel like winter was coming, but the afternoon might bring bright sun and warmth like summer had arrived.

Metropolis was always different and unpredictable which was why Sarah loved it so much. Her mind was still fixated on the incident of the other day and she felt more lost than ever before. Sarah tried very hard to understand why it was she and not someone else, but there was no answer. Without realizing it she came upon Union Square, where stood an incredible building -- the tallest skyscraper in the world -- the main corporate office Migren Inc., the name of which was already in the process of being dismantled and replaced by a new one. This building was a mesmerizing sight and at the same time alienated from itself in the shape vaguely reminiscent of the Eiffel Tower, completely made of black glass and that emanated dark energy. The giant shadow of it hung over the city and seemed to control everything around. Those were feelings that surrounded this new "wonder of the world", walled around the perimeter with installed 3D screens which broadcast the latest achievements of the corporation. On one of the walls, shown among the millions of stars a blazing sun, an inscription that first appeared and then disappeared hinting at the most powerful collectors of solar energy that in the future would change the whole world and open unprecedented opportunities for all mankind.

As Sarah was about to go into the famous café of the newly-named corporation *MAGiC*, which was rumored to prepare the best coffee in the states, her eyes fell on a small Baptist church on the other side of the square whose appearance came at just the right time. The soul of the girl was torn to speak with the Lord, and she could not skip it, not now. At this hour she was the only visitor. Humbly sitting on the pew, she plunged into her thoughts about God. Remembering like the last time, when she was in the chapel and saw an angel, she was hoping for its reappearance, but absolutely did not expect that it would happen today. Faith had taught her one very simple thing - everything had its time; she only needed humility and fortitude. Sarah knelt and whispered prayers. Evil must be sent away so the light of goodness would fill everyone and everything with love and joy. She prayed for the people close to her that everything would be fine with them and that no dark hand would harm them. She believed in the existence of Heaven and Hell, and still believed that nothing bad would go unpunished.

She cried out to God: "Lord, I am asking you to answer me. If I do everything right, is this where I should be? I'm afraid I made a mistake having left father all alone, and now putting my close friend in danger. I don't want anything bad to happen to them. I love them with all my heart and they are very dear to me. They are my beloved, as is my sister Julia. Wherever she is now, please take care of her. She is a lost soul, but she's the kindest person in the world that only needs to be cared for and loved. I beg you to help me find the right way; lead me wherever you want. You are my heavenly father and I need you so much!"

With such an emotional expression of faith, Sarah wanted to touch the cross on her chest but instead touched the multicolored beads and suddenly felt an unnatural heat. Immediately everything was plunged into darkness, as if the night has covered the whole area, and in the air were heard muffled voices, as if some kind of spirits were trying to talk to her. The walls and ceiling became covered with black flames and time slowed down, just as it happened in John's house, when the maniacal clown came for the massacre.

The girl became so frightened that she jumped to her feet and tried to run to the exit where shone a red light, but her movements were hampered by an unseen force. It was simply difficult to move at all. She still managed to get out into a crowd of people and cars but the whole picture seemed to be unnatural and somehow oddly out of tune. It was like a huge stage of theater where each person ineptly played a role. The girl froze, not having a clue what to do next, when suddenly a new energy was felt. Slowly Sarah turned her head and saw that instead of the *MAGiC* Corporation building, there was towering, giant shapeless shadow which shuddered as if was alive. It blazed with an eerie blue-yellow flame at the very top. Interestingly, none of the other buildings were turned into shadows; they just remained standing in their places, and Sarah knew that the mysterious beads were the cause. Stealthily she made her way to the crosswalk. The wind became stronger which made it more difficult to walk and the *MAGiC* shadow seemed to be a furious monster ready to swallow her at any moment. Sarah feared even more while not being able to run away from this place. Eventually the only thing that kept her hoping that everything would be all right was her belief in God. Constantly thinking of Him she hadn't even noticed how quickly she walked to the other side of the square. Only there she realized that the situation gradually began to return to what it was. The sun began to beat down as it did before, and in the end, all came back to normal.

What has just happened put a big question in the girl's mind: mainly about the *reason* and the *why*. It pushed her toward getting answers as soon as possible. A person she saw who could potentially and possibly help her was the medium. Sarah's heart insisted that this was the right decision to make and a visit to him could change everything. All her life Sarah had trusted her heart and now she was relying upon it completely.

After an amazing time spent at the rooftop bar of the hotel *CitizenM*, where she enjoyed beautiful panoramas and a few pretty cocktails, she managed to free her mind a little from all the current anxiety. Precisely at eight o'clock down she went to go see the medium at his storefront establishment. This could prove to be a very delicate situation depending on what he might have to say, and that Sarah made her a little nervous.

This time cherished door was unlocked. Inside hung an unnatural atmosphere, mystically untouchable -- perfect, yet a bit sinister. There was a peculiar odor that was not pleasant, and a special lighting -- dimmed and relaxed. At first it might seem that you had simply walked into a dark room, but then it became clear that visibility was more purposely occluded than the outside.

"Excuse me", Sarah gently walked in a small room framed by burgundy curtains, hoping to see the famous medium, whom she heard about at Brooklyn's "Jack's Bean".

There was nobody there, just candles that glowed with a weird light, so that objects were casting quivering shadows. In the middle of the room stood a low, round table, on which lay a plaster skull and tarot cards with images of ancient mythical creatures spread all around. Near the table were two old chairs with shabby leather lining, and the room's perimeter was filled by narrow shelves with everything imaginable on them: starting with dried spiders and snake's skin and ending with test tubes filled with liquids of different colors. In addition to the so-called furniture, the atmosphere was supplemented by soft music coming out from an old tape recorder located near the entrance to another room that hosted some rustling sounds. Very soon there were heard words in an unknown language. Sarah dully glanced in the direction of the tape recorder, but same time thought it was someone hiding in another room trying to scare or to simply mislead her.

"Antoine"? She called, looking into the room.

She expected to see an extravagant kind of person, a little crazy to look at and clearly shrouded in mysticism, but also promising to help. The tone of the room was set and all that remained was to have the accompanying story unfold in the cards which lay in front of her. Sarah's sight was brought to the table by the tableau of cards, and an inner voice urged her to sit in a chair and wait patiently. Whatever it was, being patient in such a creepy atmosphere was not so easy, particularly considering the events of the past two days. If it were not Sarah but somebody else, that person would surely be an inmate in an asylum and not in a session with medium. This place had its own special energy that Sarah couldn't comprehend in the moment, not yet having she crossed the threshold. It was the first time she felt the presence of something inexplicable, presence of certain spirits that captivated the room, loudly begging to be freed from their eternal shackles. They lived in the objects of the room, in the walls, and hanging in the air -- which is why there was an unpleasant smell, reminiscent of a burned-out house that stood a week in the rain. It was the smell of death, emptiness and despair. This place was much older than it seemed, which is why there was sharpened, unknown energy that pierced the surface from the heart of the planet and to spearhead up and out to Fiftieth Street, almost in the heart of New York City. This city had become a cult, of sorts, with each year becoming more and more powerful - life flocked here from all around the world, and it fed the city like a hungry child asking to eat and drink, but is never satisfied. The child was now growing up, and with it was a growing urbanism of the latest technologies. The *MAGiC* Corporation skyscraper became a newly-minted Tower of Babel, unsuccessfully reaching to the heavens.

Sarah's sight fell precisely to a tarot card with the image of a *Wonder of the World* from ancient Babylon. The tower stood at night with flaming torches on all its levels, and around it many shadows with creepy red eyes that stretched their long arms up to the sky. The girl shuddered while holding such an image; her whole body felt something terrible - a dark mark that instantly blackened her fate. One that had fallen down from the dark as an ink stain which would be quite impossible to remove. Her pure soul, defiled by events of the past, suddenly haunted her. This tarot card held something more than just the image of a mythical symbol. People do sin and always had to pay a price for their folly. Some sweeping ambitions do change things but not always for the better. Sarah heard the strong, internal warning message that is good to think about what she might do now as not to have regrets later. A sudden cry of her soul ordered her to stop and to try to understand the unknown, leave everything as it is, and go back to her father. The direction in which she was moving was not where she needed to go; it was a night road in a dense forest where one could get lost and easily perish. A place where no one would even be able to find the body. This sinister forest drew lost souls and would never let them go. It was a trap impregnated with an inescapable darkness, no light, and steeped in egregious horrors.

With a sigh the girl put the card back in its place and looked at artificial skull, feeling a palpable heaviness inside. Something told her to just get up and leave; she knew that it was not too late, but she could not do that. All the seriousness of the situation where Sarah was a slave of her own fate, filled with fear of the future and even curiosity, pushed her to the edge of her limits. Here the ancient strengths entered the game, suddenly surfaced from the depths of time, immortal, and urged her to leave all doubts behind and step into a frightening, yet firmly laid, new beginning. With leaping flames from the foul-smelling candles, she noticed that the skull seemed to start smiling. This room has become a magnet for all things mystical, calling the dead to awaken and to begin a great dance that would insanely sweep everything into its path. It would leave not a bit of doubt that destiny cannot be changed, and that the devil's fingers were ready to tickle this innocent soul, enjoying her torments as she reluctantly joined the experience.

Sarah found herself tapping the floor with her right foot impatiently waiting to meet with the medium; she had lost track of time. What could be worse than the painful expectation of the unknown, especially when, in her mind, the night was approaching with giant strides, and in fact, nothing was yet happening. The man who worked here was probably too busy, ignoring his first visitor of the evening, or maybe he just did not care about his reputation. During the last half hour, his reputation had begun to wear down to the level of the shabby wooden floor that apparently hadn't changed from the original construction of the building. And it was not only the floor, the room itself was really shabby, with wooden partitions and rickety walls, that too had become worn; they could not have been a modern style feature of the architect. It is possible that Antoine chose this place, going back to the beginnings of the Parisian lifestyle from the Middle Ages. Whatever it was, had created a wonderful atmosphere from the past. It was impressive, not because of details, but by the spirit that he was able to invite in one of the most modern places on planet.

Uncomfortably fidgeting in the chair, Sarah stood up to head for the exit but was redirected by quiet words like the ticking hands on a clock, firmly saying "NO". She lowered herself back into the chair, paused, and turned her head toward the curtained room that still emanated noises, the saliva in her mouth was absent, and girl's eyes stung from the dim light. Her soul froze in anticipation of a special moment when she would only have to breathe freely, relax and let the fate to do its job. As a result, Sarah's hid her eyes and lowered her head so that only her knees were visible. She heard steps behind her that were so smooth she could only imagine such grace and elegance from a king, but it was not.

"I sincerely apologize for such a long waiting, mademoiselle", came a sweet, harmonious voice, which immediately brought a sense of relief and allowed the body to begin to relax.

"Brown", the girl breathed out. "My name is Sarah Brown".

She immediately looked up at tall, half-balding man of about thirty-five years with a stylish, golden beard. When she first saw him, she could barely keep from laughing, not expecting to meet a psychic medium clad in a white terrycloth robe as if he just stepped out of the bathroom. His left eye twitched involuntarily which was an even more comical part of who he was. Medium Antoine wore round glasses off which the light bounced. As he moved in the darker parts of the room, nervously pacing in circles as he could not remain still, his lenses would start to ominously glow.

"I'm really embarrassed that you had to wait here for so long, almost the whole day" He apologized quite sincerely and the notes of truthfulness could be easily heard in his voice. "I suppose you have a very important thing that couldn't wait. And let me be clear: I promise to help you and even give you a discount for waiting".

"But how do you know that I've been here all day"? Sarah asked, perhaps a foolish question to a psychic medium who could possibly read her thoughts.

"Because I can read thoughts" the psychic medium said with a fully seriousness expression and looking straight into Sarah's eyes. "I know everything about you".

"What?" Sarah felt confused, then horrified, realizing that she was face-to-face with a man who could quite possibly tell her everything about her life.

"But you Miss Brown, should not worry about anything" Antoine laughed. "Fortunately, we live in the twenty-first century, and there are surveillance cameras to see who spent how much time on the stairs outside the entrance".

"Oh-h-h..." the girl breathed out with a smile, feeling silly and nearly stupid.

"But let's get back to the point" Continued the psychic medium, pacing back and forth. "I am ready to listen to you and do everything in my power to help you".

Sarah was speechless, not knowing where to start, she wanted to blurt everything out, and at the same time find out as soon as possible what curse had befallen her and continued to bring torment and burden. She realized how uncomfortable she felt as shame doused her. She knew she was doing something wrong, and that she should not be here but should instead be in the chapel and speaking with a priest and God to get the answers she sought. The hopelessness had driven her to more desperate measures. After long prayers and supplications to the Lord she did not get the slightest hint of an answer or the slightest help. Her whole life, in the last twenty-four hours, had turned into hell. If God did not want to talk to her now when she needed Him, then she would find other ways to help herself. That's why she was sitting stiffly in a chair in the center of New York City, where a strange-looking French psychic medium, was pacing around the room like a confused spider. Antoine seemed to be her last hope. Of course, there were the others, but this medium seemed to be not-so-typical and whose reputation and character held some significant mystery.

"Surely, you want to look into the hidden corners of the future" Antoine said flatly, putting his elbows on the chair so that his face was close to Sarah's.

Because of his abruptness, Sarah began to feel unsure because she didn't expect anything like this, not to mention a man who was nearly a stranger who dared to get so close to her. For her, Antoine was a kind of wizard from far-away Europe, and that fate had brought them both together on this strange evening. In fact, Sarah could only guess that there was a link between all these events that she had to analyze accurately, and surely it would take some time.

Medium Antoine had the sort of energy that made souls tremble. Sarah couldn't explain it, but she could physically feel it, and didn't even have to talk about her problems to understand she was facing the right person. At first she sat tensely, but finally something relaxed her and she slumped down a bit, completely trusting the one to whom she had come for help. This Frenchman was her light at the end of a dark road. She saw how he was smiling, how his eyes were staring at her and his thin lips were moving. He was breathing freely, naturally comfortable with himself. He seemed to have studied her without words or touches, and she knew that she must be open to him, which was very difficult for a righteous girl that had never been in this kind of intimate contact with anyone before in her life -- the kind of contact that was easier to resist than to accept.

"I need help, I just don't know whom else to ask" she uttered. The psychic medium immediately recoiled from her as if from a flame, and started walking around the room.

"I have no idea where life is leading me, but the only thing that I know it could be some place horrible, and I'm afraid" She finished a phrase almost in a whisper, feeling again the primal fear that seemed to have left her, but in fact it was just as deeply-seated as before, laying in wait, to describe it in three words.

"Another lost soul..." Antoine uttered with a certain pity in his voice. "I think you, mademoiselle, better change your seat now and take the chair in front."

Sarah found it very strange to hear such a request, both seats were the same, and the change of position seemed foolish, but nevertheless, she obediently moved over, engaging steady eye contact with the medium.

Antoine drilled into her with his eyes, diligently trying to read something in her. After a couple of minutes of complete silence, he suddenly turned around and in a matter of seconds had disappeared into his secret room. There was a rumble and fuss, and it became clear that he was rummaging through things trying to find something. Sarah pursed her lips and patiently waited, hoping that he would not be gone for the next half an hour or maybe more. She worried so much, that she began to perspire, primarily being afraid of making a mistake. She also thought that it was not too late to leave this place. What she had decided was clear, only one thing was important: that if this strange-acting medium disappeared again or continued to pace around and waste her time, she would simply walk away. Her patience was running thin and close to running out.

Things eventually turned out quite the opposite of what she had feared. The medium emerged five minutes later holding a half glass/half clay bowl filled with turquoise-colored water. It was an odd, old object, whose handles were twisted in curls in the form of interwoven stems and leaves. Its sides were painted with Greek inscriptions and images of ancient gods. Antoine put the bowl on the table and sat on a chair facing Sarah, then folded his hands on his lap with a completely serious look staring at her at rapt attention. As for Sarah this kind of session was a novelty, she did not have a clue how to behave and what to do or what to say, if anything at all. The psychic medium knew very well how his visitor felt, and therefore deliberately waited, not saying a word; his goal was to make a girl to speak up, not with questions, but to start telling her personal history.

"I saw an angel" Sarah began. "And I don't think I dreamed it. I also saw demons, and they all want something from me."

"To be honest I was expecting to hear something quite different," Antoine said. "I have already faced similar stories. Angels and demons are the favorite eternal discussion of all time."

"So, you do believe in all this?" Sarah asked with a hope.

"Yes, I believe in many things including what you have just said. The world is way more complicated than we all think; everyone needs to adapt and comply with its criteria and most importantly, remember our responsibilities. What do all these demons need from you?"

"These beads, and I want to know their purpose. They have a certain force, it is hard to explain it, it scares me."

Instantly the medium looked at the colorful beads that were on Sarah's neck, partly covered by her red-gold strands of hair. The spheres concealed something hidden, and even with the naked eye it was clear that the necklace was not an ordinary piece of jewelry. Antoine noticed them earlier, but did not want to assume anything, preferring to hear everything from girl's lips. When she mentioned her unusual artifact, the psychic took a deep breath and closed his eyes with whispering something to himself in an unknown language. At some point, Sarah felt lost because the medium was deep in his own thoughts and behaved very strangely, not explaining his actions. As much Sarah tried to focus on the ritual, it was extremely difficult to do this strictly because it was all so odd. She was already sorry that she got involved in this and was ready to just stop everything and ask medium to let her go. But then the unexpected happened.

"Quickly put your hands into the bowl!" Antoine gasped with a hoarse voice, as if he had something stuck in his throat, continuing to remain with his eyes closed.

Sarah shivered as his voice was so loud. Like getting involved in a mad dance, she plunged both hands into the slightly-heated, turquoise water. Her skin was instantly tickled by small bubbles that seemed to bring her comfort and she relaxed like during a spa treatment. At this point the medium sprang up from his place with a stunning cry, firmly grasping Sarah's hands and pressing them to the bottom of the bowl. The girl was frightened and tried to free herself, but was too weak. No one had ever treated her so roughly. She was suddenly afraid that she had fallen into the trap of a maniac and immediately regretted coming there. The nightmare continued for her. She was so scared that nothing mattered but her salvation. Suddenly something strange happened and in what seemed to be just one second, there was darkness all around with only the luminous water and Antoine's face. The medium smiled and released Sarah. She immediately jumped up, breathing laboriously as if just returning from jogging.

"What's going on?" she shouted madly.

"You are now exactly where you want to be to find the answers to your questions. Isn't this what you wanted?" The medium asked. "This is not a parallel reality; this an actual place and events that might uncover something you seek that has been hidden until now.

"I don't understand anything," Sarah said with fear.

Suddenly, she felt the cold accost her, Antoine mysteriously disappeared and an old wooden door emerged from the darkness in front of her. It was noticeable only because through the cracks along where the frame oozed the daylight, poured in a draft so cold that one could believe there was snow on the other side. Sarah walked slowly and unsteadily to the door and listened. She heard the wind through the trees that made the window frames creak and rattle. Sarah held her breath and turned back in fear, hoping to see the medium, but he was not there. Then the girl turned back to the door, feeling inside that it should not be opened. She stared at the door a minute, maybe two, not daring to open it. The draft had become so cold that she started pinching her skin and it was then that she realized, in fact, there was no other choice *but* to open the door. She gently nudged the door with her foot, and as soon as it slowly creaked open she immediately found herself in an empty room where there was absolutely nothing.

Dusk was falling outside with a sunset that filled the sky with a bright red bloody hue, plunging everything into a mystic atmosphere, as large snowflakes fell slowly from the sky. Sarah shivered and could see her breath as she exhaled, not prepared at all for the winter season. She walked to the window and glanced out over the garden with bare trees and a small lake shining on the horizon, thinly covered with ice. She knew this place, she really did, and it was so familiar. Without knowing whether it was a dream or reality, Sarah was somewhat pleased again to see the house of her grandfather in *Merry Old England*. Everything around reminded her of the past when she used to spend many months there. But that was the past, and she knew very well what was now; it was kind of a dream she deeply believed with no other explanation.

Sarah gently closed the window. The noise disappeared right away and there was only an anxious silence. It was comparable to the kind of chilling silence in a morgue when someone from the staff would leave the room and close the heavy door behind them. There was a psychological emptiness and sadness such that the girl could no longer stay there. She started calling Antoine, hoping that he was somewhere nearby and could rescue her from this terrible dream. In the end Sarah realized that the medium was not going to appear so she decided to get help from the beads. As she reached for them on her neck, she wanted to scream discovering that they had inexplicably disappeared. What could be worse than to get stuck in one's own nightmare?

Panicking, Sarah rushed to the door and the floorboards creaked unpleasantly under her feet, as if they were just about to crumble. In a horror the girl could only grasp the icy door knob desperately searching for salvation from this place. It was not as easy as it seemed; Sarah opened the door and could see nothing but impenetrable darkness. So deeply shocked, she strained to open her eyes wide enough to look into the unknown and backed away starting to recite a prayer. In her mind she couldn't understand the fact that God had left her helpless and all alone while something sinister was trying to hurt her. She was more than convinced she'd become the victim of diabolical tricks, and couldn't understand why she deserved such punishment -- especially as she always followed all divine prayers and led a pious life. It was like a curse that brought devastating pain to her heart. Were some of her past actions wrong? If so, what fate awaited those who knew nothing of God, or did torment fall only to those who believed in a higher power and connected to it by ties of faith?

She knelt on the floor near the window, giving up, her eyes flowing with tears. For her, everything that was happening seemed to be crazy and she was completely lost in something inexplicable. Sarah was alone with herself, and there was no one around to answer her prayers. Sitting in front of the open door she was staring in darkness and listening to own beating heart, whose sound now grew louder. She was under terrible stress and hundreds of thoughts were attacking her mind from everywhere. Being involved herself into a big stress where hundreds of thoughts started attacking her brain. She had not even realized that she drifted off to sleep until the silence was interrupted by the sound of water and quacking ducks. The girl slowly raised her eyelids and was momentarily blinded by a flood of bright sunlight. She squinted, covering her eyes with the back of her right hand. She began to make out exotic trees blooming all around her, whose flowers filled the air with a rich fragrance. Nearby there was a small pond with water so clear that it was possible to see the crustaceans on the sandy bottom, a flock of ducks who never stopped quacking even for a moment, and whose constant movement caused splashes that soothed the soul, buzzing bees and humming dragonflies sounded a telltale wind. It all was like a fairy tale. Absolute serenity evoked memories of a magical land, like Oz - a fairy tale that Sarah loved.

She was so deeply engrossed in what she saw that a sudden hammer thud made her flinch and instantly forget everything. It seemed as if she had been doused with icy water. Immediately she turned back around and through the lush thicket of trees, saw the brown peaks of an old mansion, and heard the far-off thud of a hammer striking from that direction. Cautiously considering her next move in that direction, the girl began to wade forward toward the mansion, pushing aside long, spiny branches assaulting her from all sides. Coated with a thin layer of ice, the ground was crunching under her feet like crisp cookies, but with an unpleasant odor of rotting wood rising in the air.

Sarah took a few more steps when suddenly a flock of boisterous crows shot up right from dry, lifeless bushes. The evil birds rose in a swirl, eclipsing everything around and began flapping from side to side, hovering restlessly, dropping down with her in their angry, demonic yellow sights. Being seriously frightened, the girl stumbled back not able to keep the balance and fell to the ground. To hide from such a hateful flock might be possible only with the wave of a magic wand. Fortunately, the winged black shadows only circled in the blue sky another couple of minutes and then completely disappeared. At the same moment Sarah found herself entangled in another thicket of bare trees.

As the sun set, it enveloped everything in a cloak of red and the ground was shrouded in a frigid carpet of multi-colored leaves. A sharp cold permeated the soles of shoes and swallowed up every corner of this once ever-blooming paradise. Like a parasite, it made its silent way up from the feet, stabbing and hacking mercilessly until it reached deep into the body. Sarah only could dream of getting back to the warmth and comfort she craved and to get away from the emptiness. Most of her life she was a lonely victim in a family that figuratively chained her to the house and did not allow to experience anything new that might be pleasing to the eye or to the soul. She was like a bird trapped in a cage, and despite all efforts to escape, nothing had succeeded. With her all-too-conservative family she was literally cut off from the rest of the world. Her sister Julia was much luckier, having spent most of her childhood with a worldly aunt, and in the end, had lived a much richer life.

Having always been closely connected with God, Sarah still longed for some idyllic existence that would nourish life and fill it with meaning, but that was a case of another time. Now she was dragged into loneliness, where she plunged into thoughts wondering if her world outlook was right. As much she tried to not succumb to any doubts, it was hard to avoid. Trying to understand what faith had given her in life, she recognized her reality of pain and suffering. She had lost more than gained, and that was sad. She felt that this was not her real place in life, and this feeling gave her a big wish to go back in time to change everything, longing to start a new and different life.

By this time the early, faint breeze had evolved into something bigger, making uncomfortable conditions even more uncomfortable. Trees began to twist and strain eerily and fallen leaves suddenly soared upward and in different directions. They seemed to come to life, as if possessed by evil spirits that haunted them and interrupted their former peace. The hammering did not stop even for a moment, and only grew louder. Sarah had no idea who would be there in the middle of nowhere, and the strange feelings prompted her not to be too curious and not to try to understand the impossible. In the simplest of words, life had taught her to not invite trouble; sometimes it is useful to simply lie low.

Sarah knew that the search for answers would not lead to anything good. Reluctantly she maneuvered through the thicket, looking around and wincing every time a surprising noise came from anywhere around her. It seemed that terrible imaginings lurked everywhere, waiting for the right moment to attack. If earlier the girl did not want to believe in anything like that, after the events of the previous day she was completely susceptible to accept even the unthinkable.

Taking another step forward the girl suddenly noticed a track of red leaves. They were red not because of the color, but because of fresh, red blood that did not yet have time to clot into a dark, purple hue. Worried, Sarah quickly looked away and tried to figure out what was going on. There on the right, at a distance of two yards near the bushes with the long needles, lay a large basset hound, breathing heavily.

"Ronnie, my dear" Sarah recognized her dog.

A horror froze in Sarah's eyes. She ran to the dog and put her hand on the warm body. The dog whined. The basset's sad eyes were now filled with even more sadness. He barely raised his head and could only wag his tail. At this point, Sarah saw that under his head was a pool of blood.

"What happened my sweet, what happened?"

Hot tears started flowing down Sarah's cheeks. Seeing that her dog was literally dying, she came into a sick and indescribable state of shock. She started shaking and grabbed Ronnie trying to turn him onto his other side. But when she slightly lifted his head she broke into an irrepressible cry. As if scalded by hot liquid, she drew back and fell back on a carpet of dry leaves; the other half of basset's head was a runny, bloody mess without skin or bones. It seemed that someone tore out a huge piece of his flesh-meat and left a bloody hole or had punched his skull with a hammer. Poor Ronnie suffered, and Sarah knew it very well. Her heart agonized because she did not know how to help him or to ease his pain.

The dog whined again and tried desperately to sit up. Sarah sobbed even harder and crawled to him. The brave basset stood up on shaky legs and looked at his mistress. Sarah imagined she saw tears flowing from his eyes. Unable to keep balance, Ronnie fell back down to the ground and whined. It took two more minutes before his labored breathing paused and then he stopped moving.

"Ronnie, Ronnie" Sarah wept heavily, leaning her head against the lifeless dog.

Life delivered another painful and bitter test; first the loss and then the tears, always the same. Sarah could not stop herself. She was crying and crying until her all her tears were spent. This continued until all around was clouded by the arrival of dusk. The girl was lying next to her beloved dog, trembling, and unable to squeeze anything else from herself. Her eyes became clouded with a white veil and an unknown power began to take her to a completely different dimension. She did not understand or have time to even notice how or when she had eventually lost consciousness, but when she did...

Something was rocking Sarah, as if she was on a large swing, and she could only hear the faint whistling of the wind. She was pulling forward, then back, and her body felt an incredible lightness, as if she had turned into a feather. Slowly she opened her eyes and tried to realize where she was and what she was doing. All her current memories suddenly shifted out of the picture. The first thing Sarah found was that Ronnie had mysteriously disappeared, and the only thing left from him were the same bloody footprints on the dried leaves. Sarah jumped up from the ground looking around. Her heart was pounding heavily, as if she had drunk four *ristretti*; she knew that something strangely sinister was going on here. Having decided to not tempt fate, she backed away toward the mansion from where she had heard hammer blows. The girl did not believe in ghosts or zombies, but now more than uncomfortable, strange thoughts began sneaking into her head, most of which concerned life *after* death. What Sarah had feared most finally happened. A rustle came from the side bushes, accompanied with a vicious growl. These were sounds that normally made by wild beasts before pounce on their prey.

"Ronnie?" Sarah called her dog and began slowly to retreat from the bushes.

It took her only a few steps before she entered the vast meadow in front of the mansion, where she saw lights both outside and inside the windows. It was a gray and nondescript building, whose windows of which were obscured with thick half-rotten planks, and old walls blackened by time and covered with moss. In front of the entry into house in the middle of the narrow path was a stone well, and a man in a brown hat who stood next to it. He was dressed as a farmer in a plaid shirt, blue overalls, and dusty black leather boots, battered by years of service to their master. The man was pounding with his hammer on the wooden cover of the well and did not seem to notice Sarah.

The girl decided not to attract attention, and furtively drew closer to the house, continuing every now and then to look back in fear that the beast from bushes would show up, but luckily, it did not. Instead there was another problem - the hammering became so loud and intolerable to Sarah that she could no longer think about anything else but how to avoid screaming from the pain that now assaulted her eardrums. With each strike to the cover of the well, more dust particles and chips flew outward on all sides, irritating the eyes. Not wanting to hear that pounding any longer Sarah stepped back. A dried twig made a piercing crunch, stirring the silence of the scene. Sarah paused, but continued staring at the man attentively memorizing his appearance and hoping he would stop in his crazy actions. Like if the man had read her thoughts, he abruptly stopped hammering and slowly turned his head toward her, like a robot. The hammer fell from his hand to the ground and stuck in the crumbly soil.

The man's fatigued face was grim, not expressing any emotions, just like his absent surroundings. Sarah's intuition told her that he had probably spent many years near the well, without moving from the spot -- without moving one step. She swallowed hard and thought about her next decisions. She had some anxiety, wishing to turn into stone or become invisible. Most of all, she preferred to not see his face and never make an eye contact. But it happened, and she had to do something.

"Grandpa" She whispered, being terribly nervous. "What are you doing?"

"Are you blind?" His garbled voice was heard from everywhere. "Your sister is severely ill, she was poisoned from water of this damn well. Apparently, something leaked in from the pond. Damn."

"Julia is sick?" Sarah blurted out, not believing what she just heard. "Where is she?"

"In her room... where else" The man said grimly. "She will never come out of there, do you hear me?"

"What are you talking about?" questioned Sarah.

"Look around" Shouted the man with an inhumane voice. "What did you wake up from this fucking pit?"

Sarah's eyes widened in horror, realizing that it was not her grandfather and she was not at home. In a matter of seconds, the well's lid started shaking as if someone were trying to get out. The sky overhead abruptly acquired the look of dark-blue paint and seemed ready to collapse in on itself at any moment. Sarah was stunned, wanting only one thing – to make this nightmare disappear. The trees around the meadow suddenly gyrated and bent unnaturally to one side, as if forced by an invisible hurricane or tornado. At the same time, the gentle whistle of the wind had become much stronger until the sound was similar to the cries of raging demons in the depths of an ominous thunderhead, accompanied by occasional hot flashes of jagged lightning. All of it was like the beginning of some sort of apocalypse which decided to punish this land, lost in the depths of the sinister woods and thickets.

"Grandpa, what's going on here?" The girl cried out in fear.

The storm that began instantly reminded her of last night drive from Blackwood to New York City, when the night was inundated by wind, rain, and lightning. Already feeling like she was in one nightmare, another one was ready to begin, but in fact that was not the case at all.

"This is all because of what you have done; you're forever damned," Angrily the man drew up his hefty hammer and forcefully struck the cover.

At that moment all of nature seemed to explode. The earth shook and writhed, surely orchestrated by giant underground worms. The sky burst into endless streams of rain, and the house shuddered so violently that it seemed it would take only a little bit more to be smashed into splinters. Scary sounds were coming from everywhere; Sarah thought this must really be Hell. Howls, crackling, creaking and croaking - all swirled together creating a real nightmare born of insanity. There was no place to escape.

"No, no, I do not want to be here" The girl wrapped herself in hysterics.

She took only one step back when her leg suddenly was grabbed by a hand that shot up from the loose ground and pulled her leg down to the level of her knee. She could not comprehend the full horror of what was going on because it all happened so fast. Sarah struggled to escape from this terrible captivity; she fell to the ground and started clutching desperately at the grass with slender fingers. She screamed -- madly and desperately -- with tears in eyes, calling for help. Sarah had not invoked the name of her grandfather, but Antoine, who so cruelly left her here all alone to be torn to pieces by monsters. She hoped that psychic would appear and everything would stop. But it never happened.

Out of the forest came more howls of wild beasts, forcing her heart to quiver in a most primitive sense. In a flash of lightning the girl saw that her leg was being held by a pair of blue arms whose multiple hands began to spread over the field like spiders stretching their long, thin legs. There was only a guess left to whom they could belong. With no further doubt in her mind, Sarah knew that this horrible place was a cemetery whose living dead decided to suddenly end their sleep and take revenge for their deaths.

"Leave me alone" Sarah screamed and twisted her foot madly to try to escape.

Either it was her anger or the last remnants of her strength, but she eventually escaped from their clutches, still unsteady, she rose to her feet and ran to the house as fast as she could. Like worms writhing in the rain, the rotten blue hands continued to appear around the area. Appendages like these could only belong to a drowned man. The howl of monsters did not cease even for a second, continuing to flood the whole area with fear. It felt as if it was a madhouse. Sarah ran, as fast as she could wishing only to get away from this nightmare. She barreled into the house and only then all the noise instantly stopped as if someone had shut off the sound.

The girl immediately fixed her eyes on the large wooden door adorned with an ornamental metal handle in the form of a snake that was covered by rust, inviting a break in to the empty mansion. The front of the door was covered in blistered and cracked white paint, even yellowing in some parts. It made sense since it had been a long time since anyone had taken care of this place; it had been left to the mercy of time and the elements. Sarah wiped away her tears and gently reached forward. Carefully she turned the handle with a trembling hand. The lock clicked and the door slowly closed with a heavy creaking sound. In a matter of second the room filled with streams of dim, dead light.

It seemed that no one had lived there for a long time: the floor, walls, ceiling, and furnishings were covered with dust and cobwebs. Despite its state of apparent abandon, every part of the house stored memories of the years when it was still occupied by its owners. Sarah remembered absolutely everything; all the details had been so familiar to her. She felt if she'd been sent back into the past. The only thing she didn't remember was why her grandparents' house had deteriorated into what it was today. It was now something reminiscent of a dark, cold and empty charnel house.

Sarah shivered and clutched her forehead, believing that all of this was a bad dream and she urgently wanted to wake up from it. With great difficulty she found courage to slowly, but quite steadily, walk up on the creaky wooden stairs to the second floor to her sister's room - the place where she found herself for the first time right after the session with Antoine. Sarah was afraid to breathe and felt a terror that fully permeated the space and could escalate at any moment. Black walls, shabby tapestries, uneven floors, and weird noises - it might have scared anyone else to death. Sarah was surprised that she had enough strength to go on. She did not have to ponder long; it was obviously her thirst for life that kept her going. Whispering prayers and holding the railing with her left hand, the girl continued walking upstairs. With each creak of the stair step tread, she shuttered but continued on, finally arriving at the landing.

The second floor appeared as a nightmarish vision: there was a long and dark corridor with boarded-up doors on the left from which came a smell of rotting flesh. Dusty, creaky chandeliers swung from side to side, throwing dancing shadows on the faded green walls. A blackened brown rusty door stood at the end of the hall that no one had opened for a hundred years. Sarah winced imagining that the chandeliers were swaying from the touch of evil, unseen ghosts, and she was afraid to make a single step forward, not wanting to incite the fury of anyone or anything.

Sarah drew a deep sigh. But then, next to her right hand, the curtain on the window suddenly fluttered and captured her attention. In a desperate state, she moved quickly to the window and forcefully pulled back the curtain; thankfully no one was there. She preferred to act quickly rather than to hesitate further interaction with the collective horror stored in every corner of this abandoned place. Outside behind a half-broken dirty glass, one could see the dusk had lit everything. The figure of the grandfather was still standing near the well, without moving and without saying a word. The trees were no longer swaying and finally calmed down, slightly arching upward. It seemed that the windstorm had never arrived; the weather returned to normal. The blue hands had vanished leaving no trace, and the land was flat, without any bumps or broken pieces. Sarah paused to be sure her eyes were not playing tricks on her as she tried to wake again into a calm reality. Realizing this reverie could not continue any longer, she began to pinch the flesh of her palm, but couldn't feel anything but pain. Feeling helpless she wanted to scream out loud, but there was no voice to use. She wanted to flee without looking back, to… no matter where, to somewhere, anywhere else, and never see this place ever again. Precisely at that moment, Sarah found herself on edge because of muffled sobs coming from the next room.

"Julia, is that you?" Sarah asked loudly, immediately inclining her ear to the door.

"Yes…" Came the weak voice from behind the door.

"Oh my dear... "Sarah broke in her voice," Do not be afraid, I'm here, I'll help you to get out".

For Sarah it was simply impossible to understand that her younger sister was trapped in this room. The fact made her feel sick and forced her to realize that her grandfather was a true monster, because only monsters could do such a thing to their own kin. Sarah frantically tried to open the door but it would not cooperate; it was firmly boarded up. After many attempts to open it she eventually gave up realizing that without any additional tools the barricade would be impossible to breach.

"Wait, I'll run to get a crowbar and free you!" Sarah said loudly. "Everything will be all right, I promise".

She ran headlong into the basement where she remembered all the tools were. She could not fathom how her grandfather could have ever locked up her younger sister. All of this seemed insane. Sarah quickly entered the kitchen and then went down into the dark, damp dungeon-like basement. Fearing for the life of her little sister was now overpowering; Sarah did not care about anything else that could possibly happen to her. The instinct to protect her loved one awoke inside her and the rest was no longer of any consequence. Somehow in the absolute darkness she found the big cabinet with tools and grabbed a crow bar hurriedly returning to her sister. Sarah still had the feeling that someone was watching her among the odd noises and dancing shadows. She again took the familiar stairs when she heard a sound like someone running on the first floor.

"Hey", she called out loudly, making a desperate attempt to rid herself of fear.

Carefully and defensively, she held the crow bar in front of her and came up to the second floor but she couldn't see anyone. As before, the chandeliers were still swinging, as a cold northern wind blew through the broken window. The incessant hammering was still coming from the outside, but the room itself was silent. Sarah called out to her sister again, but no answer. In a panic, she brought the bar to the door and started detaching the boards that blocked it. There were crackles and creaks, and curving, rusty nails flying in all directions. Once the last board was freed from the door, falling with a thud to the floor, the hammering from outside also suddenly stopped. Sarah quickly ran to the window and saw that the whole area outside was covered with snow, and the spot next to the well was now empty. Meanwhile, the house continued to maintain a steadfast silence without evidence of any disturbance. Sarah was looking around when she heard a menacing growl. At the end of the corridor stood the basset hound, bearing his teeth, his body covered in blood, and mysteriously staring at his mistress with haunting, glowing yellow eyes.

"Ronnie?" called out the frightened girl, knowing full well in the depths of her soul that her words did not mean anything to the beast. She knew that this was not her dog, not anymore, but instead some demon who had invaded his body.

The girl was now frightened of her former dog that had once loved her so much. Her last desire was to anger the beast with any wild movements, so she slowly moved toward her sister's room, carefully positioning her hand on the door. Keeping both eyes firmly planted on the dog, Sarah took a deep breath sincerely hoping that everything would be all right. The basset began barking loudly and sending saliva spewing through the air as he launched from his spot toward her.

"Aaaaaaaahhh", Sarah screamed and ran into the room, shutting the door firmly behind her and holding it shut with all her might.

The dog began to bark and howl loudly, scratching and struggling to get inside. Thick claws were literally tearing the wooden door to splinters.

"Calm down, you, horrible creature!!!" shouted Sarah hysterically.

It seemed that Ronnie listened and understood those words. He calmed down in an instant and was eerily quiet. Sarah held her breath as she put her ear to the door. What she could hear was only the whistling wind. It felt like there was a real blizzard rising outside, but nothing inside.

"He's gone… I can feel it" suddenly there was a thin voice.

Sarah turned back and focused her sight on the corner of the room. There on the dirty stone floor cowered a brown-haired girl. She had a tear-stained face and was shaking pitifully, while looking up at her sister. To her left Sarah could make out a cast iron mug filled with yellowed water.

"Julia, what's happened?" Sarah ran to her sister and hugged her tightly.

"Grandpa locked me here and said he said he would never release me because I am possessed by an evil spirit" the brown-haired girl blurted out as she burst into tears.

"Hush… hush… you're in safe hands now" Sarah began to calm her little sister, gently stroking her hair. "We just need to quickly and quietly get out of here. There is something wrong with grandfather; he is not at all himself and I suspect he is very ill. Come with me; I'll take you away from this horrible place".

"But what if he comes after us"? stammered Julia, glancing anxiously at the door.

"He won't, but if he did, I would not let him hurt you," Sarah reaffirmed her promises. She knew that there was not much time to waste and they needed to keep moving. The man who was supposed to be her grandfather was not outside anymore which meant that he possibly was somewhere in the house. It did not portend anything good.

Two girls, clasping each other's hands stood up, when a loud clap, as if someone set off a powerful firecracker, pierced the air. The front door opened first with a crack and then began to further open quite slowly, as if being urged by a persistent draft. Sarah was very afraid Ronnie had come back, and prepared for the worst. She did not want to have to deal with an aggressive demon-dog. Nervously she picked up the crow bar with one hand and took a position in front of Julia to shield her, expecting being pounced upon by a mad monster at any moment.

"Is it Ronnie? What happened to Ronnie?" Julia's eyes filled with tears. "Is he hurt?... dead? Is he trying to hurt us?" little girl asked Sarah, with a face that showed complete shock and the child's lack of understanding.

"Yes, Julia, our precious Ronnie is dead. I will explain things later. For right now, we just have to watch out for who has taken his place" stammered Sarah. "We need to get out of this damn place. Let's go to Aunt Emma's".

After attending a couple of minutes of silence Sarah considered that the demon-dog wasn't there - or at least she hoped not. Sarah pulled the perplexed Julia into the corridor and, as it turned out, at just the right time. At the end near the rusty brown door appeared grandfather's silhouette in a shabby hat, and fiercely holding the hammer in his hand. His face showed an eerie pallor, like a dead man, or a ghost -- not a man.

"You are not going anywhere, you naughty girls" his hoarse voice sounded like thunder. "I will not allow you to leave this house, you will stay here forever!!".

"No! I am not staying here!!!" Julia screamed and wriggled out of the hand of Sarah and ran down to the first floor.

"Julia, wait!", Sarah screamed.

With big steps grandfather walked toward her, hollowly stepping with heavy heels on the creaking floor, and with all his strength striking a hammer against the walls. It seemed he was possessed by something dark and sinister that was forcing him to destroy everything in his path. His blows to the walls forced concrete shards and splinters to scatter in all directions.

"Because you disobeyed me, I will make you learn your lesson", shouted the man.

Sarah was enveloped in primal horror. Without waiting for a demon who had taken possession of her grandfather's body, she threw the crow bar aside, whirled around and rushed headlong to the ground floor. Behind her, there was a twisting sound as the stair rail demonically bent forward; before her the front door unexpectedly slammed shut. At some point, it seemed to her that her grandfather was getting very close, and she let out a chilling scream.

"Julia! Julia!", Sarah screamed as loudly as she could, seeing the young girl running farther and farther away. "Wait for me... I beg you...STOP!!!!".

The brown-haired girl did not turn back, and Sarah had nothing left to do but follow Julia's trail in the snow. It was better than waiting for her enraged grandfather to reach her and continue swinging his deadly hammer in all directions. Sarah was very afraid of losing sight of Julia who was moving away so quickly she decided to continue shouting her name. For a moment Sarah slowed down near the well which caught her attention. The wooden cover was now adorned with long, sharp nails spiking upward which seemed so strange. It was just useless to try to understand anything else, and her main concern was to catch up with Julia. She heard a wild sound which turned out to be coming from the well's lid. Without any reason, it flew up in the air and was followed by thick clouds of white steam and the sound of a malevolent animal's growl. The area began to be enveloped by a mysterious mist. Sarah hardly noticed it, or the frigid conditions, as she ran quickly past the snowdrifts that had formed.

Stopping at any point now would no longer be a choice since she had momentarily lost sight of Julia. Sarah continued running forward deep into the garden. In these severe weather conditions, any delay could bring on fatal hypothermia. She had already begun to cease feeling her arms and legs, as well as feeling the stinging effects of the bitter cold. She did not notice that she began crossing the once familiar lake which now had a thick crust of ice. If the snow was not a reflective, crystal white and the moon in the sky had not shone in all its fullness, it would have been hard to distinguish anything at all in the thick evening twilight. All traces of Julia had vanished. Sarah came to a screeching halt, not knowing where to go next. Desperately she began to call her sister so loudly that the plaintive echoes resounded throughout the whole area, but there was only silence in return. The tears flowed down her red cheeks as she felt helpless and fell to her knees with a clouded consciousness, not seeing any way back. She felt as if she were a snowflake adrift in an ocean of snow and ice, and the wind was pushing her from side to side. She stopped, trying to understand the reality before her, staring blindly forward. A strange knocking sound came to her attention. It was not grandfather's hammer but something else coming from under the ice somewhere in the center of the lake. At first it seemed to be a hallucination, but then it became very clear and very real. She abruptly stood up, shaky and shaken, unable to control herself. Her head felt like it was impaled by icicles as wild pain shot through her entire body. It was just not possible for Sarah to stand still or she would die; a strange strength and curiosity pushed her to move forward.

While looking through blurry, narrowed eyes to the center of the lake, she took a few tentative steps forward at a time, making sure that the ice was strong enough to support her. The snow was crunching under her feet and the ice sometimes was crackling dangerously. With each step, it got worse and worse. Sarah imagined that the icy abyss would cover her head and suffocate her under the water, with no one to know what had happened or where she had gone. Her fear was well-founded because at any moment it was exactly what could happen.

When Sarah reached the place where heard the knocking, she cleared the snow on the ice so that what became visible was the icy, bluish floor. It was such a strange feeling to hear such purposeful sound from below. Sarah squatted down and began to stare deeply into the icy window, hoping to see something -- but what she could see in the dark of the night? The water suddenly lit up and from the depths she could see the body of a brown-haired girl.

"Julia, NOOOOO!", Sarah cried and drew back. The ice parted under her feet in an instant, and she fell into the dark, unknown depths of the lake, blacking out.

"Come back", Sarah heard a familiar, far away voice.

She awoke to find herself in total darkness. It was so cold and empty but it was not under the frozen lake. It was larger and full of echoes like an underground cave. Here and there could be heard dripping sounds. Like small bells the drops were beckoning her. As she stood up, it seemed as if she had somewhat awakened but was still not fully aware of this reality. She started looking around, trying to see at least something. The picture she held in her mind was of her dear sister whom she loved with all her heart and who surely needed protection. Shouting Julia's name, Sarah was trying to understand what was going on, but the darkness did not dissipate. She started walking slowly -- to nowhere -- crying intensely like she cried after her mother's death. Sarah now found herself on a soft, unstable floor that made it very difficult to stay balanced. Continuing to repeat her sister's name, her voice gradually lowered, lessened, and became a wheeze. Her head was buzzing from the empty darkness and she had to stop walking. Once again, a familiar voice was heard:

"Come back"!

Only now, Sarah *was* able to recognize the voice. Her memory was coming back to her and she stopped crying. She knew that the psychic medium was somewhere close by.

"Antoine"! She screamed desperately. "I beg you, I do not want to be here anymore. Please, Antoine".

With her plea, there was a sudden clap of thunder and rain started pouring down in torrents. The poor girl felt like a mole, having never been in such a dark place before. Everything seemed so real and yet she was still completely confused, trying to understand what was real and what was a terrible dream. It seemed to her that she was now in some kind of grove because she could hear the movement of tree limbs and rustling leaves. Continuing to call the medium's name now, not Julia's, Sarah understood that everything else at this point was useless. This seemed to be the only solution to finding a real way out. One step at a time she moved forward, off in the distance, she saw a bright lightning strike. It lit up the area, indeed a dark forest, which did not look very inviting. With outstretched hands, trying to avoid what she could not see, the girl carefully inched toward her mental picture of the forest up ahead. She walked for a very long time but still had not reached the tree line. Sarah felt worried that in the darkness she had been going the wrong way. She needed another bolt of lightning to guide her way.

"Lord, if you hear me, please, show me the way", Sarah whispered, while still filled with great fear. "Don't make me stay in this evil place".

As if by the wave of a magic wand there were several rapid lightning strikes. They lasted for only a few seconds, but shed enough light to see that nearly right in front of her was not a forest, but a dozen extremely large, ferocious coyotes. The hair on their necks stood on end and Sarah just opened her mouth and began to back away, not having the slightest idea where she could hide. Her first thought was to question why she had received such a response from God who was supposed to protect her. Her head filled with thoughts of a painful death if the beasts pounced on her. She was sure they were eager to tear her into pieces, scattering her blood in all directions. The indescribable horror gripped the poor girl and wherever she turned, there was nothing but complete darkness. Having lost all hope, Sarah ran forward in haste under the canopy of thunder, rain, and lightning. Surprisingly with the next flash of lightning she saw a deep crevasse in the ground into which she nearly fell. She stopped abruptly and skidded on the slippery ground not easily able to stop herself. She fell into the mud, striking her knee on a rock just before the precipice which would have sent her plunging straight down. Crying out from the pain she rolled over on her back. Looking up, she saw something hanging over her -- the sinister face of a terrible clown with blurred makeup and gore in the corners of his mouth. He smiled mischievously and glared down at girl lying helplessly in the mud.

"No... no... NO!" Sarah cried out in panic and crawling backward when the clown jumped at her and tightly grabbed her shoulders.

In a wild terror, Sarah seemed suspended in time, not believing that she could survive the moment. She seemed to be on death row, where there was no justice, and whatever truth there was in anything, none of it mattered. Her shoulders were being held so and tightly, squeezing what remained of the life, out of her. She could not even draw a breath and let out her last scream.

Suddenly, everything ended. She opened her eyes and saw that she was in the medium's salon. Antoine was sitting beside her on the arm of the chair and looked at her pitifully, finally stopping shaking her shoulders, trying to wake her up.

"No, no, no, no!" The girl burst into tears, looking at the medium.

She was never as frightened as she was in this moment, feeling as if her life had been robbed from her, cursed and forever locked up in a most sinister place. The first thing Sarah thought was that it all seemed too real to be simply a bad dream. Another one like this she would not survive.

Antoine waited patiently, as he knew it was necessary to give his visitor the time to release her emotions, to calm down, and to return to the present. He also knew something that Sarah could not have never imagined: his consciousness was paralyzed, so much so, that for the first time in his life he felt a great loss of how to react.

"Did you find the answers?" he asked inquisitively when Sarah stopped sobbing.

The girl was calmer now with her head bent forward and remaining completely indifferent to what was going on, completely engrossed thinking about something else.

"I... I do not know" Sarah whispered powerlessly, raising her eyes to the medium and still trying to be sure that she was in the present time's reality. "It was worse than I could have ever imagined. You did not warn me -- do you hear me? -- you did not warn me, you son of a bitch!".

"You were plunged into the past, were you not?" The psychic medium began to focus the conversation.

"Yes, I saw my past, and I would never want to return to it ever again".

"You should not. The question is, have you found the answers you sought?"

Sarah clutched at her neck to see if the beads that were indeed missing as she thought. What a surprise it was to feel them lying obediently where they had always lain. They had never disappeared; not in this reality. Only now she fully believed that all that had happened was just a bad dream.

"No, I did not find the answers" she spat out the words to the medium. "I re-lived my past, and I don't understand why I returned to that day" Her voice was full of anger and despair. Wobbling on the edge of a breakdown, Sarah tried to restrain her emotions.

"You returned there for a reason because it was an important moment. Believe me, if that day had not significant to your life, you would have never plummeted into it again. You do not have to answer me here and now; my advice is simple - try to figure out exactly what really happened that day, how it changed your life, and whether or not there is something in it that continues to haunt you?"

"I think that…" The girl began.

"Shhhh" Antoine put his finger to his lips. "Do not answer now. Come back when you have *your* answers. Only then I can help you."

"To help with what? To save me from more insane persecution from an array of maniacs?" Sarah became even angrier.

She suddenly had a feeling that she was wasting her time in an incomprehensible, endless ritual that had no result. There was only pain and terrible memories of the past which had lain hidden in her unconscious for many years. She felt betrayed wanted to get away from the salon as soon as possible. Injustice seemed to have once again greeted her as an old friend.

"Thank you for your time and help," She said, barely able to restrain her anger and abruptly rose from her chair taking a something from her purse. "I hope you accept credit cards?" she said, presenting the plastic money.

"I will not take payment for this session," Antoine said calmly. "Save it for next time when you come back".

"I do not think that there shall be a next time." Sarah interrupted, she could feel herself shaking on the inside.

The psychic medium only smiled enigmatically and wished her a good day. The girl fought herself, but at the same time had a strange feeling that everything had happened for a reason. She turned around and walked quickly to the front door. Once outside in the street, she shivered from the cold that had arrived while she was with the medium. Sarah wanted to return home as soon as possible. Despite bad memories about the clown that broke into John's house, she felt safer there with her dear friend than here now all alone. She successfully hailed a taxi, managing to give the driver the address in Brooklyn. Sitting on a back seat she was watching the night avenues flooded with light, tourists and smoke, whiz by her. Streets that were full of energy; streets teeming with life that would never stop.

This was the reality in which the defenseless girl found herself on the first day of her stay in The Big Apple. A collision of memories, people and situations both real and imaginary, and other events that simply had no rational explanation. Experiences alarming to the mind, frightening to the bone, and all with dark warning signs of the threatening shadow hanging over humanity.

CHAPTER 2: NYC TALES

There once was a prince. He was a dark-haired, tall man with blue eyes, and a snow-white smile whose expressive facial features emphasized his regal perfection. He was also clean-shaven and smelled so inviting that it could entice one to jump into his arms. His name was John and he lived in New York - the greatest of all the kingdoms where stood the tallest tower in the world and from which everything was visible, even places far across the sea. Although he did not rule the kingdom, his status granted him full access to all its treasured rooms. His status also afforded him quite considerable power. Many beauties wanted to become his beloved, but he rejected all, pledging his heart to the one who was unfortunately indifferent to all his courtship. She came from a simple family - neither noble nor of renown to anyone. But it was neither nobility nor money that was his interest. It was her soul, clean and kind, her brown hair, and big brown eyes whose external form complemented her inner beauty. This wild flower, named Julia, had beautiful pink petals, a strong green stem, and a few sharp, hidden thorns. The prince needed to take care as he tried to win the flower as his own; admiring the beauty while avoiding the prickly thorns. He firmly believed that sooner or later she would become his one and only, so he was ready for any test she put forth. Coincidently, Julia's sister was his close friend, which in the end gave him many advantages. Particularly so that by sheer chance she moved into his castle for a short time. Brief, but there nonetheless.

Sarah knew the whole truth. She knew that Julia was not easily swayed, and that she was not wooed by John's courtship -- no matter how romantic it seemed. Feeling that time would ultimately guide everything, Julia left for an internship in Paris. A well-known house of *haute couture* offered her a once-in-a-lifetime opportunity that she could not refuse. Sarah couldn't say that her sister was exactly focused on climbing the social ladder of the fashion world, but that was indeed coming to pass. Julia was a very sensitive and kind person, but the moment John started his courtship, it was clear that she was not yet ready for anything serious. Julia thought of the many people she knew who sacrificed their life dreams for an ultimately unhappy love. She was very aware of her feelings for John, and that if love was true and sincere, it would not wain in a year or two of separation.

"Is there any news from your sister?" John attentively looked at Sarah, hoping to hear something about the one for whom his feelings smoldered.

For Sarah this was an odd question because she believed that John and her sister had maintained a strong connection. She was very fond of her sister, but after Julia went abroad even they began to communicate less and less frequently, mostly because of Julia's employment which left her little free time and also because of the long distance and time difference. It was both difficult and sensitive to answer exactly why their communication had devolved from connected conversations to brief, uneventful chats. Sarah really did not have a clear picture of the life Julia was living since she had practically isolated herself from everyone by leaving for another country.

"All good, " Sarah managed to say, feeling confused and guilty that she couldn't say more about her sister, whom she supposedly knew as well as the five fingers of her right hand. Sarah knew it was no one's fault, just that it was an unfortunate, bitter reality in which sometimes relatives don't really know each other as well as, for example, a mother could know her own child.

Her gaze fell to John's hirsute arms, which were crossed on the top of the table. A faint smile appeared on her face; the man noticed and smiled in reply and asked what was going on. The girl immediately became embarrassed and a little uncomfortable. She responded with something distracting about just being glad to be with him this day which had turned out to be unusually sunny and quite soulful.

After all the events that had taken place in Blackwood and at the salon of the psychic medium a two good months had come and gone. December now arrived and Sarah found a job at *MAGiC* Corporation's coffee shop. For quite some time she had not slept properly, always having nightmares, with unfound fears in close pursuit because she was so afraid that one night the sinister clown could return. She had to take sleeping pills which caused her to have frequent mood swings and a perceptible low-grade depression. Her anxiety eased only after a few weeks had passed and she began actively searching for employment. With John's support she found a job in a very familiar setting.

Life had finally begun to get better and she hoped that her dreams might once again come true; they needed only perseverance and purpose. After so many prayers the Lord finally heard Sarah, intensifying her faith. She found a Baptist church near Brooklyn where she went every Sunday morning, or if she had to work, she always tried to go attend the evening service. Convinced that all her misfortunes happened soon after she took possession of the mysterious beads, she decided to stop wearing them. The evening when she returned from the psychic medium Antoine, she hid them in her suitcase, deep underneath some clothes so as to not to touch them anymore. Her relationship with father, who first had worried deeply about his daughter, finally seemed to return to normal. After visiting his *little girl* and making sure that everything was in all right, he worried no longer. The only negative point to this story was that those notorious thugs from Blackwood had never been found. The police had not closed the case, even though they had no promising leads. Thoughts about those men briefly concerned Sarah, but not for long once she considered how well she had assimilated into the city; even the devil himself could not find her.

"The last time I talked to her, she mentioned something about coming back to New York City for a fashion show at Elena Barbella's home and place of business," John said.

"My sister always keeps everything as a secret until the last moment" Sarah said with some noticeable resentment in her voice.

She was a bit angry about not speaking much with Julia during her absence. Sarah knew that was just the way of her younger sister and she loved her in spite of her shortcomings. They were connected by so much more than just by blood ties. She was very glad that Julia had been brave enough to take big steps in life, all thanks to the fact that she grew up with a maiden aunt in the most fashionable city in the world. Being part of Lena Barbella's show was a privilege and a wide-open door into the highly-regulated and restricted world of fashion. Sarah hoped that the meeting with her sister would not be long in coming, and would serve as a step toward reuniting the family. The only meaningful solution to fill the gaping hole in the family relations was to have faith and patience.

Not forgetting for a moment the harm that had come to her, Sarah thanked the Lord every day for saving her and showing the way to a completely different life and world, with good people now surrounding her. Feeling reborn she lived a new life, fully confident that she had passed her biggest test. Despite the complicated schedule and intensive work, Sarah was happy in her own way as she lived in the city of her dreams. Multicultural, always evolving, and never stopping for more than a moment, this city grew deeply into her heart. Sometimes Sarah would spend hours in some nice coffee shop (Jack's Bean was one from the short list) just watching the unfolding of metropolitan life, or walking along her beloved and treasured Hudson River. Often, she'd walk down from Central Park to the river's bank that offered amazing views of the city and where it was possible to dive head first into her infinite thoughts. Sarah especially liked to sit on the benches in The High Line when making plans for the future. Heavy on her mind was the search for an apartment because she did not want to overstay John's kindness. Although he was her friend, she planned to move into a new place of her own by spring.

The fall days flew by into the coming winter. The nights grew darker and the temperature of the air kept fluctuating causing her to have headaches. Winter was much closer than it seemed, which made her mood vary as well. Sometimes the girl wanted to leave everything behind and go back to Blackwood, while in other moments, she was inspired by the world she saw all around her that somehow gave her the strength to continue living there regardless of her difficulties. Sarah was swimming in the ocean of her thoughts about her life goals and had literally lost track of time. As if in a trance, she sat with her eyes closed until she heard a voice:

"Baby, you are wanted on the floor".

Sarah looked up and saw in front of her a slightly plump brunette with glasses, twenty-eight years old, holding a reproachful stare. It was her colleague from work, Barbara Shors, whom others secretly called "Ashtray" because she used to take too many annoying smoking breaks thus pissing off her co-workers. Sarah, however, had built quite a friendly relationship with her. They had become pretty close friends and often would meet up to spend time together in the City doing shopping, going to the movies, or just walking around while talking about everything.

"Oh" Sarah said in surprise; she had not noticed that she had dozed off on her break. "What time is it now?" She felt suddenly stressed.

"Don't worry" Barbara laughed. "You still have at least five minutes".

"Well, you really scared me" Sarah said checking the time on her phone. Quickly she got up from a chair and proceeded into the hall without even listening to what else Barbara was trying to tell her. Sarah was always punctual and did not do well with even slight delays. Sometimes people would ask her if she was born in Switzerland, where everything was supposed to operate like clockwork.

Once Sarah got back to work she saw her manager, Kate Johnson, who was standing behind her desk stubbornly re-counting orders for the next day. She was a young blonde woman also of twenty-eight, who had recently moved to New York City from Chicago and quite easily discovered a good start for a future career. She was familiar with big cities, and she had quickly "found her place". It was she who hired Sarah into her first position. From the very first day and initial encounters, they got along very well. Nevertheless, at work Kate remained a person of principles, first paying great attention to professionalism with her colleagues and only then considering possible friendships. Kate had also became "a lead". She, among all the other managers, arranged the very competitive coffee art competition for baristas from all around the globe. The annual event also attracted many new customers and made The *MAGiC* Coffee Shoppe one of the main attractions in the City.

"Sarah" Kate said, not taking her eyes off the papers. "Table 11 is waiting, and there is no one to wait on the customers".

"I'll take it; no worries." Sarah said, as she headed to the table next to the window with a beautiful view of the City.

The first thing that caught her eye was the soot-black hair of the customer, a little long and unkempt, descending to the collar of his equally black coat. Seeing him only from the back, Sarah felt that she would be dealing with an unusual person. Approaching him cautiously while walking around the table, her smile disappeared as she came face-to-face with this stranger. It was rather shocking to look this man in the eye. She saw his pale skin and gloomy dull look and immediately wanted to serve someone else -- anyone else -- but he. His appearance reminded her of a vampire from ominous tales. If his skin were a little bit paler all of his veins would be clearly visible through his paper like skin. Sarah considered that this kind of unhealthy appearance might mean that the guy was simply ill, but the only sensible thing to do was to ask was if he wished to order something.

"What is your name Miss?" He asked in a deep, low voice.

"Sarah", the girl responded, remembering she had forgotten to put on her name tag.

"Nice to meet you", the man said and held out his hand. "My name is Igor".

"Nice to meet you too", Sarah said, being gripped in his uncomfortably strong handshake. She quickly tried to release her hand. She abruptly asked, "Are you from Europe?"

"My parents were from Eastern Europe, but I was born here in the States, in New York. Surely you are from another state, no?"

"I'm from Pennsylvania".

"I'd say we were neighbors then! ... And what brought you here? -- if I may ask such a personal question? You don't have to answer."

"Living in New York has always been one of my goals, so here I am."

"Isn't it amazing when dreams come true?" There was a strange and very unpleasant energy in his voice.

"Of course", she said tentatively. "It's why I'm happy" Sarah was ready to change the subject.

"Excellent. I haven't seen you here before. How long have you been working in this coffee shop?"

"Oh… about a month".

"Welcome. I hope you like it here."

This phrase totally confused Sarah. She had no idea with whom she was speaking, but she was certain that it was someone from management. Only now, when she had a closer look at him, she confirmed one of her earlier assumptions that he might be a worker: under his half-opened coat was an icon of the *MAGiC* Corporation in the form of a black star on his shirt - the kind only worn by employees of the corporation.

"May I offer you something sir?" These words automatically flew out of her mouth.

"Just a coffee. Black. No sugar".

Returning in a rush to the desk and interrupting Kate from work, Sarah asked her if she knew the customer at the Table 11. Kate squinted forward and then said that it was Igor Miltent, second in command after Migren Litsiona, who was the head of the *MAGiC* world-wide corporate offices. He owned a collection of world-renown restaurants and cafes, which were also under the quiet auspices of *MAGiC*. In a word, he had just as much power in his hands as Litsiona did.

Sarah at first was speechless once she has learned about Igor; she did not expect to have a real conversation with one of the most important people on the planet. For her this was tantamount to a spontaneous meeting with the president of a country. Of course, she had heard of Igor Miltent many times over, but she did not remember what he looked like. Every time he appeared on television his face was obscured for some unknown reason. Some shadow would always fall directly on him and make his facial features not clearly visible. Sarah instantly felt a great responsibility in terms of service, at the same time she decided not to change anything in her behavior and to just simply be herself. Nevertheless, she was aware of the importance of the situation and could not afford a tactless reaction. Serving the coffee to Igor, she considered the importance of letting him know that she was glad to work in a coffee shop with such a stellar reputation, where the management created the most comfortable work conditions, where respect played a significant role, and where care was shown every step of the way both inside and outside the company.

These seemingly ordinary details allowed the creation of the best service, friendliest atmosphere, and the delivery of full-flavored, quality coffee -- famous all over the planet -- all of which were important criteria when Sarah was in search of job.

"I'm very happy to hear this Sarah", Igor smiled. "I hope you feel good in New York." he said dreamily. "I can only imagine what it took to change this one-time "little Blackwood" into a huge metropolis. Good luck. Do not hesitate to contact me if I can be of any help to you."

Throughout the day Sarah pondered how Igor Miltent learned that she was from Blackwood. At first, she tried to assure herself that he, as the director, had unlimited access to the dossier of all who worked in the corporation with something as simple as a mobile application. But even if it was so, why would he know such an unimportant detail such as what town she was from? No matter at what angle she approached the question, she never found an answer that made sense. In her mind's eye was a frozen image of Igor as he was leaving the coffee shop. He had glanced at her, and it was one of the most bizarre sights Sarah had ever seen in her life. It seemed to her that his eyes had turned black, like ink, as if life had left them, and it literally scared her. Sarah wanted to quickly forget all this, believing that it was only her overactive imagination prompted by the events from the past. Late into the night, her mind kept seeing the same picture: Igor Miltent with his pale skin, cold smile, and deadly black eyes. This image was plastered into her brain and it was impossible to chisel it away.

Sarah was even afraid to fall asleep thinking that nightmares would again invade her reality; strangely enough, though, there were no nightmares. She did however have one very odd dream. She dreamed that Julia, John, and she were together somewhere in the mountains on a hill from which there was nothing to be seen except an endless forest valley below. At some point they needed to get somewhere. It turned out that the only way to proceed was on a tiny, narrow path along an overhung cliff. The mountain side of the path would sometimes crumble sending rocks and small boulders careening down onto the path, obstructing the way, or tumbling down to the valley floor. There were also weak, unstable points along the path itself making the journey even more perilous. After one such shift in the path Sarah began to feel herself sliding downward but she grabbed at the mountain wall to try to hold on. She noticed three, tall, yellowish stones, covered with cracks protruding from the edge of the cliff. Sarah was very scared to take even a single step but she knew that there was no other way. She had to push herself forward somehow. Her greatest fear came to light as the ground under her left foot began to disintegrate further. Sarah screamed as it started to drag her down.

"No-o-o" She cried and extended her hand to John. "John help me!".

John miraculously caught Sarah but couldn't keep her hands clasped in his as the terrified, screaming girl slipped closer the very edge of the cliff. She wriggled and squirmed managing to grab the short clay middle stone of the trio. It looked sturdy enough but it suddenly began crumbling into small pieces causing her to lose her grip. Sarah thought that this was the end. She was hanging over the cliff of a terrible gorge, and the last hope for which she was clinging to life was literally slipping through her fingers. Her voice exploded into a desperate scream.

Sarah woke up with a sudden, shuddering start. It was four in the morning and once again her sleep was abruptly interrupted. She felt there was not enough air in the house and it felt so stuffy that she decided to get up, get dressed, and go to "Jack's Bean" which thankfully was open, even at this hour. Since the events with the maniacal clown it was her first very early morning visit of this place that became to her very special - a part of her every day routine. Thinking that perhaps she wasn't scared was wrong. Bad memories still occupied her mind so that the entire way down the street, she would constantly look around her. Fortunately for her there was no one in the street and once she got inside the cafe she would feel safe. Again she took her flat white and picked her favorite spot near the window from where she could see the most of the street with its beautiful nightlights.

Suffering under the aegis of her nightmare, Sarah tried to consider some possible interpretations but without any success. She used one dream interpretation website after another trying to find meaning, but almost everything she found was of little use and no solace. Eventually she gave up, put her phone aside and looked at the barista bar. Lily was standing there, holding her head in her hands and leaning on both elbows, staring blankly at the TV screen delivering a mindless infomercial about weight loss. It was not clear whether she was hearing anything at all, as the sound was muffled by the unbearable drone of the fan. It seemed that the barista girl was in a different dimension, hypnotized and completely detached from reality.

"Lily..." Sarah called, but soon realized that she had not said loud enough, since the barista didn't even flinch. "LILY!" She repeated, much louder this time.

"...What?..." She threw an empty look at Sarah.

"Lily, have you ever thought of asking the boss to replace this terrible fan?"

"...Amelia..."

"What?"

"My name is Amelia, not Lily."

"But... I thought your name was Lily!?!"

"It was last month -- but this month I prefer to be called Amelia."

Sarah felt completely confused. She had always known this girl by one name and to now call her something different was a big surprise and more than a little weird. She could only guess at what name barista-girl might choose for following month.

"Yes, I told the boss once" Amelia looked up at the ceiling trying to remember something, while at the same time catching sight of the cobweb in the corner where a little black spider was sitting peacefully. "... uhhh...It was his grandmother's fan. Apparently, it has great sentimental value to him."

"And was the TV also hers?" Sarah asked, deepening the already perplex conversation.

The phone next to her vibrated and displayed a text message that took all her attention and might be one of the happiest moments of Sarah's life.

The message was from Julia who had made up her mind and would be arriving in New York in exactly one week. Sarah didn't expect such a wonderful surprise, especially so early in the morning. The girl was consumed by what she read over and over. She mentally started to count every second, imagining what would happen when she finally met up with her sister after such a long separation. The following six days stretched out into an eternity as the wait felt unbearable not only to her. The same was true for John. The guy noticeably brightened up, and the fatigue on his face disappeared. One could imagine that the message from Julia was a magical elixir for everyone.

Finally, the day had arrived. Sarah had planned a special dinner in advance and from the start of the morning was on pins and needles impatiently waiting for the long-awaited moment. She even came to the airport an hour before Julia's scheduled arrival time. Sarah really hoped that the plane would somehow miraculously land earlier than it was scheduled to do. It was a childlike thought of pure excitement. Unfortunately for Sarah that didn't happen, but when she saw on the arrivals screen the word "landed", her eyes flashed with incredible love and joy.

When Julia first came out of the baggage claim area Sarah could not believe that she was actually seeing her sister. Over the past year Julia had changed incredibly -- and in a much better way -- primarily in terms of appearance. The fashion world helped her a lot. She was a tall, thin girl, who had just turned twenty-four years old. Julia had a mane of chestnut hair which tumbled smoothly onto her shoulders, her mouth was surrounded by bright red lips, and her face was framed by expressive hazel eyes, rich with lush liner. The more you looked at her, the more apparent was her beauty. She looked like a model from the cover of a magazine, dressed in a tightly-fitted white dress with black stripes, cinched at the waist with a wide black belt. Even in her stiletto heels, she strode quickly over to her sister, with her hands stretched out in unabashed joy.

"Sarah!" She shrieked with joy and caused many of the passengers looked around.

The two sisters fell into each other's arms, overwhelmed by tears of happiness. This had become an unforgettable and soul-touching moment for both of them. John was not able to be part of the "welcoming committee" because he was working, but promised to come to dinner right after his workday was done. The entire time they were in the taxi, the girls chatted incessantly just like in the old days. Julia still could not believe that her sister had finally come back to New York City for good. For her this was the best possible news because they could see much more of each other and really be together again. They both cried, and laughed, and recalled so much from their shared past. There were moments when Sarah believed that now her life could be even better than she had once imagined. At the entrance to the house, Julia unexpectedly pulled out VIP invitations for her sister and John to attend the fashion show, taking place at a private party in the mansion of Lena Barbella - a famous US fashion designer.

"I will finally get to present my first big collection!" exclaimed Julia.

"Unbelievable! I know how hard you've worked to have this day finally arrive" joyfully cried Sarah.

She was completely delighted. Ecstatic for the success of a person so close to her; she was more proud than ever of Julia and her accomplishments. Right away she held her sister tightly and whispered in her ear how happy she was for her. They went up to Sarah's room, and as the two best friends they were once again, sat down on the bed and continued their incessant chatter. Julia took out a pile of cosmetics and perfumes, little trinkets and gifts from Paris, and handed them to her sister. They spoke for a very long time and covered many subjects. At some point their conversation turned to the family, remembering with nostalgia and the painful joy of what it was like when their mother was alive.

"Please tell me that you brought photos of mom with you?" Julia asked with great hope in her voice; she really wanted to look at the one she loved so much who was no longer there in the flesh.

"They are always with me!" Sarah said, hopping off the bed and take a large suitcase out of the closet. "They must be here somewhere." she added and started rummaging through the clothes, when she finally came across the beads. Julia of course noticed them. Her eyes flashed with curiosity, and she immediately wanted a closer look. The beads were somewhat different; some energy emanated from them that drew her in. Sarah certainly knew the truth, and therefore did not want Julia to touch the beads at all. She would need to come up with an excuse not to show her something she considered sacred and even dangerous. Sarah could not find the words, and decided nothing terrible would happen if they were held briefly by her sister. Of course Julia was madly delighted to touch the beads, but when she did, her body became drenched in cold, as if she were naked somewhere in Antarctica. With such an unexpected feeling the girl tossed the beads on the bed in front of her and stared at them with wide open eyes.

"What just happened" She stuttered.

"What are you talking about?" Sarah didn't understand.

"It's so cold in here, and these beads seem to be frozen," Julia said, visibly shaking and clasping her arms. "They're not made of ice, are they?"

"No," Sarah laughed oddly. "You must be just tired after such a long flight."

"Maybe ... Put them on. I want to see how they look on you. Odd as they are, I think they are very stylish and they will be perfect for the fashion show."

Sarah just smiled, put on the beads, and praying nothing would happen. She was very nervous, afraid that something similar might happen to the first time she experienced the inexplicable, mystical power of this artifact. She was sure if it did, it would mar her relationship with Julia. The last thing she wanted was to involve her sister in something unthinkably terrifying. The beads were just that powerful. Much to her surprise, she did not feel anything unusual at all. Sarah sighed with relief and flashed a genuine smile.

"The day after tomorrow I want to see them on you in the show!" Julia said clearly. "And now..." She picked up the package from the floor. "...this is for you!"

"What is it?" Sarah asked with surprise.

"Open it and you will see," Now it was Julia's turn to flash a genuine smile.

The girl began to unpack the bundle, her eyes glowing with childish curiosity. What she eventually found made her happy. There was a small letter in which Julia had written how she valued her sister, and the letter was attached to a one-of-a-kind, stylish red dress,

"I spent a month and a half planning and creating. I made this just for you! I've never stopped thinking about you, dear sister," Julia said.

These words touched Sarah so deeply that tears welled up in her eyes. They hugged each other and the tears continued to flow without restraint. This was truly a happy moment for them to share. After they unpacked everything and stored all the contents, they took a little time just to enjoy each other's company since they were in no rush. It was an incredible time that brought wonderful memories to life as together they enjoyed photos of their mother. There were happy and sad moments at the same time; Sarah and her sister both missed their mom who was deeply loved and remembered.

Since Julia's return the family reunited, strengthening their bonds of joy, love, and peace. Finally, the pain of separation that had existed for quite some time was now in the past. The two girls again felt a strong connection between them that neither would ever allow to lapse.

Later in the evening they headed into Manhattan with a first stop at Julia's apartment. Time was short, and soon they had to leave for trendy "see-and-be-seen" Polo Bar, just south of Central Park. John was supposed to meet them there after work. Julia's apartment was a gleaming two-bedroom jewel on the 26th floor of East 60th Street at Park Avenue. She shared this gem with Nadi Levenshaut, her German friend who also worked in the fashion industry as a makeup artist. They had met at university five years ago and since then had stayed close friends, two years ago became roommates.

"I'm so glad to be home; I can't believe it has been a whole year!" Julia said, releasing the deadbolt of the front door. "I texted Nadi earlier and unfortunately she's in LA at the moment, but you will definitely get to know each other very soon. She is taking a redeye so she can be back in time to work with my models in the show."

"It's all so new and strange," Sarah exhaled. "I know so little about your life in New York".

"I know," Julia said with a sigh. "Those were difficult times for all of us. I just could not be in a place where absolutely everything reminded me of mom. I just couldn't take it ..."

"Trust me, I understand perfectly," Sarah nodded. "There no fault; I'm sure mom is very proud of you now!"

"Thank you," Julia said with a smile, but Sarah clearly noticed the sadness in her eyes. She knew that Julia wished their mom could be with them to celebrate such an important life event.

This was Sarah's first visit to Julia's apartment. She found herself in a large, bright, and well-designed living room, fragrant with the smell of flowers, and windows that looked straight out onto Central Park. Here, from the twenty-sixth floor, opened up a stunning panorama of New York City. Many people would dream to have such a view.

"Voilà… Welcome home!" exclaimed Julia.

"…WOW… I cannot believe that you live in such a beautiful place!" Sarah's eyes became as large as saucers.

"I told you about my place many times, but you were always so busy. Now you won't have any excuses not to come by since we live in the same city!"

Sarah laughed. Julia immediately pulled her around by the hand, impatient to show the whole apartment to her sister. There was a workshop area with at least a dozen mannequins, a loggia with the fantastic view of the City, and a small garden with the restful sounds of a miniature fountain. One could stand at the balcony and look out over the city of millions of dreams, spending days and nights dipping into unlimited inspirations for living. Back inside, Sarah saw Nadi's workroom full of every possible cosmetic facial product and the bathroom that looked like a fancy spa. The last room was Julia's. There were many dresses and shelves filled with all kind of textiles and fabrics, also there was a big floor-to-ceiling window giving a sumptuous view of the finery of 5th Avenue. But it was not the view nor the expensive materials that caught Sarah's eye, it was a picture on a nightstand. In it, Sarah, her mom and Julia were smiling, wearing Christmas scarfs and hats, and holding in hands that were full of big yellow maple leaves they had gathered from the ground. Sarah remembered that moment as if it were yesterday. She didn't say anything, but just smiled holding back her tears. She secretly wiped a few that did manage to form in her eyes.

"I love you Julia," Sarah held her sister. "You will always be my little sister, and I'm happy that you're finally back!"

"I missed you a lot," Julia admitted. "And I am sorry that we didn't talk much to each other, you know it was not about you?"

"I know," Sarah nodded with a smile.

The girls spent about fifteen more minutes looking over everything there was to see, only stopping their visual inventory when they realized they would soon need to leave for dinner. Another special moment was looming on the horizon.

John was already at the table impatiently waiting for Julia to appear. He was completely lost in his thoughts, detached from everything and immersed in quiet, soothing music. In fact, he was actually a little nervous, understandable for someone separated from a loved one for a long time. Tonight was very important to him. It was not the first time he tried to pursue Julia romantically. He was on the right track, but he had only partially succeeded. Once Julia left for France he was afraid that everything might change because of the distance. Nevertheless, he continued to believe that if there was love present, it would not disappear despite the distance. He believed that tonight could change his, and perhaps their, destiny.

He was abruptly distracted from his thoughts when his phone vibrated. A message came from Sarah who said she and her sister were on their way and would arrive in about 20 minutes. After the text message came in, the "low battery" red light came on; there was only six percent left. The guy swore under his breath and began rummaging through his messenger bag trying to find the charger. It was nowhere to be found. As he put the searched bag aside, the phone vibrated again. This time it was a call from work.

"Yes, Indigo," John answered.

"John, we need you now, it's urgent. Please come."

"What happened?"

"We have to reprogram the elevator into the laboratories. The system refuses to respond to our auto-reset signals. We can't generate a new access code. Nobody's here to do it."

"Call the guys from the 35th floor."

"Greg got sick and went home. Robby is out on a call and I'm afraid he will not come back anytime soon. It's really urgent John; you're not far from the office, are you?"

"Damn ..." John felt himself becoming unavoidably angry. "Well... I'll be there in about twenty minutes. Don't forget, I told you about the importance of this dinner tonight."

"I do remember. Believe me, it won't take long with you here. You're the best, my friend. I'll be waiting for you. We'll be outta' here in no time, I promise" Indigo was very happy that at least his troubles would be over.

John immediately sent a message to Sarah, apologizing that he was urgently needed at the office and would return an hour later. As soon as the text was sent, the phone went dead. John stopped the first taxi he could hail and asked the driver to deliver him to the *MAGiC* building as quickly as possible. Fortunately it was not far away. Once the taxi driver dropped him off in front of the mile-high tower John looked up and fixed his gaze on the antenna whose red warning beacon pierced the distant sky. The bright light periodically filled the black sky with prominent bloody shades as it revolved, giving John goosebumps. He had seen the antenna many times before, but tonight it looked so ominous that it gave him a chill. If one compiled a list of the most sinister corporations in the world, most would say that *MAGiC* would undoubtedly occupy the first line. Running up the stairs, John found himself in a spacious, golden hall with white columns and a black glass floor – a space ripe with a mysterious atmosphere. As soon as John stepped onto the floor there was an illusion that he could easily lose his unsteady balance.

Indigo was already waiting for him here in the hall. He was John's deputy who usually worked in the early evening or on the overnight shift, hence his constant state of exhaustion. He was a tall guy with black hair, a closely cropped beard and a nose like a bird's beak. With his odd appearance, he seemed like he might be a somewhat detached person without good communication skills. In simple words: his energy was off-putting. Among the whole *MAGiC* team, the only person with whom he could stay on quite friendly terms was John. They were probably the only ones in the company who worked so ideally together: each performed his own functions, never shirked his responsibilities, but most importantly everything was based on trust and the fact they could always rely on one another.

"My good friend, thank you for coming, I could not have done this without you." Indigo began to shake John's hand.

"Okay... okay Indigo... Let's do this. I don't have much time. My dinner, which is all about Julia by the way, will not wait.

"I can imagine how excited you are" Indigo said.

"Oh, I am. She just arrived today and she's already on the way to a restaurant where I'm supposed to be now."

"All right... all right," Indigo said and rubbed the palms of his hands together. "We will try to do everything as quickly as possible. Thanks again for coming. And now to business. The bottom line is that today they will again test "ENTAL-B", and just recently there was a failure in the elevator system."

"What the hell. I thought it was already tested and proven."

"I do not know all the details my friend, but the elevator to the labs inexplicably self-reprogrammed. I think it's in the panel. Not really sure."

"Let's go see," John suggested.

In principle, he could guess what caused the issue. Something similar had happened when he first started working for the corporation. And if this was anything like that, the solution could be found in the next half hour which was quite acceptable. He was growing more impatient to get back to the restaurant and be with Julia. They went up on the wide staircase to the public elevators and walked to the back side where they stopped near the elevator exclusively intended for top-level personnel. The elevator was huge; capable of accommodating as many as thirty people. Depending on the level of security access, it worked differently in various sections and was intended exclusively for the management.

"Hey guys," A voice was suddenly heard.

John and Indigo turned around and saw Igor Miltent right behind them. He stood leaning against the wall with a coffee in his right hand. There was the definite impression that he was in a state of alcohol inebriation evidenced by his staggering gait. On the one hand, it seemed funny, on the other - unpleasant. The director of the huge company looked completely unprofessional in front of his colleagues. Nevertheless, he didn't care because he was the director, and everyone else was one of his subordinates.

"We have excellent specialists and engineers working here. I don't want to call on third-party companies to repair what we can repair ourselves. I'm sure you understand what I mean. This fucking elevator must be working by 9:00 pm."

"We'll do our best, sir," Indigo said.

"I'm glad," smiled Igor. "Thank you, Wishep, for coming here after your work hours. That's real loyalty".

"No problem, sir" John smiled.

"I hope that there won't be any further problems tonight, as I said, it must be operational by 9:00 pm," Igor said coldly, turned around and walked away.

"The solution is simple," Indigo said and called for the elevator. "Go to the office and disguise the source code so it will fool the system into generating a new temporary code, while for us it will still operate with the old one."

"Not exactly what we need," John shook his head as he entered the newly opened elevator, starting to inspect the control panel.

"What should we do then?"

"If you run a new code, it must be done from both ends simultaneously - from here and from the main computer. If not, it will fail again. Let's do it differently - I'll go up to the office and rewrite the code. You open the panel and erase lines "b" and "y". This will allow the system not to block itself when the new code is launched."

"That's a great idea - and why you make the big bucks!" Indigo said happily, immediately realizing the solution of the problem was the right one.

John again went into the main lobby and up to his office, thinking through the code and the steps to rewrite it. He was about to go to his computer when he noticed he was in the midst of a rather chaotic scene. Papers were scattered on the floor, and the window was opened with a dank wind blowing in from outside. The guy was dumbfounded, not expecting to see anything like this. He was more than sure he had closed the door and window before leaving, but now he began to doubt himself. Contemplating what happened when was not important now. He slammed the window shut, quickly sat down at the computer, and dialed Indigo's number.

"So, how's everything going?" John asked.

"The signal sends, but the elevator won't drop below the tenth floor. Try replacing "h" by "e"."

"Okay," John answered. "Give me a minute."

Indigo highlighted the control panel by his phone, simultaneously changing the settings, following John's instructions to the letter. There was a continuous squeal as the small lamps were constantly changing color, at first green, then red. Realizing nothing they had tried so far was working, Indigo asked to erase the erroneous line and enter additional functions for a repeated identity request. He got the go-ahead with yet another kind of code that on the second go-round did not produce an error. John obediently followed all the recommendations of his partner, biting his lower lip and tensely waiting for the full loading of the new code hoping that this time the system would not reject it as a virus.

"Uploaded!" Indigo shouted, then nervously waited for the result. He knew for sure that if this idea did not work, then they would have to change the entire order of the protective protocol for the system as a matter of urgency -- and that would take hours.

Lamps on the electronic panel changed color one by one from red to green, building more and more hope, when the last one remained red. Indigo was so angry he wanted to tear his hair out. He knew perfectly well that failure would not have played well. Igor Miltent would not have accepted this kind of defeat, despite all of his or John's qualifications and previous successful contributions to the corporation.

"So, how is it now?" John's voice was impatient.

"One moment," Indigo said, nervously reviewing the final execution of the jerry-rigged code. He could not afford to blunder, not today. "Reduce the weight on the door, and increase the time to scan the card. One of these two functions should be the final solution."

"I think you're wrong," John said. "This only doubles the waiting time for the elevator. We don't need that. The error returns every time when it comes to reading the third line. If I make it mirror, it will be read as the second, by default."

"I hope you are right," Indigo said.

John began to copy the lines of code, while still monitoring the time, he realized it was quickly running out. He knew for sure that if this option did not work, he would have to choose between work and the relationship he was eager to resurrect. It's unlikely that Julia would accept his absence at dinner in some positive way. After spending a good fifteen minutes he asked Indigo to link the last two lines into one and restart the code. All the lightbulbs on the panel once again turned red, and then one after another began to switch to green light. Indigo froze, unable to even breathe. When it came to the last light, it again remained red.

"Damn it!" Indigo became completely exasperated.

"What's wrong?" John asked, confronting his worst fears.

"It looks like we still have a big problem," Indigo said with disappointment when suddenly the last lightbulb suddenly changed color and the panel completely lit up in green, and the elevator itself started to buzz with power.

"John... John... you will not believe it," he almost screamed in happiness. "It works... this damn elevator works! We did it!!"

"Yes!" John said through a wide grin. He was happy, like never before. "Uffff," He felt the perspiration run down his tense forehead. "Double check if it works properly all way down the line and let me know - that's all I need to know."

"No problem. You saved me -- you saved both our asses."

"I hope the worst is behind us. By the way, did you go into my office any time tonight?"

"No... Why?"

"Somebody caused a hell of a mess in there. Feels like someone was trying to dig through my things. Hell, maybe it was just the wind, who knows..."

"It does sound strange. If you want, I'll check the cc cameras. Weird. No one else has access ..."

"Yeah, please do and let me know."

"Okay. Will do."

Indigo scanned his access card through the slot in the activation panel. The elevator squealed into action and the doors obediently closed. There was a descent of forty floors, which was equivalent to descending into a coal mine. Since the elevator was not a high-speed model, Indigo had to wait for at least three minutes before the doors slowly drifted apart, opening the way into a dark corridor filled either with steam, or fog, and a faint blue light.

"Laboratories", announced the computer voice from the operating panel. The lamps in the elevator blinked from the power surge. The man shivered because the whole scene was somewhat frightening. Not that he believed in ghost stories, but still it just left him feeling uneasy. What did cross his mind was a memory of a rather frightening childhood fairy tale about a dungeon where a mad king was performing supernatural experiments which did not end happily.

Indigo had never been on this particular level before. He knew that the creation and testing of many new products for the corporation took place here, but he had no direct access because everything here was held in strictest secrecy. He had never seen the people who worked here. They were those who, according to the "official version" from the corporation, never existed. Every day they came to work as civilians, with completely different names, and would easily become lost among the thousands of workers, allowing them to always remain invisible. Indigo took a few steps forward, but then stopped because the visibility was simply terrible. The omnipresent fog showed no sign of dissipating. Indigo sighed heavily when his phone rang which made him flinch. Of course, it was John.

"So, how is it up there? Indigo, we really need to hurry this along." There were still several communication obstacles, even on the internal line which was iffy at best.

"All fine man, thanks again. I'll tell you more about the surveillance cameras later this evening, as soon as I can figure a couple things out."

"Great!" John replied.

Indigo's curiosity overcame him and he decided to take a walk deeper into the place even though a deep-seated, uneasy feeling told him no. He walked along the corridor to the end and found himself standing in front of a closed door which required a special admission which he did not have. A kind of disappointment pierced through to his ribs. He was drawn forward by a thirst to know what came next. He touched the panel and without any hesitation opened it up. All that remained now was to enlist the support of John.

"John, I'm gonna need your help again..." He announced on the phone.

"Oh man, I really need to get going. Julia and Sarah have been waiting for me at the restaurant all this time. I've already had four texts from them."

"I just need you to restart the B level, please."

"Lord, why do you need that? That's no quick task…"

" Just temporarily shut down the security system."

"If anyone gets wind of this, both of us are going to have big problems."

"Don't worry. I just need the access. If there are any questions, we already have the answer: we had to briefly reset the defense of all levels in order to restore the elevator to working order. That's all."

"That's crazy. You have half an hour, Indigo. I have to go."

"Thanks, John!" After these words, there was a continuous hiss and the conversation was completely interrupted a few seconds later.

After a long five minutes, Indigo finally heard a familiar squeal from the control panel as the red lights were slowly being replaced by green lights. In the dim light, it was difficult for him to even see the lines of code, but using some random patterns, he was able to generate a code that worked. A small drop-down menu screen ran numbers and letters, and then the panel squealed again and the door opened with a hiss. Behind it was the all too familiar fog, and also a very strange smell like burnt plastic. Indigo held his breath and began to move closer, practically by feel. Wisely, he had set his phone alarm so that it would ring ten minutes before the door's closing, or he would certainly have never be able to get out without someone's help.

Walking through the thick, dead silence, he intuitively knew that he was making a mistake. His mind warned him to immediately turn around and leave while he still could. It was more than just a creepy feeling, this place was like a spaceship, like in a classic sci-fi film, where some kind of monster was lurking - and maybe not just one. Indigo himself did not understand why, but simply continued to move forward, deliberately risking being noticed and possibly creating for himself more problems, not fewer. His darkest imaginings eventually proved to be true.

Very soon his eyes revealed what was hidden from everyone, deep underground in the heart of New York City. It took him a dozen more steps before he was in front of a tall door with a biohazard sign warning of what was inside. It was a huge, round glass room, from whose walls protruded metallic hands supporting cryogenic capsules. Inside each of the capsules were naked bodies sleeping peacefully or, at least, so it seemed. An instant shock grabbed Indigo by the soul. He was trembling and taking shallow breaths. He began to gasp, taking in more air to remain conscious. For a moment he had a feeling that he had been poisoned. Indigo backed away in a panic and came across the door to the bathroom. It was the place he needed most now. He ran inside and turned the cold water at the sink full force, cupping his hands and drinking greedily, as if he had just returned from a desert. "Experimental people" were the last thing he expected to discover about the company for whom he was working.

Indigo was not an expressively emotional person or someone who would get scared easily, but he was now. He looked at himself in the mirror and saw only a face riddled with primitive fear - fear about the place where he was and about what else he might discover. Being blindingly wrapped in a strange fog, he could barely distinguish himself from the mist. He reached into his pocket and his shaking hand pulled out "the pills". They were strong painkillers. The man knew about his diagnosis that required the medication, but never told anyone, otherwise he would have lost his job the next day. Unreasonable outbursts of anger, paranoia and acting like a completely different person were the features from which he suffered. Sometimes his body was shackled by a wild pain, making him want to scream and having a clear desire to cut himself into pieces. That is why he had a scar on his right cheek - a mutilation that he had inflicted on himself, while assuring others that he had been the victim of a robbery. To find his way back to normal state, he often found it helpful to console himself. He began to reason out loud:

"Boy, this is just some kind of stupid hoax, it's not serious."

"Do you really think so?" his inner voice inquired.

"No, but I can't think of anything else that makes sense. I should not have come here."

"Then why are you still here?" the voice shot off another query.

"Exactly!" He bolted up in anger hit the sink with his hands. Indigo stepped back a few paces, while still looking at his sad reflection.

He saw disheveled hair and large, bloodshot eyes. The look of a monster, for sure, nothing more. His lips twitched, and the veins on his neck and hands swelled so that if there were a vampire nearby, he would be in trouble. Indigo swallowed his flowing saliva and with his right hand touched his heart, which was pounding at an incredible speed. Usually he felt like that after abusing recreational drugs. But all that was in the past when he was in a college. As if hypnotized, he looked at himself, enveloped in a strange fog, until a human-like shadow suddenly slipped in behind him. The man shuddered and immediately turned around, but did not see anyone or anything, just a bluish-white vapor. Turning again back to the mirror, he was now face-to-face with a monster. At the distance of his outstretched hand stood a naked, hairless man of incredibly tall stature, with strange symbols all over his body, reminiscent of Egyptian hieroglyphics. His hands were riddled with scars, his mouth was carelessly stitched up with thick threads, his eyes seemed to become numb, completely absent of eyelids, and blood oozed out of each of the eyeballs. Since everything happened so abruptly and suddenly, Indigo lost his footing and slipped while trying to run away. He fell on the floor and struck the left temple of his head. In a moment his head was filled with a strange buzz that he'd never heard before. All that he could see now was filtered through a milky, white veil making the walls and other surrounding objects hardly distinguishable.

"Arghhh…" Indigo groaned in pain and crawled across the floor.

His mind was spinning, and sick feeling rose in his throat that he simply could not contain. He vomited right away. Tears sprang from his eyes and he looked around, fearful that the monster was somewhere nearby. All he could see was a poorly discernible shadow flailing in the fog from side to side in the distance. Indigo crawled on all fours straight to the exit, his body quivering and quaking all over and a crushing headache. He had only one thought: get out alive. At first he tried to phone John, but the call did not connect. Suddenly the phone's alarm went off - a sign that it was time to go back. Indigo somehow rose to his feet and wildly screamed when he momentarily caught sight of an eerie face that had disappeared as quickly as it had appeared. The guy seized the cold wall as he struggled to make it to the exit. The further along he moved, the scarier it became.

All the capsules in the glass room were now open and empty. All that remained was to determine where all those who had been in the cryogenic nightmare had gone. Walking quickly the man continued to head toward the exit from this nightmarish dungeon, when something sharp as a blade slashed his hand. He shuddered, and felt his hot blood pooling into his palm. He strained to look around and see who could have done this, he saw nothing except the ever thickening fog. He reached into his pocket to get more pills, but found out that he had used up everything. Gritting his teeth from the pain that tore through his body, he began to breathe quite rapidly, A terrible smell that permeated the room that caused him to gag and choke. He was overtaken by a deep, suffocating cough that forced him to double over and made him unable to move further. Here he was confronted with an alien feeling; it was the fear of death. Indigo knew that something terrible could happen and he did not want to die. He greatly regretted, greatly regretted indulging his curiosity, which put him in this situation in the first place.

There were only a few minutes left before the exit door would be ultimately secured. Indigo would have to be both nimble and agile to break the hell out of this nightmare and get back into reality. He knew perfectly well that he had only one last chance, and there would be no other. Expending both sweat and blood he rose to his feet, clutched his nose, and lumbered forward as well as he could manage. A warning sounded from the door panel; the voice of the computer suddenly announced that until the door would be completely locked, in exactly one minute.

"Damn," Indigo cursed both to himself and out loud.

He hastened his step when something very powerful grabbed his ankles, causing him to fall face first to the floor and hit his chin. It felt like if his skull had been shattered. Screaming in pain, he began fighting off the invisible enemy, who held him for a matter of seconds, and then simply evaporated as if it never existed. In panic and terror, Indigo crawled forward, scared to death that the creature would reappear. The computer announced that there were ten seconds remaining before the entry was secured. The man bellowed at the top of his voice, in a state of insanity that he had never known. These ten seconds would decide his fate and present the only opportunity left to escape death's clutches. With a last-moment, powerful lunge, numb to the pan that tore through his battered body, he crossed the threshold of the doors as he heard the locking mechanisms click doors closed tightly.

Exhausted and wrung out with relief, Indigo rolled over on his back and breathed more easily. In this part of the corridor the air was cleaner, but it didn't help much. His mind still remained clouded and he couldn't stop thinking about that invisible monster that didn't murder him, but simply wished to play cat and mouse until one completely gives up. Then it would be time to kill or be killed. Indigo's fear was palpable and took part of each of his breaths. He wanted to leave this dungeon NOW. His arms and legs were not cooperating from the ordeal he had survived, and it was not easy to get on his feet, but somehow he pushed on until he reached the elevator. For Indigo it felt like the night had been six months long. He wanted to get out of the damned building and out of the *MAGiC* Corporation, and never to return. With determination he threw himself into the elevator with his eyes shut and holding his breath, until he heard the doors close. He thought he could finally relax. Instead, new terror replaced the old when the call button he pressed so desperately did not work and the elevator did not budge. Full of fear and despair, Indigo began to hit the hated button repeatedly, but never got any effect. Trying to the other buttons he, he was confronted with the same problem. Nothing worked.

"God... John, you son of a bitch!" Indigo swore, and immediately dialed John's number, but in response he heard only the recorded voice message.

"Damn it, answer the fucking phone!" Indigo shouted in desperation. He flung open the control panel only to discover that it was all glowing red. That meant only one thing - he could not get out of this hell without someone's help.

"No... no...no...please," Indigo whispered, slipping down to the floor and holding his head with hands. His eyes were wide open with madness in his pupils.

After some silent, solitary prayers, a strange creak came from afar, as if something strong were trying to break open the door. Literally holding his breath, afraid of making too much noise Indigo stared at the corridor filled with fog not able to see anything beyond his outstretched hands. The creaking lasted about a minute, and then were heard sloshing steps as if someone were walking through water. In his mind Indigo prayed to the Lord to save him. Being a long standing atheist, for the first time in his life he did what an hour ago would have seemed to him stupid and unintelligent.

"My heavenly Father," Indigo said with a quavering voice, but couldn't continue. Two long arms emerged from the fog and seized his head with an inhuman, vice-like grip, instantly dragging him into the white veil. Indigo's petrified scream was heard for only a fraction of a second, and then there remained only a cold, dead silence.

At the same time John was already in a taxi on his way to the restaurant. He blamed himself the entire journey for not charging his phone while he was in the office. His only calming thought was that even though he was delayed, it was not so long and could have been much longer. What did raise his ire was the fact that ten minutes later after leaving the corporation, he was at a dead stop because of the evening traffic. He found himself only eleven blocks from his destination yet none of the cars was moving an inch. He chose the only sensible course of action that could be made: to continue on foot for the rest of the way. On route it suddenly started to rain, and of course, he had no umbrella. His day had just gotten off on the wrong foot and never righted itself. John took up a quick jog to the restaurant. What he faced was endless crowds of people, all interacting in a chaotic symphony. They all jostled and tangled *en garde* with their umbrellas, blissfully ignoring others while purposefully making their way. Welcome to New York! Life here was in a constant state of chaos, you can say frenetic at any time of a day and night and in any weather. John could not believe he finally reached the restaurant much sooner than he expected. Disheveled and out of breath, he ran inside the restaurant and the first thing he saw were two girls sitting across the room with glasses of red wine, chatting peacefully. John lingered for a moment, amazed by the incredible smile of Julia, who had not yet noticed his arrival. He turned to the mirror that hung right next to the entrance, quickly smoothed his hair, took off his wet, limp jacket, and confidently walked toward the table.

"Julia... Sarah...," He said as soon as he was face-to-face with the two girls. His words ran out, and there he stood, only staring. Rarely was he without words, but this was truly an overwhelming moment. The two sisters just looked at him in amazement, with smiles on their faces. John smiled back and without further hesitation moved to Julia, hugging her tightly. At that moment, Sarah looked away, feeling a strange mix of joy and something else: bitterness or envy or maybe just being there.

"I missed you so much," John whispered in her ear. His words merged into a light kiss and on to another reality. Julia didn't expect this or the feelings which followed. It was what she really wanted and what she had been thinking about on the flight home from Paris. Everything else in this moment simply disappeared, there was only Julia and the one whom she so missed for the last year and for whom she really yearned.

"I just can't believe my eyes that it's you!" She said happily. "Incredible, just incredible!"

"I think you both have so much to say to each other," Sarah said with a forced smile. She was happy to observe such a beautiful moment, but at the same time, great sadness pierced her heart. There was an awkward silence among the friends because no one knew what else to say, but it didn't last long. A sudden flush of joy that they were finally together overtook the moment.

The evening lasted much longer than expected. The trio had an unending agenda of topics that went on and on. For John it was a happy event he wished would never end. He listened with pleasure to Julia's stories about life in Paris and the charms of a European lifestyle. He felt as though he was taking a dream journey around the world -- finally breaking away from the work that for the past three years had taken all his time without a moment to breathe. Sometimes he just watched her without saying a word, and simply enjoying the sweet tones of her voice and her remarkable natural beauty. For his part, John spoke mostly about his street racing, which took up much of his free time and became an important part of his life. Sometimes an exhilarating rush, albeit sometimes a very dangerous one. Regardless, he loved this car craziness -- certainly more than his crazy-making work at *MAGiC*. In recent months, especially in the last few days, work had become a real pain in the ass. Julia really didn't like this kind of life-endangering hobby, but Sarah supported John one hundred percent. She knew very well the importance of doing what you love. By sharing her plans about opening her own coffee shop chain in New-York, she only confirmed that people must follow their passion, believe in their dreams, and turn them into a lifelong profession. For her it's always been about a coffee business, likewise, for Julia it was all about fashion and the only thing on John's mind were sportscars. They all were happy to share everything that at the end, it was not important who liked to do *what*, the most important thing was the reunion. Everyone's best feelings and ideas found themselves in a cozy restaurant in the heart of Manhattan.

Dinner finally wound down to its end about one o'clock in the morning. The friends agreed to meet the day after tomorrow at the fashion show. Julia had lots of last minute preparations to make, so the next day she was completely swamped and doubted that she would even have time to rest.

But, that is the way of the fashion world: an endless nonstop of "to do" lists. At their parting, she kissed John on the lips and said with a flirtatious double meaning and wished she had more time to spend with him that night. The guy just laughed in response. They were all a little tipsy, but their minds remained with them. The most important thing was that the distance between them had been erased, and this gave hope. John noticed great changes in Julia's behavior; she'd become more open and accessible. A long struggle for her heart still beat within him. Seemingly small victories like a short kiss or hugs played a much bigger role for him. He saw that Julia was moving in his direction and nothing could make him happier or truly calm his anxious heart.

The next day for John was the longest of his life. All he could think about was getting his girl back into his arms as soon as possible. She was on his mind every second, so concentrating on the real world was not so simple. In the morning, he returned to his office and decided to start cleaning up because there still a big mess. His will to complete the task vanished as quickly as it came to mind. He sat down in his swivel chair and began to compose text messages to Julia, confessing the incredible feelings that had seized him after their long-awaited reunion last night. After he pressed the "send" icon, his gaze drifted to the message that appeared on his laptop about the security system break at the lower levels of the corporation.

"Indigo... what the hell?" John swore and immediately dialed his work number.

John was perfectly aware of all the responsibility that he took last night, and even that trusted a man who eventually disappointed him. How stupid the whole situation seemed. The morning had begun so well, and now what? Hacking of the security system was a serious oversight of the protocol. This could lead to anything from dismissal to criminal responsibility. John literally seethed with uncontrollable quell. After Indigo did not respond, he re-dialed the number again and again until after ten minutes after the failed attempts, there was a voice:

"Yes?"

"Indigo, man you've got big problems."

"Sorry, it's Steve."

"Steve? Where's Indigo?"

"I have no idea, he never showed up at work, and it's been impossible to reach him by phone. I dunno. Maybe he's sick."

"Weird. I talked with him last night and he looked quite cheerful. Anyway, if see him, tell him that he's gotten himself up to his ears in crap."

"All right." Steve said.

"You'll have to do something else for me. You see where the elevator for the management is? The one in the main lobby?"

"Yes."

"I need you to go down to the elevator and open the control panel.

Completely erase the seventh line, and then copy the fifth and replace it with the original line of code. Call me as soon as everything is done, okay?"

"No problem John."

"Perfect. Thank you Steve."

John carefully gathered all of the disordered papers in a pile and turned his attention to the computer screen where the alarming message continued to flash. He just shook his head. He dialed the security chief's number and asked him last night's surveillance video recorded from opposite his office. What was his surprise when he heard the answer that the cameras had not worked that day.

"Are you kidding me?" John scowled in anger. "I need the fucking surveillance cameras to be repaired and working properly starting from now. You mean to tell me last night someone broke into my office, *and* the video surveillance system was defective? Fucking ridiculous..."

John could no longer control himself. He was completely sure that everything had been planned in advance, so that there was not a trace. He needed only to prove the fact it was indeed a break in. His office contained many important documents that were quite confidential. The last thing he wanted was for a data breach to occur. Having lost half a day of investigation with last night's circumstances, he decided to go down to the cafe where Sarah worked.

"Those beads look nice on you," He said immediately, as soon as Sarah came up to his table.

"Thank you," Sarah smiled. "If it were not for Julia, I would never have worn them."

"I'm glad you did. They look just perfect on you. You shouldn't keep them under the bed."

"I am not sure about "perfect", but indeed, they are special" The girl said. "How about things with you? You look kind of upset."

"Problems at work. Someone broke into my office, while the surveillance cameras were not working, of course, which means that it will be difficult to prove anything. And also my partner Indigo messed some things up, so I'm just about ready to throw in the towel. Damn it all."

"Are you serious?"

"I have a suspended NASA project, which is on a very short timeline, I have to finish the report for another no less important project, and all this fell into my lap at the same time. Just a lot of problems; I don't want to flood your mind with all the goings on."

"Sandwich and coffee?" Sarah asked, understanding that it was better to abruptly change the topic than to continue on the downhill, emotion packed spiral.

"Here is what I need: I need the strongest damned coffee you have with extra sugar."

"But you never take sugar!"

"I will today".

Sarah knew how busy John must be, and that he needed the freedom to dive deeply into his thoughts. His mind was built analytically, and so he could spend hours pondering rational nature of one thing or another. That's why the girl decided not to further distract him with serious conversations, instead leaving them for later this evening or even for the next day. John almost never came down to the cafe, so seeing him here meant that he needed some down time. He actually looked more than annoyed.

"As you like!" She said, putting in front of the guy a huge hot sandwich with cheese and ham, and a large mug of very black coffee.

"Thank you!" John said. "I'm sorry if I'm not in a mood you'd like to see me in."

"Don't worry about anything," Sarah assured him. "We all have bad days. Try to relax. If you want something else, I'm right here."

The guy smiled and started his meal as Sarah went to serve another table. On her way back to the counter, the cafe door opened sharply and a familiar figure appeared in the doorway. It was Igor Miltent. Sporting a generally somber look, he wanted to visit his favorite place. Instinctively his gaze settled on Sarah, who then was so distracted that she stopped in the center of the hall, looking at him in bewilderment. Igor formed a thin, eerie smile and spoke quietly so that his voice was like a hiss:

"Good day, Sarah! What a surprise to see you again!"

"Hello," The girl greeted him. "How are you doing?"

"Excellent, thank you," The man answered. "And how are you? Beautiful beads, by the way. They look beautiful on you! Where did you get them?"

"Oh, they were a gift from my grandmother." Sarah said with a false smile. "Even though she's been gone a long time, they make me think about her whenever I wear them."

"Your grandmother had excellent taste."

"Yes, she did. Thank you," Sarah replied.

"They look like a real rarity, if I'm not mistaken they should have some kind of identifying logo or trademark."

"Really?" The girl was genuinely surprised. Maybe a little too surprised.

"Can I have a closer look?" Igor asked.

"Yes, of course." Sarah said.

All this time John had been watching them from across the room. Out of nowhere, he observed that complete darkness shaded everything outside the window like a total eclipse. He then noticed Igor's sinister eyes riveted on the beads as if he had made some great discovery. John brought his attention back to his side of the café. His body flinched as if a chilling frost had arrived. He could not ignore that the darkness outside the window had dissipated in a matter of seconds. John realized another implausible fact: Sarah and Igor had continued with casual conversation as if nothing had happened. That seemed very strange indeed.

"Yes they're an antique." was heard. "These could be worth several million dollars, just for your information."

"No way!" Sarah said surprisingly.

"Oh yes; I am sure I am not mistaken." Igor whispered in her ear. "I'm a collector, and if you want to sell them one day ... I'll be the first in line."

"All right," The girl was confused and gently covered up the beads with her hand. "I'll keep you in mind."

"That's great." nodded Igor. "Wear them with caution, such things can attract a lot of unwanted and , may I say, *dangerous* attention. In any case, you know where to find me. May I sit at that table?" He pointed to his favorite place.

"Of course, of course," nodded Sarah, as she noticed John trying to get her attention. "I beg your pardon," She said politely.

"No, no," Igor answered. "Go ahead... I'm not in a hurry."

Sarah quickly came over to John who shot an incredulous glance at Igor sitting casually at a table by the window.

He asked, "Did you see that?"

"Did I see what?" the girl got confused.

"There was an eclipse, just a couple of minutes ago. Sarah, it was as dark as night."

"I don't understand John. What are you talking about?"

"Exactly two minutes ago it was completely dark outside the window, like it was night."

"I... don't think so... Maybe I was not paying attention."

"Oh, uh... ," The guy said. "Never mind... Do you know Igor? What did he ask you about?". He spoke in rapid succession.

"Hey, hey, hey... slow down," Sarah laughed. "Why are you so agitated?"

"I'm just asking, that's all," John said meekly. "He's my boss, you know - and yours too, by the way."

"He liked the beads I'm wearing. He said that they could be worth a couple of million bucks, and he would have even considered buying them."

"Are you serious?"

"Yes. No joke."

"I can't believe it!" The guy's eyes flashed dollar signs and he smiled, briefly forgetting all the worst parts of the day. "I did hear that he collects antiquities. Who would have thought that your beads would interest him. If he really does make a firm offer, you must take it. And don't give away the store cheap! Make him pay top dollar! Who knows, this could be an answer to your prayers.. Who else could make that kind of offer?!"

"I really will think about it, John. We'll have to discuss it further."

"Sure."

After Sarah served Igor the coffee and sandwich he ordered, she tried not to meet his gaze. She was uneasy and her inner feelings told her that something was wrong with this picture, there had to be some kind of catch. She thought about this unceasingly all day long giving her little if any rest. When she finally got home, she went straight up to take a hot, relaxing bath with plenty of bubbles and fragrant oils. Out on the street it became sharply colder, a downpour began, and the wind rose. Quite typical New York weather. Sarah luxuriated in the bath with her head on a towel and her eyes closed in sheer bliss. Slowly inhaling and exhaling the therapeutic steam, she wasn't thinking about problems, or family, but instead of her long-standing dream, about the City -- her City -- where she had finally moved and had more or less arranged her life. She thought about what luck had finally fallen into her hands; at last, the opportunity to live where she had always wanted. The half-open bathroom window suddenly rattled from the wind and abruptly interrupted the girl's thought-conversation with herself. Reluctantly she rose and secured the latch, and turned on the whirlpool jets in the tub, completely immersing herself in a world of total relaxation. She lost track of time and did not realize how much she needed to sleep.

The next day was supposed to be very busy, and therefore it was important for Sarah to be at her best, both physically and mentally. She needed to be rested so she would be full of energy. So, that's why she drank a "all natural" - and horrible tasting - potion to help her fall asleep that would take about 30 minutes to work. While waiting for it to take effect, the girl tormented in thoughts whether she must patiently wait in bed or have a short visit with John. Without much hesitation, she eventually decided to go down to the living room where John was sitting behind a book that had all of his attention. It was not quite like him to be lost in a novel, just because he was always loaded with work. When he did finally come home he would be completely exhausted. But that was not the case today. He was glad that he could find time for what he always liked to do in those rare moments when his life was not so chaotic. Peering into the room as she descended the stairs, Sarah saw the guy peacefully sitting and reading, while soft, soothing classical music set the background mood. She smiled to herself, not really wanting to distract her friend. Quietly, she turned around and headed back to her room. But John had indeed heard, or felt, her. Not distracted from the book and without turning his head, he calmly said:

"I'm almost done... you can keep me company if you like."

"Oh, do you really want me to join you?" Sarah asked. "I was just coming down to say good night."

"Please join me." John said as he put the book aside. "I just need to ask you about something, if you're not too tired."

"I'm not too tired," Sarah said, again descending the staircase.

At that moment for some unknown reason, she felt uncomfortable standing in a robe before John. He was not fazed by her attire. For a few awkward moments they did not say anything to each other, between them there was a certain palpable energy; a true sense of connection. The only words that Sarah could find now was to ask John how he was feeling after such a hard and nerve-wracking day. The guy just laughed.

"A little better compared to the beginning of the day, I'd say. It's good that I finally found time to read a little."

"What are you reading?"

"Ole Smith's Reincarnation."

"Hmm-m-m… interesting," Sarah said. "What's the book about?"

"About the evolution of human consciousness and construction of a new society. Actually, it's a pretty deep story about when people decide to choose a different path of mental and spiritual development and fulfillment."

"So… is it something historical?"

"Not at all, it's a fantasy, it is a story written from our perspective. It starts with the establishment of governments and societies, and progresses from there until now. What is personally interesting to me is whether is there really another way of being, without violence and without wars. Is there some kind of "golden rule" that can really work for all of us?"

"Sounds like some way-out, new-age, philosophy to me."

"Well, it's kind of… Listen, I wanted to ask you about tomorrow."

"Yes?" Sarah sat down in a chair, clasping her hands around her, as it suddenly became cool.

"What time do we have to be there?"

"It starts at seven o'clock, which means we should be there about an hour before."

"Okay. So, do you want to go there together or meet at the Barbella's mansion"

"We can go there together, of course."

"Perfect, but I'll have to stop by the office for a couple of minutes before we head out."

"That's absolutely fine with me."

"Great." John sounded relieved. "A nightcap before bed?"

"No, but thanks. I took a sleeping potion so I don't think it's a good idea."

"Sleeping potion!? Lord, why would you need that?"

"I really need a good night's sleep to be in shape for tomorrow."

"Taking that stuff is a bad idea", John said as he shook his head. "Are you having nightmares again?"

"No, not anymore."

"Are you sure?"

"Yes John, I'm sure."

"Then what's the matter? Is it because you can't stop thinking about becoming a millionaire?"

"… John… that's not funny. I am not going to sell the beads."

"Why not?"

"Because. Does there have to be a reason?"

"Sarah, don't get me wrong, I am not pushing you to do anything you don't want to do. I understand, especially if they're a family heirloom…"

"They're not a family heirloom."

"Then what's the problem?"

"The fact is that this is not just an ordinary necklace. These beads contain a power that I cannot control."

"What do you mean, *power*?"

"The day I saw the angel, I just had to listen to what I was told. It gave me these beads and said that I should protect them at all cost."

"What??… Are you being serious?"

"I am sorry, John, I just can't revisit those memories right now."

"I'm sorry," John said apologetically. "I didn't want our conversation to take a turn in this direction... I really didn't."

"Everything is all right. Life goes on. The past is the past. But today at work Igor, Lord, he behaved strangely! I mean, I felt like he wanted to seize the beads right off my neck!."

"That's why I was pretty worried when I noticed his weird behavior while you two were talking."

"I'm sure I'm just being paranoid; I need to get rid of such crazy thoughts. I can't suspect everyone. The responsibility that has been given to me from above is a heavy burden. I wouldn't wish it on anyone. You have no clue what it's like."

"I believe you. Have you ever thought why you've been singled out, or *chosen*, and not somebody else?"

"I think about it all the time. I haven't come up with an answer that makes any sense."

"Would a higher power really entrust you with something so important? And why would they make it so difficult and dangerous for you? Honestly, you'd be the last person they'd pick for something like this -- and I mean that sincerely; I don't mean to offend you."

"Maybe you're right, but what if I really *was* chosen. Look at the Virgin Mary!"

"Quite a stretch. If that were true, someone would have come for the beads long ago."

"Have you forgotten? Someone already DID.., twice!"

"Then hide them somewhere far from the eyes of others."

"Pour me some whiskey," Sarah requested.

They talked about the truth and fiction of religion for another good two hours, until eventually they realized that it was a dead-end conversation. Trying to convert one to the other's idea was just impossible. Close to three o'clock, the girl quietly dozed off right in her chair. Completely relaxed, she suddenly felt a shiver, her eyes were tearing and her hands and feet lost control, as if they no longer belonged to her. Still completely unaware of what was happening, the girl slowly opened her eyes. In the blink of an eye, she was completely underwater, and above her head huge sheets of ice fused together. Layers of terribly icy water enveloped Sarah in its arms and was not going to let go. What could be more terrible than being under water without any way to escape? Sarah was gripped by panic and swam up toward the iced-covered surface and began banging with all her strength to break through. All her attempts were useless; the icy death-sheet would not break. Only a few seconds remained before the oxygen in her lungs would be completely exhausted. The girl was trying to push the ice upward, to find the hole through which she fell, but all efforts were futile. It was the end, at least so it seemed. The water around suddenly sparkled with bright white light and warmed, as if a huge heater had been working up from the bottom. Feeling mortal terror, Sarah could not process everything that was happening around her. Her life could end right here and right now, but from the depths emerged a faceless shadow that immediately swam upwards. Either it was a shadow or something else. Sarah started beating her fists against the ice with even more feeling, as if she were in a cage with a lion. But all her actions had no effect.

She had finally run out of all life-force, including her precious oxygen. Sarah felt as if her whole body had been stung by a legion of jellyfish. Her mind began to swirl and her thoughts became meaningless. Completely submitting to the will of the Lord, with half-closed eyes, she began to slowly sink down into the unending water when she saw another shadow suddenly appearing on the surface of the ice. Then there was heard a loud crunch. The ice broke easily into pieces, and there appeared the figure of an old man in a hat. With a powerful jerk he rushed to the drowning girl and firmly grabbed her helpless, outstretched hand and pulled her up to the surface.

"Lord, grandfather, No-o-o!!!," Sarah hardly squeezed out the words.

She suddenly awoke and saw that John across the room was dozing off on the couch with his headphones on, hands hanging to the floor. What happiness it was to see him so peacefully, blissfully asleep, like a child, right there in front of her. Such a picture made the girl a little calmer and washed away the nightmare she just dreamed. John slumbered so innocently that she did not want to interrupt his sleep. His calm face showed an extraordinary ease which erased from her memory anything bad. Being in complete silence with someone who always had held a special place in her heart caused Sarah to feel an unusual connection to him. This was something she couldn't explain. At some point, she even regretted that Julia had returned so soon. But who knows what could happen in the future? Everything was possible.

Sarah focused her sight on John's lips and his stubble. She listened to his rhythmic breathing which ignited a spark in her that she had kept in her heart all her life, because she was not sure if this opportunity would ever come again. Not at all like herself, she went up to him and, squatting down, touched his manly hands, gently squeezing them in hers. The only thing she wanted at this very moment was to embrace him and feel the warmth of his body against hers. Sarah's heart began to pound. She touched his surprisingly warm chest, and then brought her face to his lips and she gently laid them upon his which met in an indescribable, magical sensation. She wanted this moment to go on forever. A moment she could not even dream of had become a reality. If only it could have lasted a whole night, but John suddenly opened his eyes and stared at Sarah with great incredulity.

"What are you doing?" He asked weakly, continuing to be half asleep.

Without saying anything, the girl rushed headlong upstairs into her room and closed the door behind her. Clambering under the blanket, like a child afraid of monsters, she was most afraid to hear John's steps and then a knock at the door. She mentally scolded herself for what had just happened and for the shameful thing she had done. She grabbed the beads from the table and began twisting them in her hands, biting her lip and looking at the door with fear. But after an eternal half an hour John did not appear, and Sarah could breathe a sigh of relief. This was the first time in her life when she wanted the morning never to come. The shame she experienced was equal to the most terrible sin imaginable. Continuing to slowly trace the beads, she suddenly felt a burning sensation in her fingers. Time seemed to slow down as if it were about to stop. The space became bathed in a veil of red light and objects seemed to have been deliberately rearranged. The door of the room suddenly opened by itself with a slow, eerie creak, which was particularly strange given the fact that it had never creaked in the past. At first Sarah thought it was John, but no… there was no one there.

Cautiously rising up from the bed and again putting on her bathrobe, she carefully walked to the door, trembling from the terrible pictures she had drawn in her head. She knew she could expect anything. Instinctively returning to the night when the two thugs made their way into her house, Sarah only wished that this wouldn't happen again. She whispered her prayers to herself and gingerly looked out into the corridor. It was empty, only the chandelier, for an unknown reason, was swaying above the stairs. With tip-toed steps Sarah moved to the railing and looked down. She caught a glimpse of someone downstairs who quickly passed into another room. The poor girl both hoped it was John, but worried if it were he. Deeply embarrassed about what had happened, she was nearly ready to go back into her room, but noticed that a light coming from the first floor was on, and brighter than usual. Despite her intuition telling her not to go down there, Sarah decided it was right and rational thing to do. The girl was little scared, but ready to go and check on the mysterious light. But just then, she heard laughter from the outside. It seemed as if there was some sort of celebration going on with voices pouring out from everywhere. Bewildered and wondering who could possibly make this kind of noise in the middle of the night, Sarah immediately went downstairs to the front door. No matter which direction she looked through the peephole, nothing was there to be seen. Then she went to the window in the kitchen and looked through the blinds. So strange… the street was flooded with bright sunlight as if it was the best part of summer. While the area remained completely deserted, she still heard a continuous stream of joyful voices. Was it another dream?

Sarah returned to the door and went out into the street, expecting to see crowds of people, but no. It was empty, as before, except the sun was unusually shiny in the otherwise night-black sky. It was not an eclipse but something completely alien to this world. She did not feel fear or trepidation. To the contrary, it was all so fascinating: the sky softly filled with warm sun rays which were pleasantly tickling to the skin. Sarah was rapted in reverence like coming face-to-face with a great work of art. The street smelled of fresh cut grass and blooming flowers, all carried by a light breeze. The leaves rustled and the trees themselves playfully swayed from side to side, in the background she could hear the sounds of people, whom she could not see, dancing and playing games. The girl clearly felt them, even though they were not visible, but again, it did not frighten her. She seemed to be in a vivid dream, the most beautiful dream in her life. Absolutely without any particular reason, she laughed out loud. Her soul was happy and it made her want to dance. Without realizing her actions, she continued down the street with delight, watching frozen drops of rain in the air, glittering like diamonds, and there were thousands of them. It was a real fairy tale.

Rejoicing like a child, she was running along the street, with her eyes closed in a state of bliss, inhaling the invigorating air and spreading her hands out in both directions. She did not even notice when ahead of her appeared a luminous figure from nowhere. She was still running when her inner voice told her to open her eyes and look straight ahead. Sarah didn't expect to see anything that would bother her, but then she noticed *it*, and she stopped abruptly, looking and trying to understand who or what it was. At first, it was difficult to recognize anything at all, but soon Sarah recognized this figure was the one whom she had once met and who in fact, had handed her the mysterious, multi-colored beads that possessed such special power. The naked golden-haired girl was approaching quickly, as smoothly as the boat on a lake of very still water.

"I was looking for you, praying for you to return every day," Sarah burst out with joyful words.

In the next instant, an invisible force tied her body up so absolutely that she could neither open her mouth nor turn her head. The creature, whom at first she thought she recognized as a friend, was approaching and glowed so brightly that to look directly at it was terribly painful. Sarah's joy was quickly replaced by a looming fear of the unknown. She did not have time to really take in the situation when the plastic, mannequin-like body was already in front of her at arm's length. Such an eerie, yet mystical sight. Sarah started breathing heavily, like she could not catch her breath and her whole body was contorted. If earlier she believed that she could easily meet "it" -- even if it was an angel -- she doubted it now. Again, unable to say a word, she could only wait for further interaction.

"Never take them off!" Shouted the voice in a strident, dissonant tone that was both frightening and imploring.... "Because nothing else can save you. They are your only protection from evil and the only protection for the rest of the world as well. Be careful!"

Immediately two hands, hot as fire, seized Sarah by the neck. The girl's eyes instantly bulged and wild pain pierced every part of her body. No matter how much she wanted to scream, she could not squeeze out even a sound. Obviously, she could not resist this higher power. Already beginning to lose consciousness, her eyes rolled back, and there would be nothing ahead, but dead silence and emptiness.

The angel's hands suddenly released her and she fell to the ground. She noticed that her neck stopped burning but it felt as if the sky crashed down upon her head. The darkness returned and again it began to pour. With her head pressed to the asphalt, Sarah cried deeply, unable to move and not understanding why she was cursed with misfortune and why the angel had hurt her. She tried to hide the beads as best she could but her efforts were in vain. What was she supposed to do with them? Wear them so everyone could see them and put herself in great danger? If this was the ultimate plan and she was to become a walking object of sacrifice, then she was ready to give herself for the sake of the God and all those whose souls she could save. Feelings of fright and despair took over her being. She cried without stopping until she heard the sound of a car horn blaring at her. Her vision was flooded by bright headlights and her ears were filled with the screech of the brakes. Sarah helplessly managed to lift her head and heard the door slam. Then she heard a sound of the some's heels, after which a woman with glasses ran up to her, who was probably fifty years old. She had a very worried look on her face.

"Miss... are you all right?" The woman was clearly panicked as she gently used her hands to lift Sarah to an upright position.

"Yes... yes... I think so," The girl said with a pliant tongue, trying to take in as much air as possible. "I'll be fine, but could you please help me to get up."

"I can call an ambulance," The woman said.

"No, thank you, that won't be necessary. Don't worry," Sarah shook her head and she struggled to keep the balance. "Thank you for your help, but I have to go."

"Are you sure you'll be ok?"

"Yes, I am all right."

"Where do you live? I'll help you at least to get home. Being in a such state out here all alone is very dangerous. It chills my blood thinking about that maniacal clown who showed up in our neighborhood just a couple of months ago. So terrible… so terrible."

Sarah's only thought was that this woman who so generously offered her help had no idea that the maniacal clown actually had appeared in her house and tried to murder her and her friend John. It was only by the will of God that they both survived. It all could have ended tragically on that night.

"That's my house, that's my house," These were the last words Sarah remembered as she staggered toward the front door.

At first the wind was buzzing in her ears, the rain was splattering on the ground and thunder rattled the sky. As time went on, Sarah just breathed more and more calmly. All her anxieties subsided into the background. A sound like a mixture of thousands of voices kept repeating in her mind that she must keep the beads on at all times for her own safety, that there was no turning back now, and that time could not be stopped, and it will probably get worse before it gets better. The girl understood that this was all so crazy. The most terrible thing was that she felt she could not do anything about it. Why did God leave her to be terrorized by inexplicable forces? She read the Bible all her life and constantly went to church… and now she asked herself "what for???" It only resulted in pain and suffering. Sarah held a contentious back-and-forth conversation with herself, posing and then answering questions. Random words, disconnected phrases, and various numbers began to bombard her mind, her soul was tormented and did not find peace. She was crying, very much, being lost, unhappy and alone. She felt dead, and it just could not be worse.

She stood in the midst of a large flowering garden. It was very hot, despite the fact that there was a faint breeze that occasionally broke the stillness. At the sight of all this wonderful beauty, a conscious feeling of delight flourished from the depths of her heart. Sarah looked around. She saw foliage hanging from every tree, little birds jumping from branch to branch, butterflies fluttering in the air and the wings of dragonflies whirring as they made their way from destination to destination. All this was so enchanting that a sudden spate of laughter from the thickets made Sarah prick up her ears to listen. She soon heard the laughter again and immediately moved in its direction. After a couple of minutes, she found herself in a meadow near an old, classic mansion, similar to one about which legends could be written. There was also a well nearby, and on a lounge chair was a girl with chestnut hair who was sunbathing. Sarah took a good look at her and decided to slowly approach.

"Julia?" She couldn't believe her eyes.

"Sarah? I thought you went to the pond."

"What pond are you talking about? I don't understand what I'm doing here." Sarah rummaged through the disconnected depths of her consciousness, realizing that she had returned to what she had managed so hard to leave before, only now there was no Antoine to help her.

"Sarah are you all right?" There was a short pause. "Stop it; you're frightening me," Julia said, rising from her chair. "If you're thinking about going back to the States, there's very little time left before the move. Mom said that she needs to settle a few important things and then we can go. I hope it will be New York! I don't want to go to dad's house; it's so boring there."

"Who told you that we are going to dad's?"

"I am just saying…"

"Did mom, by the way, specify what exactly she has to finish?" Sarah really was searching for answers to some unasked questions she could never figure out in real life, but maybe she could in this dream.

"I do not know," Julia shrugged. "Maybe grandfather could tell us."

"Where is he?"

"In the house. By the way, this morning I read some interesting stuff about this area."

"Oh really? What was it??"

"Apparently many centuries ago, at exactly this place, stood a large castle that also served as a fortress. Some terrible things happened; the king and all his courtiers were killed in one day and the fortress became a haven for dark forces. The only survivor was the king's adviser, who recounted the story."

"Sounds like a fairy tale," Sarah said.

"Like a *scary* fairy tale" Julia added. "The whole thing is an "unofficial historical fact". Nevertheless, if we believe it's true, then we're now in a place in which every corner is saturated with supernatural forces. Unknown energy is hidden in these very lands!"

"It seems to me that this mansion is long dead and that we must get out of here. I don't understand what pleasure grandfather gets from living here alone in the middle of this wilderness."

"Hey, *dark forces*, where are you?" Julia yelled down into the well.

By her behavior it was clear that all this mysticism excited her childlike imagination. She deftly dropped the bucket down into the well and began shouting out different phrases, hoping to get an answer. For obvious reasons, no one answered her, but this did not deter her.

"Since when did you start being interested by ghost stories?" Sarah asked concernedly.

"Sometimes it seems I hear voices -- especially at night when everything is silent."

"Julia, I already told you those are just nightmares. You must stop reading horror stories, especially before bed."

"You sound like mother."

"I might sound like mother, but I'm talking like your sister," Sarah boiled.

"A sister who is not always there...," Julia broke off and, having scooped up a cup of water and in one gulp, drank it down.

"What are you doing? Sarah got mad and ripped the full bucket of water from Julia's hands and threw it down the well. "It's dangerous to drink unboiled water!"

"Go away!" Julia cried. "Why did you come here?"

These words rang out in Sarah's head with an unpleasant sound and she felt uneasy. Immediately the dream-time passed into the deep, cold autumn. The surroundings were dark as a late evening and from behind the bare trees was seen a frozen pond. The first snow was slowly falling down from the sky and all around it was as quiet as in a cemetery.

"This water is somehow charged with magic, I feel it with my whole body, "Julia confessed. "I knew it, I knew it!"

Suddenly she trembled and burst into a coughing spell. Her legs gave way and she almost fell, but luckily she held onto the edge of the well. Frightened, Sarah immediately ran up to sister and wrapped her arms around her.

"What happened?" She asked nervously. "Are you okay?"

"Something is stuck in my throat," Julia uttered with great difficulty and tears forming in her eyes. "It's getting hard for me to breathe. Sarah, please help me."

"Granddad!" Sarah cried out with all her might, and in a flash she felt numb, her voice was gone, just like that.

Not only could she no longer make a sound, but her body stopped obeying as if it had been paralyzed. In a matter of seconds, she again moved in dream-time. This time Julia was not there, next to her stood her grandfather, beating on the well lid with his heavy hammer.

"I don't understand what's going on..." Suddenly Sarah regained her voice.

"Can't you see, I'm hammering a well," Came the stern reply. "Your sister is very sick. She was poisoned with water from this fucking pit." Apparently the poison has leaked into it from the pond."

"Julia is sick?" Sarah said with horror. "Lord!"

"Why did you let her drink this water?" Grandfather shouted so loudly that it became really creepy. It was not a human voice, but something completely different.

Overhead, black clouds covered the sky, making it as dark as night, and the trees suddenly began to sway from a strong wind that did not exist. It was such a strange feeling because Sarah knew that she was in another terrible dream and could not do anything about it. She was scared to imagine what might happen next. It all seemed to her if she were reliving the same moments that she wanted so badly to forget. Her nightmare memories were some of the most terrible in her life. For many years she had tried to rid herself of them -- and she nearly succeeded had she not made that visit to the psychic medium. Otherwise all these events would have slipped deeply into the past. Sarah began to retreat in fear when she noticed some humanlike shadows that had slipped between the trees in the garden.

"Grandfather, what's going on out there?" Sarah whispered in fright while looking around.

"Grave critters… you who woke them up. Why did you let Julia drink this goddamn water?"

"She did it on purpose when I wasn't paying attention…"

"You could've done whatever was necessary to stop her if you had wanted to, but you didn't, damn you."

"I am not like you!" Sarah shouted out in anger.

Immediately there was silence. Sarah looked into the furious, bloodshot eyes of her grandfather and couldn't believe that it was he. It was someone else, but not he. Stone facial features, lifeless glassy eyes, arms held tensely with prominent veins, and tightly clenched teeth - all this suddenly appeared in a man to whom such things were not inherent.

"Where is Julia?" Sarah asked.

"In her room... where else?" The man said angrily.

Time advanced forward again, and Sarah this time found herself in Julia's room. The girl with brown hair was sitting on the dirty floor in the corner. Her whole body was trembling. Next to her stood an iron mug with yellowed water.

"Something weird is going on with grandfather," Sarah said breathlessly. "We need to leave right now. We have to escape from this place."

"Do you think the story about the *dark forces* is true? Do you think an evil spirit has possessed our grandfather?"

"I have no idea, my dear. All I know is that now he frightens me and I do not want to spend us another minute here."

"Grandfather thinks I deliberately poisoned the well."

"You're crazy!" Sarah flared. "...He's gone crazy. He told me a completely different story. Give me your hand, we must leave."

"What if he notices us?"

"Well... that could happen," Sarah hurried. "Enough talking, Julia," She was very nervous, afraid to imagine what would happen if the old man suddenly found them on this floor.

They quietly walked out into the corridor when at the very end, next to the brown door, appeared the ominous silhouette of their grandfather with a hammer in his right hand. It was nothing but the shadow of a maniac from horror films, the outlines of a monster that had lost its personality and whose main vocation was to bring violence and murder.

"No you don't..." His throaty voice sounded like thunder. "...you're not going anywhere. You hear me?"

"I do not want to stay here any longer!" Julia shouted and escaping from her sister's hand ran downstairs to the first floor.

"Julia, wait!" Sarah rushed right after her.

She got outside and saw the retreating figure of Julia. Without losing a second, Sarah began to trail her and shout her name. A damp wind blew, snow fell from the sky, and mysterious shadows continued to dart between the trees. The well lid flew into the air with a whistle and clouds of steam started blowing out. Sarah did not even pay attention to it; she did not care. More than anything in the world she wanted to catch up with her sister. Fighting her fear, she moved into the garden.

"Julia, don't be foolish… Stop!" she screamed, "What's wrong with you?"

Peering at the barely perceptible outline of the garden ahead, Sarah flinched in horror, seeing those who before this had hidden behind a mask of darkness. Empty, dark souls wrapped their arms around the trees and looked at approaching girl with black, dead eyes. Their faces were curved in the likeness of a grin, and their jaws protruded far forward, as if they had been contorted with a blow from a hammer. Sarah stopped, covered in sweat, not knowing what to do next and afraid to make a move. She did not have a way forward or back. Closing her eyes and almost crying, she began to quickly recite prayers and when she finished, she saw that the sinister silhouettes had disappeared as if they had never existed. God's blessing - the demonic creatures went back to Hell.

Despite the terrible cold, which was stinging her entire body, she continued to stoically make her way into the garden following the footprints left by her sister. She was shaking with an unprecedented chill, as when one has a fever, but knew she had to stay strong if she wanted to save herself and her sister. If this feeling continued much longer, she wouldn't be able to take even one step further. She did not look forward anymore, just down to her feet. After a long span of fifteen minutes, the trail suddenly was lost. With great difficulty, Sarah looked up and saw in front of her familiar the snow-covered pond. Looking around, she began to call out to Julia's name, hoping that she would respond, but it all was in vain. She collapsed to her knees, losing all hope at this point, unable to cry or cry any more. At that very moment she heard a tapping from under the ice somewhere in the center of the pond. Initially, the girl thought it was her imagination, and that it was a sign of impending death, but a little later and listening attentively, she realized that the strange knock was real. Still somewhat confused, she soon got up to her feet and gently stepped onto the ice at great risk, to begin moving toward the source of the sound. Moreover, she was afraid that her grandfather would chase after her, and then one could only guess what he might do. At that moment, a voice sounded in Sarah's head. It was not her voice -- but someone else's -- ordering her to stop. This is what she did just before the ice under her feet unexpectedly started to move and the water beneath it lit up. Sarah screamed out as the ice broke away and she fell into the water, immediately seeing the body of Julia that had emerged from the abyss.

For a few seconds, she had to endure the most frightful moments of her life - this was when death breathes down your neck, when there seems to be no hope for salvation and when there was only an empty blackness ahead. The ice pieces did not wait and instantly fused above her head, and Sarah's body began to cramp from the cold. Sarah wanted to utter a silent scream, but could not. She grabbed her sister's pale arm and began to try to break the ice, but all her strength was completely sapped. The water for no reason became warm and started to send up bubbles. There was a whistling sound and a cloud of scum rose from the lake's floor. From the shadows incomprehensible creatures emerged, reminiscent of electric eels, whose energy began to pierce the two girls. Everything blurred in front of Sarah's eyes. There was not enough oxygen and she practically stopped breathing. Using her last ounces of strength, she struck heavy blows to the ice covering. An instant later the girls were grabbed by someone's hand that dragged them through the ice to the surface. Choking and coughing, Sarah suddenly saw her grandfather swinging his foot down hard, trying to break the ice. The man in his broad-brimmed hat struck it several times more broke through, and pulled out lifeless Julia.

There was nothing more terrible than seeing her own sister not showing any signs of life. The old man immediately began artificial respiration on Julia, while watching him alternate between compressions and breaths, Sarah watched but could not say a word. She was beside herself with confusion and practically dying of exposure. It seemed to be the end for dear Julia, but fate, apparently, decided otherwise. The girl with brown hair suddenly spewed out water in a deep cough, gasped for air, and opened her eyes.

"Julia!" Sarah cried out with great relief and rushed over to embrace her sister. "You frightened me so!! Lord, don't do that again, I beg you."

"Ohhh, my dears," The man started crying and held both of his granddaughters in his big arms.

Once again everything melted away, and Sarah found herself sitting with Julia on an empty beach. The bright orange sun was slowly sloping down toward the horizon and almost touched the watery surface. The waves lit up with magical light. From a distant shore came the call of birds. The bluish waves started to inviting the two girls to join the rhythmic game.

"I never dreamed that I would ever move to New York, especially after mom's..." Julia couldn't finish her phrase. "I still cannot believe that we are here... I miss you Sarah. I wish you could move there with us."

"I missed you too Julia, but you knew, I couldn't leave dad all alone..." Sarah said with deep sadness.

"The most important is that we are far away from that house."

"So terrible. My blood still runs cold when I remember what had happened even though it was years ago..."

"Indeed."

Only now Sarah noticed what a frightened look her sister had on her face. She just wanted to forget about what had happened as soon as possible. The problem was that the nightmare she had passed through did not leave her in peace. Its remnants haunted her every time she went to bed, and it would repeat endlessly, even years later. Trying not to drown in the sea of abyss, Sarah had turned into religion, which her father tried so hard to earlier impose on her; it had been tremendously helpful after her mother's tragic death. Knowing that all this was a big trial, Sarah believed God was again testing or preparing her for something bigger than was yet unknown.

She was awakened by the sun that was flooding her face with light and made the room as impossibly hot as if summer had somehow mysteriously arrived. For a few minutes, the girl just relaxed in the blankets and watched what was happening around her. How the shadows moved slowly along the walls and ceiling, the birds fluttering among the bare branches, how the sound of rustling branches came from somewhere above the roof, and the rhythmic sound of passing cars on the street. This mixture of the familiar, ordinary and domestic reminded her that she was living in the present. Sarah stretched involuntarily and looked at her watch. It was just about two in the afternoon. The memories of last night returned to her like an electric shock, which immediately put her into great anxiety. Thoughts about what she did to John felt like her soul was tainted, and she was perfectly aware that she had made one of the biggest mistake of her life. She didn't want to see him now; she was sure she could not survive it. Sarah also felt the same about her sister. If Julia found out about what had happened, Sarah could not even imagine the consequences. She thought about simply not going to the fashion show, but that would stretch the relationship with her sister to the limit -- and not for the better. She could not let the regret of the moment affect her whole being. Confused and lost, she suddenly noticed that her phone began to vibrate, and on the screen appeared Julia's picture.

"My God... not now," Sarah said nervously, realizing that she had no choice but to answer.

"Where have you gone? I called you a thousand times?" Came an angry voice.

"I am sorry, I did not feel very well last night. I was awake most of the time."

"Ohhh, I'm very sorry to hear about that... What happened?" Julia's tone dropped immediately.

"Apparently, food poisoning."

"My God, that is the last thing you need. I hope you are feeling better now."

"Yes, much better," Sarah said. "I need to take a hot bath and then everything should be fine."

"Are you sure you will be all right?" Julia was concerned. "If you feel sick I don't want you do force yourself to go to the show... I'd understand"

And now Sarah felt so guilty, that despite all her worries, she couldn't ignore Julia's very important day. She would not forgive herself if she put her selfish concerns as the reason to not go. It would only make her sister sad -- sad on a day when she deserved to be shining with happiness.

"No, I believe I can make it to the show!" Sarah said firmly.

"I hope so! Please take care of yourself and, if possible, if you really feel well enough, I need you here before the show. I need some help. But if you can't come earlier, that's absolutely fine with me."

"Before the show? Like what time?"

"Five o'clock, if you can. One of my girls fell sick so I've had no time to look for a replacement. I need someone who will help the models to get dressed. If they had to do it themselves, they simply would not be able to cope."

"Okay, then I'll be there at five o'clock!"

"I love you Sarah! Take your time, see you later then."

For Sarah this was a good sign. Clearly John did not tell Julia anything, and in principle, why would he do that anyway? Glancing at the beads glowing in the sunlight, she touched them with an apprehensive hand, remembering to the smallest detail her meeting with the angel who literally ordered her to keep the beads with her. As before, she felt a burning sensation around her neck and a feeling that she was suffocating. As if scalded, she immediately took them off, lay them on the nightstand, and hurried into the bathroom. Having entered into the hot water, she plunged into thoughts about things more positive than what she felt when she woke up. She tried to forget about everything that happened last night, but still her soul was tormented with pain. No matter how she comforted herself, saying that it was all because of the alcohol, that everything was not as scary as it seemed, John's face kept popping up in her mind and did not allow her to concentrate on anything else. There was only one way out.

After her bath, Sarah poured herself a large glass of white wine and began to style her hair while listening to some music. Looking at herself in the mirror, she hated the face that looked back at her, smiling and secretly scoffing at who she saw. Restraining herself from self-loathing as much as possible, she suddenly let out a scream of anguish. Yes, she just screamed and struck at her reflection with all her strength. The impact caused the mirror to crack, and a few fragments cut into her palm. The blood gushed out and Sarah grabbed a towel and clamped the wound. She ran into the room and sat herself down on the bed, sobbing desperately and hating herself with all her heart. She wanted to disappear without a trace and never return to this world. Despair, which so tightly bound her, seemed it would not let her go. Through Sarah's sobbing, the beads -- the hateful beads which acted more like a poisonous noose than a protective amulet, again appeared in her sight.

"No, no!" She screamed hysterically, grabbing them off the nightstand with a bloody hand, and threw them against the wall. From the impact, the chain on which they hung stretched so tightly that it could not stand the pressure unlatching the clasp, and the multicolored beads tumbled onto the floor, spreading out in all directions.

"God... God... My God," Sarah cried an ocean of tears and fell onto the bed, her face buried in a pillow.

She needed to process her feelings, but, as always, as usual, she was running out of time and had no idea what to do next. After crying for a good thirty minutes, she finally relaxed, unable to even move. Fashion show? No, not now, she did not even want to think about it. Why was all this happening right now? Why not later? Why did the Lord hate Sarah so much? She did not find answers to any of these questions. She lay there in the house of a man she loved with all her heart, and she could not even admit that to anyone but herself. She was alone and, apparently, she deserved it. She did not deserve happiness, at least not in this life. Sarah wanted to disappear, but didn't know how. Gradually she slowed herself down, her breathing leveled off and she raised her head. The sun no longer shone through the window and the room became noticeably gloomy which meant only one thing - the day had begun to decline toward sunset.

The cut on her palm of the hand was burning unpleasantly, and it was still bleeding, though not as much as when it happened. Sarah winced. Exhausted, she struggled to get out of bed. Her muscles twitched as she crouched to the floor and began crawling on her knees to collect the beads. Fortunately returning them their previous state was not so difficult. Carefully fastening the chain, Sarah put the beads on the bed next to the prepared evening gown, hurried into the bathroom to get herself ready, and to treat the cut. She glanced at the clock and thought that she had plenty of time, but somehow it was nearly four o'clock and almost time to leave the house.

As she was dressing, what came to mind was a fairy tale about a place that now lies buried by the sands of time -- and all because of the fact that time was misused. The city, called Nine, had become rather famous in a surprisingly short time, primarily because of all the great masters who lived there. Nine was many years ahead of its time, with its incredible creations about which there were no less incredible rumors. People from all over the world wanted to see the famous Nine, and those who visited this place once in their lifetime, spread the word and created picturesque legends. It was here that there were amazing glass bridges which shone every night bathed in moonlight, as well as musical alleys and fiery fountains. Here, also, so-called *living houses* were constructed, that were slowly moving on the perimeter and *shadow theaters* in which performances were staged depending on the position of the sun in the sky. Among other things, the city was famous for its light, airy clothing and rejuvenating springs that kept the inhabitants from ever growing old. It was a real paradise. Everyone was happy, and nothing could be better.

Nine's prosperity lasted a very long time until the day when the power-holders had decided to cash in on all those who, in fact, made some financial contribution to the city. Deciding that their ideas and creations could no longer be free, so they started making money on everything the city had to offer. The costs became astronomical and no one could afford to take advantage of the wonders of the city any longer. As a result, a disastrous financial crisis ravaged the city, and everyone who lived there either became rich or impoverished. The latter simply could not afford a luxurious life any longer, and therefore left Nine. Sadly, this included many great minds and masters. Here is when the advisors to the rulers came into action, recommending them to temper their ardor and to think about all those whose lives they'd destroyed. They implored them to start caring about the city itself first and to stop thinking about their heavily-laden pockets. Even though it was not possible to win the eternal battle over greed, everyone who lived in Nine believed that even without foreign help they could rebuild and reestablish Nine into a more powerful and possibly even the richest city in the world. And that was what happened. The glory of Nine's wealth traveled at the speed of light and scattered around the world, and was what made spiteful ill-wishers focused an eye on the famous city.

What happened later could easily be assumed. Almost all the foreign outsiders threatened war. The inhabitants began to panic and to build fortifications, which for many years they never had to consider; they just spent all their time relaxing and having fun at their pleasures. Their downfall finally came. Having wasted so much time, they now lacked what was so necessary. They began begging all those who had left Nine to return home but there was not enough time or ability to protect the city. For so many years -- even centuries, they had created a paradise on earth which was now literally collapsing right before their eyes. The enemies proved to work very fast, overtaking the city in one day. They utterly destroyed it, plundering and killing all those who had remained there. Nine was swallowed up by its own greed, sins, ignorance and blood of recent past generations. Time had spared it for centuries because its people had always cared about it, but when their progeny neglected such a great city, time became its number one enemy. Up to the very end, the inhabitants of Nine did not realize this. When the great catastrophe was over, there was nothing left but for the sands of time to swallow up the ruins of the great city. There was only a desert and nothing else.

Time was no longer ticking in Sarah's favor either. Not that all was lost, but now the years of the tender innocence she had shared with John, in her mind, were gone. She felt the same as the people of Nine must have felt in their last hours, namely, that she had wasted so much time distracted by people and things that her actions lead to a loss of forward momentum and even a regretful act.

She was always so hard on herself. How much easier it would have been, she thought, like for those in Nine, to have paid attention and to have acted while there was still time. She hated the bitter taste of loss in her mouth, realizing that from this day forward she would not only have to act, but *live* differently. And although it was not possible to erase the past, it might be possible to renew her life and finally start fully living. Sarah had to admit that she had been existing as a survivor, not as someone who lived their life in the present. If she hadn't spent so much of her precious youth concentrating on her secret feelings for John, making sure everyone else was safe and cared for, and otherwise wasting time dreaming and not doing, she could have built a more productive and authentic life. Until this epiphany she had created instead a life of self-imposed limits. Sarah could no longer escape the blowing sands of time that stung her face, reminding her that mistakes were to be learned from, not repeated. What was done - was done; in Sarah's new consciousness the only path was to move forward.

Sarah resolutely put on the red dress given to her by Julia and obediently adorned her neck with those most colorful beads. She did not want to go to the show at all, but she remembered how important it was for Julia to see her there, especially on this day. Nor had she had not forgotten what the angel told her last night: to always wear the beads. But most of all, it was her heart that truly prompted her to wear the beads. The last few moments had seemed like a dream; the girl didn't even remember how she had gotten back to her room. She sent a short message to John saying that she needed to be at Lena Barbella's mansion much earlier the planned and went down to the street to hail a taxi.

Even before leaving the apartment Sarah had drunk enough to make her head spin. The entire time she was in the taxi she was still so full of emotions that even the cognac could not suppress her busied mind. At some point during the taxi ride she lost consciousness and came to her senses only when the driver gave her a nudge on the shoulder at the end of the trip while trying to wake her up.

"We have arrived, miss," He said in a disgruntled voice; he was impatient to get her out of his car which now had a unpleasant smell of alcohol.

"How much?" Sarah asked, opening her eyes with difficulty, still being in only a half-reality.

"One hundred twenty three dollars."

"Here's one fifty," She drawled. "Keep the change."

"Thank you, miss."

The taxi driver helped Sarah to get out at the main entrance to the six-story classic mansion that was in the East Village. In front of it were parked many expensive cars, it was crowded with journalists and photographers, and random passers-by. This event was second only to New York Fashion Week. Sarah's attention was immediately drawn to the gargoyles that guarded the roof of this Victorian house. One of them, probably the scariest one, towered high above the main entrance. Light showed from every window with the shadows of the guests moving back and forth against it, like a ghost-ball. Sarah was enveloped in strange, multiple sensations. On the one hand, she was happy to be there, where ordinary people were in fact not allowed to enter, on the other hand, this place and event itself frightened her. She felt something dark was hidden in the depths of this ancient house. With a shaky gait, she approached the gates but was stopped by a security guard.

"I'm on the list" She said and showed the invitation.

"Your name, please?" asked one of the guys.

"Sarah Brown," She replied with an unusual air of superiority. "Is there a problem?"

"Not at all. Just checking," Said another guard and, stepping aside, started talking on his shoulder-mounted radio. Sarah felt very uncomfortable, thinking that perhaps there was something wrong and that she was not trusted. A wave of nausea only added to her thoughts of turning back and returning home. Either it was because of the alcohol or the situation itself. Sarah knew it was a mix of both. She could feel her rising anger and thought she might explode. A minute later, security returned and wished the girl a great evening and promptly apologizing for the inconvenience. It made her feel a little less anxious but no more than that.

This was the first time Sarah felt so extremely unwelcome company. She knew perfectly well why it was so; she was not a famous person and no one had heard of her. People like her who penetrated fashion's inner circle were always treated in the same way. Wanting to quickly hide from the tormenting eyes reporters and others who were curiously looking at her, she rather climbed the marble stairs to the porch and dialed Julia's number.

"I'm at the mansion. Where are you?" She asked nervously squinting at the people crowded in front of the gates.

"You arrived already?" Julia asked.

"Yes, I'm on the porch."

"Come inside, I'll be right there."

Sarah turned to face the entrance, when the smiling butler smoothly swung open the door and kindly offered her entrance to the main hall. There were many beautiful people specially invited for such an auspicious evening. Among them there were celebrities, from actors and musicians to politicians and businessmen. In addition, there were a lot of personnel serving everyone. There was such unprecedented fuss you would have thought that it was a royal reception. Yes, and, by the way, Sarah felt a little like a real Cinderella. Slightly embarrassed, she took a glass of champagne from a waiter who come up to her with a tray and, thanking him, went to the window where she stood next to a marble replica of a statue of Venus.

"Here you are!" A familiar voice was heard, and Sarah saw a girl with chestnut hair emerge from the crowd. "Oh, my God... you look amazing!"

"Thank you!" Sarah's response was a little slurred.

"Sarah, have you been drinking?" Julia was surprised. "And what happened to your palm?"

"Yes, I have had a couple of cocktails... oh that, just a minor accident, I tried to move a flower vase to another place, but I slipped and fell down, bringing the vase with me..."

"Oh, I'm so sorry!" Julia hugged her sister tightly. "I hope the cut is not serious. Let me see."

"It's all right, do not worry! Better show me what you need me to do!"

"Sure, sure, come with me."

Julia took her sister across the lobby behind the main staircase where there was a small elevator. They immediately went to the top floor that seemed more like a backstage, where there were even more people. Almost all of them were models for the show. The two sisters did not even have time to get out of the elevator when a tall blue-eyed blonde ran up to them.

"Julia, I was looking for you everywhere!"

"Nadi, May I introduce you to Sarah!" Julia said with a smile.

"Sarah!" Exclaimed the blonde and rushed to the confused girl with embraces. "I am so glad to meet you in person!"

"Thank you, Nadi," Sarah said, realizing that in front of her was Nadi Levenshaut, one of Julia's close friends. "I'm very pleased to meet you. Julia has told me a lot about you."

"Julia and I have known each other for a long time, for ages, and she's a terrific and talented person. Can you believe what she has achieved? Presenting her first collection in New York! It's incredible! I'm just so happy to be with her on such a special day!"

"Thank you, Nadi," Julia blushed. "So… why were you looking for me?"

"Christy and Veronica will not be able to go with the opening, so I'll have to find replacements for them both."

"Oh my God," Julia breathed out. "What happened?"

"There's been a little accident… I think Christy had a nervous breakdown. Earlier they argued and really went at it. She actually attacked Veronica."

"This is crazy!" Julia was shocked and couldn't find any other words to comment on the situation.

"I know," Nadi nodded with a smile, in fact feeling guilty for what had happened even though it was not her fault. She did not want anything to spoil the day for Julia.

"Well, I think we have to do something -- and fast", Julia said trying to talk and think at the same time. She needed a second to figure out a solution. At first, she looked at Sarah, then at Nadi, and then to the crowd of half-naked skinny models rushing to be on time for the show. "Hey girls, we're gonna shuffle the deck a bit," Julia's voice was louder than ever before -- full of power and energy to make everything work perfectly despite the circumstances. "Kate... Melanie... you'll have to fill in for the opening. Nadi, please take care of them."

"All right," said the blonde. "Girls, let's hurry," She spoke in staccato. "See you later Sarah, there's just a bunch of things to do."

"Yes, of course," The girl nodded.

"Come on, I'll show you your stuff," Julia called out to Sarah, and led her into a small room with tons of clothes. "Everything has been already marked a long time ago, I mean that everything is prepared for each of them, most of the dresses have a back zipper and they will just need help to get it on."

"And how will I know who must wear what?"

"Don't worry, they'll know. Okay?"

"Yes, sure," Sarah smiled.

"Thanks so much once again for agreeing to help! If you need anything, I'm right here. Just call me on my cell phone. You are a lifesaver Sarah!"

Julia immediately walked out of the room and left Sarah alone. She had plenty of time before the start of the show, so she took one of the dresses and carefully held the dress in front of her as if she were one of the models, and admired herself in the mirror, turning to the right, and then to the left. The muscles of her whole body uncontrollably tensed up. Her eyes twitched nervously, and the pupils widened and were bloodshot. In her head there was a storm of incomprehensible words and voices of thousands of people. It was simply impossible to understand and caused Sarah serious

C.L.O.U.D.S. Part One

discomfort. She shivered when her phone chimed out a message that had just arrived from John, who briefly replied: "No problem." This only added to her confusion. She staggered, took a deep breath, and leaned against the wall. In a fit of panic, she threw the dress on a chair and touched her beads with her right hand. All around everything lit up with a bright light, flickering like sunlight, and became incredibly distinct. She relaxed a little and opened the door to let in more air. The first thing she saw from the half-open door were the unusually beautiful and slender models looking like they had just come off the covers of all the fashion magazines, or maybe even more, they were real angels. They all seemed to be glowing and smiling, and they were really a pleasure just to look at. Sarah watched them with fascination, and her body began to slowly recover and calm down,

Suddenly from the same crowd emerged the very model, Melanie, that was supposed to open the show. She noticed Sarah looking at her, and then her face and body-transformed into something inhuman in a matter of seconds. With her new appearance she would do no more nor less to scare anyone to death. This model had red eyes, round and dilated, and her face was covered with thousands of wrinkles. It was hard to believe that the beautiful girl turned into a hundred-year old hag from a scary fairy tale, whose face was blackened and charred as if from a fire. Sarah held her breath when the ominous old woman quickly moved toward her. The girl didn't expect anything like that and backed away from the door before she could close it. Suddenly the door was forced open and inside came something she recognized as a demon.

"Help me," Sarah screamed hysterically. She stumbled and fell on the floor, when the demon grabbed a pair of dressmaker's scissors from the table.

"What's going on?" The door swung open and there appeared frightened faces.

Sarah just burst into tears, covering her face with her hands, as if someone were going to attack her.

"I beg you, don't touch me, Lord save my soul!"

"What happened to you?" Julia's voice was full of anxiety.

139

Then all the voices merged into one general rumble, and Sarah could no longer understand what was going on around her. She also heard Melanie's voice saying that she just wanted her to undo the top buckle on her back of her dress. Then Sarah felt someone's hands lift her and carried her out. After that, everything seemed like a dream state, and she later woke up on the couch in front of the fireplace, where the fire was crackling soothingly.

"You must stop drinking alcohol," Said a voice.

"What?" Sarah unexpectedly half rose up and saw a short-haired woman with black and white hair, smoothly laid straight to the shoulders, dressed in all black standing near the window.

Once the woman noticed that the girl had awoke, she approached her with quick steps and sat on the arm of the couch, as if she did not have enough room, and looked reproachfully into Sarah's eyes. Sarah felt unprecedented discomfort. She just didn't understand the situation, what had happened, and why she was here now. The only thing she could clearly confirm about herself in that moment, was that she was indecently drunk.

"We've all gone through this," The woman said. "There have been worse situations, but the main thing is to understand that it is time for this to stop."

"Who are you?" Sarah asked weakly and completely rose up to be in a sat position.

"My name is Christine. Christine Barbella."

"My God," Sarah flinched, not wanting to be in front of anyone, let alone this stern-looking woman. "I feel so ashamed..."

"Listen to me... What's your name again?"

"Sarah."

"Sarah, you have to tidy yourself up and forget about being nervous over things that are not really important. You understand that this evening is very special for my daughter. I don't want everything spoiled after so many days of preparations."

"I didn't have any intentions to spoil or…"

"You have not spoiled anything *yet*, my dear. Now you have to pull yourself together and support your sister on such an auspicious day. Don't you agree??"

"Of course I want that! Julia, where is she?" Sarah abruptly stood up from the couch.

"Hush," Christine took her hand. "She's very busy right now, and I do not think you should see each other before the show."

"But, she is my sister!"

"It doesn't matter how she's related to you. The principal thing now is to stay conscious. You are my guest, and I will be very grateful if you will respect my opinion of the situation. Look, the show will begin in less than half an hour. You have about thirty minutes to pull yourself together and come down into the main hall. I know you have a reserved VIP seat in the first row, but I do not think it's a good idea to sit there. I am afraid you will just distract your poor sister. You can choose any place from the fifth to the tenth row, but not closer, okay? You're an intelligent girl, I hope you understand. And remember, you are doing it not for me but for your sister. If you really care about her, do what I ask."

Sarah was confused and so uncomfortable that she wanted to escape and never come back. This world of fashion was so far removed from anything that was even vaguely familiar she wondered what she was doing here at all. The answer was actually very simple: Julia needed the support of her loved one, Sarah loved her very much, and would do everything possible for the sake of her sister's well-being. Even if it were something in which she was not the least bit interested - like this ridiculous fashion show. Looking intently into Christine Barbella's eyes, she nodded, not wanting to utter a word to this arrogant woman who disgusted her. The woman only smiled, having achieved the necessary answer, and quickly left the room.

She had reached her limit; Sarah could not hear such humiliating things. She knew the truth, what happened was not a vision or the consequence of an overload of alcohol. This time it was real. An evil spirit possessed the body of that young model and wanted to do something terrible to Sarah. Only by pure luck was she still alive. If everything had happened differently, Lena Barbella's mother would not have said such things.

The girl was burning with a desire to leave everything behind. For the first time in her stay in New York City, she wanted to return to her father's home. Suddenly her eyes were open to how the city was full of injustice and humiliation, everyone cared only about themselves, not paying attention to the inconvenience or pain caused to others. Now it revealed its dark self as a city of sharks - either you eat or you'd be eaten. Sarah grew up in a completely different environment, and this abominable attitude towards others, was alien to her.

Deciding not to succumb to her overwhelming emotions, she forced herself to go into the bathroom and give herself a fresh look. It took some time, but eventually she looked and felt like her old self. And now came the moment of truth. She walked along the corridors, trying not to look around, just lowering her head and looking at her feet. She was ashamed and uncomfortable, she could not do anything with this. Rather than waiting in the main lobby as she was instructed, she went to the show room which was already crowded with people and bumped into one of the visitors to the event.

"Ohh, I am so sorry", she said as she looked up at the person.

It was then that she saw his pale face, like a vampire from a horror movie. If Sarah knew someone with such a face, it must have been the only person on the planet - her boss, Igor Miltent - who happened to be here and now. What a strange coincidence that she ran into him and not somebody else. It was possible to think anything. Was he spying on her? Had he deliberately sought her out because he needed beads? ... Beads, yes of course! Nevertheless, Sarah couldn't allow her mind to wander so quickly so she reacted with the usual surprise anyone would have shown, having met someone totally unexpected. Seeing her confusion - even the fear in the girl's eyes - Igor only smiled and gently touched her shoulder.

"Don't worry. In such a crowd of people contact is unavoidable. He said. "It's a surprise to see you here, Sarah!"

"I'm here because of my sister – she is a designer."

"Ahhh, I see, I see! This is a very prestigious event; your sister must be very talented if she succeeded to get here."

"She is a professional and she knows her job."

"Excellent. What else can I say? This is a beautiful dress on you. It is your sister's handiwork?"

"Yes. It's an exclusive gift to me!"

"Well, now it is clear to me why your sister was invited to share her designs in the show. No doubt in a couple of years her name will be known to everyone around the world."

"It's very kind of you to say such a nice thing, I'll definitely tell her," Sarah promised, feeling the pride for Julia growing inside her, slowly suppressing all the unpleasant emotions that weighed down her heavy heart.

"I said this not to merely impress you. Your sister is immensely talented!"

"What you say is true, and thank you," Sarah's words sounded forced. "I really would like to continue our conversation, but I need to go..."

"That's okay. I'm in a hurry to get to my seat for the show as well. I suppose we're headed the same way. In any case, we will have time to talk on another day, right?"

"Most definitely."

Suddenly, in front of her, another visitor came out of the crowd with a really eerie look. He looked as if he were sick with something very serious. He was taking very deep breathes as if he did not have enough air and silently stared straight ahead with a stone face, but it was unclear at whom. Under his eyelids were bags, as if he had not slept for several days. His eyes were particularly and oddly bloodshot and, showing how inhuman they really were. This look with which this monster - and he could not be called otherwise - met with the girl was not friendly at all. It was the look of a predator, a hungry beast, who was not thinking about anything more than its prey. Among other things, there were bloodied, scabbed-over bruises on his neck, which gave an even more frightening appearance to him.

"Indigo, there you are!" Igor said. "I was looking for you. I wanted to have the pleasure of introducing you to this young and beautiful person Sarah Brown!"

"It's nice to meet you." Sarah reached out her right hand, feeling her heart begin to pound faster, and she was not comfortable being in his company at all.

What she first felt was a strong handshake, became infinitely long. It was getting stronger, and at some point, her hand was gripped by pain. With an eerie gaze, Indigo looked into her in the eyes, and then slowly moved to the beads. He was instantly being interested in them, there was no doubt. He half-opened his mouth, then clenched his teeth with such force that they creaked, and his nostrils began to swell with incredible force. Really becoming frightened, the girl somehow extricated herself from the handshake and quickly merged into the crowd of people scurrying into the showroom. The whole nightmarish day had turned into a big disaster. Sarah just hoped that it would all be over soon, when suddenly she saw John ahead of her. She sharply turned to the right and imperceptibly slipped into the depths of the row and hid, sitting down in the first available space.

Sarah knew very well that something was wrong with her, but she did not know what she could do to stop it. She cringed, as if she had been gripped by frost, and she closed her eyes. She whispered to herself in prayer, begging God to take pity on her, forgive all her sins, and to give her a chance to live a normal life. In this state she was ignoring everyone and everything, and stayed that way until the lights in the room were extinguished and the rumble of voices slowly came to silence. Bathed in bright spotlight, a small girl, with a black hair and expressive black-lined eyes, took the podium. It was Elena Barbella herself. At first, she thanked everyone for coming to her evening, and then she said a few words to her family, thanking each member, and in the end, she listed all those who helped her with the organization of the event. After a speech that lasted just over five minutes, she finally announced the show was "officially open".

There were applause but Sarah sat frozen and confused, still feeling herself as part of something grand. In her head, voices were heard again and one of them, more expressive, insistently telling her to leave this place. But no, the girl could not bring herself to do it. She sat motionless and looked at what was happening on the stage, unable to pay attention to the details. Before her eyes there were only flashes of cameras, exclamations from the audience, and the swirling colors in the play of stage lights paired with the music created for the event. Sarah wished she could enjoy the evening like the others in attendance, but the voices in her head did not subside, and were not going to subside. At some point it became unbearable and she thought she would lose her mind. Not able to stand it anymore she pinched herself with all her might, hoping that it would shift her attention to something else. As if waking from a deep sleep, she saw the models slinking down the catwalk, some of whom she remembered from having met in person. Undoubtedly, this was her sister's proudest moment. Sarah could only guess about Julia who was now surely breathlessness, carefully watching her creations in their debut. The girl glanced at her phone and saw a dozen missed calls from John and Julia, as well as text messages. Ignoring these, she put the phone in her purse and continued to watch the show. Deep in her soul she was overwhelmingly worried about her earlier actions. Even from where she was seated now, she saw that John continued to keep a open place for her. Such emotional pressure forced her to stand up and made her ready to move to the first row. Sarah was confident that this was the most correct decision; she could no longer hide herself. She had to act decisively, throwing all fears aside. New York was not intended for the weak.

Somehow, having made her way to the third row very close to John, she suddenly saw that somebody was watching her. From the first row, Indigo turned his face to her, and in the dim light his already red eyes seemed now more red. Like a demon, he was staring at her. Sarah immediately stopped, not daring to breathe, petrified, as if a rabid dog had bared his teeth at her. At the same time, she saw that Julia noticed her, standing at the podium, and also John, who for some unknown reason turned around almost at the same time as Indigo. Immersed in the depths of immediate despair, Sarah did not see a way out of this situation. She could do nothing but trust God and do what He wanted from her. Yes, she already did so, and what were the results? Constant doubts and fears of the unknown. She simply had no idea how to go on, or whether there was any meaning in anything.

The red-eyed monster, Indigo, took several steps toward the aisle. Sarah instantly remembered the words of the angel that the beads could actually save her from all evil. Without thinking, she touched them. In a matter of seconds, as if an explosive wave ran through all around, the power of the beads changed everything. Where there was a passage, now there was a continuous row, the runway now stretched from the left side, and the spectators sat opposite. Only now Sarah realized that she was in front of the audience, where everyone stared at her in surprise. She saw John, and even Igor Miltent, who jumped up from their seats, not understanding what was happening. Sarah seemed to be in a different dimension, where there was no point in trying to figure things out, because there was no explanation. It was necessary to flee far away from this terrible place. Understanding that to take the usual way would be difficult, Sarah took a desperate step. Running on the runway, she rushed straight to the backstage area and in passing, almost knocking down the dumbfounded models. From the audience came a disgruntled rumble. The music abruptly stopped.

"What are you doing? You're acting crazy, Sarah!!", Julia shouted angrily.

Sarah collided with her sister, completely and unintentionally knocking her to the floor. Thinking that things might take an even more serious turn, she ignored absolutely everything and everyone. All she wanted was to get out of this place once and for all. However, it is unlikely she would have been allowed to do this. Everything reminded her of a nightmare in real time. Running out of the first door on her way, Sarah ran into an empty corridor with giant Victorian windows on the left side, and burning candles on the right. For a moment, the girl thought that she was in a medieval castle, but that was just a feeling. Imagining where the main entrance could be - and the way out - she rushed straight to the very end where a statue of an ancient Greek warrior stood ominously with a spear in a right hand pointed at an imaginary victim.

"You have something that does not belong to you," Blasted a voice sounding like thunder and heavy with anger.

Sarah turned her head back and saw Indigo who ran after her into the corridor. His body was anxiously shivering like in a fever and lit by an ominous red light. He was more like a shadow than a man. The girl was not sure if she were alive or not. She might be only two steps away from something terrible that could mark the end of her life. Defenseless, she was still unsure if one more another spark of luck would help her leave this place alive. Supernatural forces brought her into confrontation with the unknown, and there was no way out, or rather there was only one... Sarah remembered the words of the one she considered to be an angel, but now she was not sure because angels surely do not deceive, except for this one. That creature had convinced her that the beads would protect her and that everything would be fine, but that was all untrue. The girl seemed to be in some momentary chaos, in which every movement passed with great difficulty. Slowly retreating, she continued to look into the eyes of this demon, who could certainly not be a man.

Suddenly all candles on the walls were simultaneously extinguished, as if ghosts had blown them out. The smell of smoldering wicks filled the space, and the corridor became gloomy as in the darkest rainy day, except for a strange, blood-red light emanating from somewhere unknown. It was unusually cold and a frost began to burn Sarah's skin. The girl intuitively felt that something very bad might happen in the next few seconds. She squeezed the beads very tightly in her hand, as if it were the cross she used to help her in the past. She slow began to retreat to the end of the corridor. She made a quiet, quick maneuver, when suddenly the floor shuddered. There was a tremendous sound–as if something very heavy had crashed down. Sarah turned sharply and cried out as loudly as ever. Directly in front of her stood the statue of the Greek warrior, who had stepped down off the pedestal and come to life. Cold marble and demonic forces were intertwined into one. It was one thing to see this in fantasy movies, and quite another in a real life. The boundaries of reality were eroded and Sarah knew one thing - she could no longer escape and that no matter what step she decided to take, she would still be the focus of all the evil that could be found in this world.

It's hard to describe the feeling knowing that death is inevitable, and then a miracle happens. The statue glowed with a bright white light, and the girl was sure she heard anguished screams in the background. The warrior's whole body fell apart and the spear in his hand, along with his arm under the influence of an invisible force, flew through the air and reached Indigo with great speed. Indigo dodged the projectile by moving to the window, so easily that the whistling spear grazed the air next to his head, without even scratching him. At the same time in Sarah's head a barely audible voice sounded and warned her to flee. She climbed over the debris of the collapsed statue and rushed to the end of the corridor stairs which led down to the exit, but a sharp pain raced through her entire body. Despite the pain, she went on without thinking of stopping, when a human-like shadow seized her, not allowing her to move. Something similar had happened to the girl a long time ago in the mansion of her grandfather, when she tragically fell through the ice and the mysterious shadows that rose from the bottom of the lake and pierced her body with pain.

Sarah screamed wildly, feeling as if her entrails were being pulled out - a pain that the human mind was incapable of imagining. She no longer saw Indigo, just the shadow which he had become. Starting to quickly weaken, she was limp, just in a few seconds she was squeezed out like a lemon. Having lost all thoughts and ceasing to feel her own body as if she were one of the living dead, she—was about to— collapse to the floor when suddenly-a bright flash of white light appeared. Then the very creature that spoke to her last night merged with the shadow.

"Run!" She heard. "There won't be any other chance."

The invisible force that bound Sarah earlier, evaporated, giving opportunity to escape. To escape? Sarah had no idea how much more she had to breathe in this world, yet she obeyed the voice in her head and ran away from here, from the place where something quite out of the ordinary was going on. Hearing sounds similar to discharges of electricity, as if giant cables were beating each other, she only begged God to save her soul. But anyway, all her expectations were not justified, it seemed, everything became worse. Just in one second the space was enveloped by pitch darkness, that even your own hands could not be seen. Sarah more than ever now believed that she was in some kind of parallel reality, and not even in a dream. And when she only thought about it, she hit her head against the wall. Further there was no passage. Restraining the cry of pain, she clumsily grabbed the wall and by short steps headed to the right, where as she remembered there should have been steps going down. And she was not mistaken.

"Sarah," She heard about halfway down toward the exit.

The girl's heart jumped at the sound of a familiar voice that revived and awakened something in her, giving her a strange new feeling of hope. Sarah's lips tightened, because she wanted Julia to run after her, and turned around expecting to see her sister. She imagined herself throwing her arms around her and John, and they would all get out of this nightmare together. Instead, as the darkness became less obscure, something appeared that resembled a human being. Initially, Sarah thought that it was somehow an aboriginal, because his naked body covered with tattoos. When she saw his red eyes and his mouth, sewn with thick threads, she decided he was some other kind of entity. It was-another demon who came after her, thirsting for her blood and soul. In part, he reminded her of the clown that had appeared right in front of her at John's house a couple of months ago. She could never forget how she stood silent and motionless behind the glass panel of the front door in a torrential downpour, while the clown pierced her soul with his dead gaze, knowing full well why he had come. There was nothing else left for the girl to do but touch the beads. Once again a bright red light flooded the area. The demon disappeared, and the way downstairs suddenly became distinctly lit, as at dawn. Sarah struggled, afraid of losing the moment to escape, and crouched down. She could not escape the sound of distant screams, terrible and full of despair - voices of those you might think were tormented in fire. Her mind could not imagine what was happening there. The nightmare, which was no longer a prisoner of her mind, became a reality touching everyone and everything. Sarah could only imagine the terror experienced by those who screamed so wildly, but also about what could have happened there. It seemed that there was a real massacre going on. Not feeling like herself anymore, she ran out into the street ignoring the shocked people outside, and continued far ahead to the other side of the road. She turned around only when the screams ceased. Elena Barbella's mansion was now completely enveloped in darkness and dead silence.

The girl was panic-stricken, like that night at John's, when the clown brought death with him. She wanted to call her sister and John when she realized that she had dropped her phone somewhere in the dark. For her, it felt like the end of the world. She had two ideas fighting in her head, each vying for the next step, as if it was an angel and a devil. Should she go back and try to find people dear to her, or just run away because the danger was too close? She spent more than five minutes outside, when she saw security run into the mansion. A few minutes later she heard shooting. The windows of the building were expanding and Sarah could clearly hear how dangerous the situation became as they began cracking and swelling under the pressure building up from the inside. One second later they gave way, raining down shards on everything. The sound was like a violent explosion. People fell to the ground screaming, just like Sarah. Like fiery hailstones many small fragments fell on her, and a sickening burned odor permeated the air.

Different thoughts spun around in the head of the frightened girl. She knew that staying here would be a foolish and costly act, but at the same time she could not allow herself to leave her sister and John in trouble. As if stung by an angry wasp, she jumped up from the ground and raced to the entrance of the mansion, when she was blinded by a brilliant flash of light. She put one hand over her face and put the other one forward when she heard a familiar voice:

"You WILL NOT go there!"

This voice sounded hostile, which only added to Sarah's confusion surrounding the situation. For her, the salvation of loved ones was the only thing that mattered, in fact, everything else was unimportant. Now she was simply wasting time, but what could she do when she was hindered by cosmic forces? She did not say a word but persevered forward when something invisible twisted her hands. Without any physical contact, something supernatural seemed to tie her up.

"You're a fool, if you think you can do anything that comes into your head. I tell you, you WILL NOT go there! These beads, they were almost taken by evil forces. Unfortunately, they now know where to find them. There is only one last option for me, Sarah. You must forgive me. You know it is not about us, but about the millions of innocent souls still living on Earth".

"What option?" the girl became angry. "I need to help my sister and my friend.

Let me go!"

"I am sorry," the voice said. "There is so much that you still need to understand, about which you have no clue. I helped you to fight the demonic clown and that was fine, but this, I can't fight. It is more powerful than the both of us put together. We cannot risk everything simply being led by our emotions".

"What do you mean "the both of us"? The girl didn't understand why the angel would compare itself with her as if she had the same strength".

There was no response. The voice disappeared and Sarah wanted to run into the mansion when suddenly she became weightless and quickly floated upward, being blinded by an incredibly bright white light. Something very powerful grabbed her beads and stretched them so hard that Sarah lost any chance to save them. Her body was twisted with fear and pain in her neck, but it lasted no longer than a long, painful moment, and then there was darkness again. Sarah slowly opened her mouth to gasp for air when she had a feeling as if in that moment she existed outside of her physical body. It was an alien feeling that somehow let her know that all her memories, emotions and feelings were suddenly taken from her. The girl forgot almost everything and felt as if her life had been erased.

Her body was limp and she found herself lying on something solid. There was a noise and the smell of exhausts. Undoubtedly there was a busy road nearby. Sarah barely opened her eyes. Continuing to remain in a vegetative state she, to her great regret, could do nothing more than to lie there helplessly. It seemed to her if all the energy had been sucked out of her body. The girl was lying on the steps under the eaves of one of the buildings, the rain was pouring down a little farther ahead, obscuring visibility. On the opposite side of the road cars were honking their horns, having gotten stuck in a traffic jam, and all of the city lights were reflected in different directions alternating between red and green. There were no passers-by here, and those who occasionally appeared from the haze would quickly leave.

Sarah coughed and grabbed her stomach. Her dress was soiled by mud, and her hands were scratched. Trying to get up, her body suddenly brought a terrible cramp. Her muscles collapsed and she fell helplessly, striking her face against the pavement. She did not even have the strength to cry, her teeth clenched in pain and she moaned. There was no use to try to remember how she got here and what had happened. Her head was buzzing and her thoughts were jumbled. There was only one thing that the girl could now feel, and it was not the pain, but realizing that perhaps she had lost her soul. This was the strangest feeling that could never be described, but which would certainly feel terrible. Sarah felt that her body had become only a plastic shell with a hollow, empty interior.

As if receiving terrible news, her heart almost stopped and she was staring blithely at the soggy road. Strange as it may seem, something reminded her of the past, but she could not understand what it was. It was not even *deja vu*, but something else, as if she had been here before, but in another epoch. Memories in Sarah's head began to seem uncontrolled and disconnected from each other, involuntarily emerging into her consciousness. In the depths of her mind she could not cease asking herself where her soul had gone, without consciously expecting an answer. Deep in some kind of trance, she lost track of time, not knowing how long it would last, when suddenly the door next to which she lay unexpectedly flung open.

"Miss Brown!" Came an anxious, familiar voice.

The girl felt strong hands carry her into the building, where there was a familiar smell of candles, different spices and oils. Whether it was its warmth or its quiet atmosphere, for quite a strange reason, Sarah gradually felt herself come back to life. She was lying on her back on a firm, little sofa, looking up at the ceiling. It didn't last long. Soon she moved her gaze

152

to the side, understanding and remembering that once she'd been here and had promised not to return. But Sarah found herself back in the salon of the psychic medium - for better or for worse.

"What happened?" asked Antoine. Yes, it certainly was he. "I well expected your return, but not like this."

"What am I doing here?" Sarah asked weakly and only now saw the one who spoke to her. Immediately a feeling rose inside her that they had known each other for many, many many years. She vaguely remembered that one day he tried to help her, but with what she had no recollection.

"We know each other…" Sarah whispered.

"Yes, of course!"

"NO, we've known each other for a very long time."

It was the first time Antoine was confused as he tried to digest what he had heard. He suddenly thought that it was he who was at a session with a medium. He was consumed by the strange, unheard-of force that came to him at the sight of the weakened girl. Then it became clear that even his gift, passed down through many generations, could not help in any way to understand the true essence of what was so clearly feeling. Suddenly it became unbearably hot for him. Cautiously he began to watch Sarah with some degree of suspicion. She turned and somehow rose, all the way showing her half-lifeless condition. That's how she felt herself, more likely a puppet than a person. With difficulty leaning her elbow on the chair, she finally took a sitting position.

"I can call a taxi." Antoine said.

"I need your help," Sarah said in a urgent voice. "Help on a spiritual level."

"I am afraid you need to ask for that kind of help in a church."

"No, I meant another spiritual level."

"Seriously? What kind of spiritual level?"

"You know what I am talking about."

"Yes, I am afraid I do… Well, and how far can you go?"

"I don't know the limit. Something strange and scary is going on in this world and I am very concerned about it."

"Why do you want to know the unknown?"

"Because it concerns my very existence."

"Then we'll have to meet on another day," the psychic medium said, looking into the girl's eyes, attentively reading her emotions and realizing that she needed a good rest. He could not afford to conduct a spiritual reading with her now because it could be very dangerous for someone in such a weakened position. Such rituals required a lot of energy, which Sarah did not have today.

"I'm ok for the time being."

"I am afraid it's impossible."

"I will double your usual fee!"

"It's not about the money. Diving into the other world requires very specific preparation, and it does not happen as easily as you think."

"I'm afraid I won't *have* another chance. Please, I beg of you!" Suddenly she rushed toward the medium and grabbed his arms.

Everything that followed happened very fast and there was no time for thinking or understanding anything that was about to happen. The shocked medium startled and jumped back. Now there were voices in *his* head -- all sorts of sounds, and he could no longer concentrate on anything. In a fraction of a second, Antoine felt strange things: the objects around him seemed to part ways and then he unexpectedly felt like he was pelted by water. Then came first a hot wind, and then a cold one. Now deeply settled in a trance, Antoine flew through time and space, he was dragged somewhere downward into the blackness with no more than an array of a million stars playfully winking at each other. This state was not unknown to him, but this time it was different. Without realizing it, the medium had himself become a patient.

All of his unusual abilities were discovered in his youth when he began to see things that were not visible to the naked eye. The first serious test for him was the so-called "spiritualistic" meeting with his best friend Emma. It happened twelve years ago and turned out to be something he would never forget. Both of them were then twenty years old, and life seemed to be so easy that you could freely talk about absolutely everything, even to making jokes about serious matters. Emma wanted to know about her future. Obsessed with the idea of finding a boyfriend, she persuaded Antoine to help her. Despite his lack of experience, he was eager to help his friend with her idea -- only because for him it was something like an adventure. But there was one thing he did not know nor count on -- once he had looked into the depths of his friend's consciousness, there was no way back to *un*knowing. After sending her into a trance-induced nightmare, he ultimately blamed himself for her death: while he was in the trance, he saw a car crash that would happen about a year later, and which he could not prevent. Having known from his trance full well what would happen, it literally broke his soul and gave him no peace. All he could eventually think about and hope was that the visions he saw were not real, that this was just a mistake, a strange dream that had nothing to do with real life.

Whatever it was, the outcome happened in all its tragedy, and Antoine had a terrible time accepting it. He isolated himself from the outside world not having the faintest idea of how to continue living. All he could do at that time was to try to understand his abilities and understand whether it was a gift or a curse. The answer was not long in coming. Very soon after the death of Emma, he began having dreams in which he could experience people on a higher plane. Realizing that to hide from which he was destined was impossible, he decided to seriously engage himself in a form of "spiritual therapy". He sincerely believed that this could help many people, perhaps for the first time, to fully understand themselves. Professional intent came to him not immediately, but it did come. As often happened in these kind of cases, there was a price for such mystical talent. Antoine left his ordinary life, left his friends and completely immersed himself in the work. He began to live his own world, which in his opinion was the most real.

Over the past ten years, Antoine had experienced the deepest levels of the human mind and soul with a depth that he could have never imagined. What happened this evening, when he touched Sarah's hands, caused him to reevaluate the scope of his standards. It was such an alien and strange feeling. He didn't expect to feel anything like that at all. The last time he had spiritual contact with Sarah, nothing so monumental had happened. But now it left a big question in his mind of why and how things had happened this day. As it happened in life, things and events would take over on their own; sometimes good things, sometimes bad. When Antoine felt his patient's energy, a kind of *third eye* opened for him that could see things beyond the conventional.

Antoine was pretty sure he saw a future, a terrible future, in which there was no place for anything alive. He had a vision that cast a strange violet light, which gradually extinguished, leaving millions of stars instead. Then the cold wind began to blow, lifting dust into the air, and the earth was empty and dead. His body felt like he was there, but even he had no idea where he was. The vision was short, but memorable, and then it was replaced by an even stranger one. As if looking through a lens, Antoine saw a sun-drenched, cloudless blue-sky day in New York City, without warning, turned red, and a chorus of voices sounded full of dull but panicky screams: "*Hypnovillions, Hypnovillions*, they'll kill us ". After that, everything abruptly disappeared.

"I have no idea what any of it was or meant," Antoine said, distractedly, looking at Sarah, then to the floor. "But this is something abnormal. I do not know how to explain what I saw."

"What did you see?"

"Scary things. Some kind of cryptic message, I would even call it a warning."

"A warning? About what?"

"If I only knew…"

"I need to understand all of this…" Sarah uttered with desperation, feeling that she was losing focus for any meaningful interpretation. "I believe I am here again with you for a reason. If that truly is the case, then I need the help now before it's too late.

"All right – all right," The medium put his hands forward and looked away, as if afraid to look directly into Sarah's eyes.

"Last time when I was here you told me that I would return, so here I am!"

"We'll have to use a spiritual contact board," Antoine said coldly. "I've only used it twice, and neither time was a good experience.

Yes, the medium did consult the spiritual contact board twice in his life. The first time was the case with Emma, and the second time was an experience with his father who wanted to know how far he would progress in his career. All the novice medium saw then was the joyful face of his father being consumed by fire. He could not explain this, but he incorrectly interpreted the vision as fiery, strong success in his father's work. And everything happened, just as he had foreseen. A couple of months later, his father was mercurially promoted and included in the Council of Directors. Unfortunately, his first Council meeting was held at the World Trade Center on the morning of September 11, 2001... After that, Antoine promised himself to never again use that demonic board, from which his experiences only led to death.

"Come with me to another room," He beckoned Sarah darkly. For the first time in a long time he felt afraid and feeling great responsibility. He would never intend to harm another innocent soul.

Sarah obediently followed him to another room which always remained hidden from the eyes of the others. She only hoped that finally she could get at least some clear answers. As a result, she was in a small room that could hold two people at the most. Surrounded by mirrors, capsules and various herbs, Sarah sat down at a small short table where lay a–spiritual contact board with a circular flat stone, with the Eye of Ra painted on it. The girl tensed, as the unknown scared her. She had no idea if she was making the right move or another mistake; her heart was more inclined to the first. As if at the dentist's office, she anxiously tapped her right foot on the floor, bit her lower lip, and looked contemptuously at the medium. Antoine closed his eyes and breathed deeply. Preparing for a session was an uncommon and energy-intensive exercise. Sarah understood this perfectly and patiently waited.

"Think carefully," whispered Antoine, "about whom you want to call. The *world of ghosts* is very dangerous. You must be very careful with words and actions."

"I want to call the guardian angel," The girl said.

"Lean your right hand against the stone and close your eyes, trust the energy that surrounds us," the medium said and placed his palm over Sarah's hand. "Mentally ask what you want to know, and only speak about the most important thing, only three words -- no more."

"All right," Sarah said and closed her eyes.

She began to feel uncomfortable in the room's complete silence. She was worried that nothing would turn out well, that eventually she would have to return home with nothing and continue to live in fear that at any moment something terrible could happen. That evil would undoubtedly return into her life and try to inflict as much pain as possible -- not only to herself, but to those closest to her -- she began again to think about her grandparents, her father and mother, and her sister Julia. She wanted nothing to happen to any of them. All these strange and very vague visions had the potential to bring her family history back to life.

"Relax," whispered Antoine. "Do not think about everything; just focus on the main thing."

It was not easy to fulfill what seemed like such a simple request. Sarah asked herself what was more important for her, and eventually she settled into the thoughts of her mission in this world, why she kept the mysterious, colorful beads, and why the angel did not come when needed. If she were preparing a list of questions, then it would be infinitely long. The biggest question that worried her was if she could ever return to normal life. Slowly moving the stone on the spiritual contact board, Sarah wanted to receive at least some sign from the one whom she felt imposed such a heavy burden on her. At some point she began to feel that she began to hear voices, but then everything returned to normal. As a result, long minutes of movement of the spiritual stone back and forth were wasted. Disappointment? Yes, especially when real answers were being sought. Sarah desperately wanted and needed God's guidance here and now. But as usual there was silence. Feeling herself abandoned and defenseless, she succumbed to disappointment - primarily in herself, in her naivety, that she thought she was able to talk to the Almighty.

"I need *freedom!*" Sarah said it out loud.

"...Freedom?" She heard a voice come back, but it was not Antoine's. She could not tell if the voice was either a male or female.

Sarah opened and sharply focused her eyes. She moved away from the table and saw that she was sitting in a desolate place where there was only dust and a gray sky so low that it seemed to be possible to touch it. There was an empty feeling all around, at least all *seemed* to be empty, and the psychic medium, as usual, had disappeared as if he never existed. If the last time the girl plunged into her past which was a place that reflected where she spent her childhood, this place was something completely different. She stood up and looked around in confusion believing that she had missed something.

"There are a lot of secrets here," The same strange voice she heard before came to her ear.

Sarah let out a shocking sound when suddenly in front of her appeared a human-like figure. Its features were almost impossible to discern due to its bright glow. There was no face and no body, only outlines. The energy that was coming from this creature was so strange that it rendered Sarah speechless. She felt a surprising calm in her body. She had never felt this before, even in the church, but she knew it was something from above. Transfixed, she gazed at the figure, involuntarily smiling and losing track of time. Her mind almost seemed to be cleansed and she could not think of anything except what she saw right in front of her.

"Who are you and what is this place?" She uttered the words with great difficulty.

"Welcome to Gray World - the world of ghosts." came the response. "You are the first of the Living World to be here. I know what you need."

"If so, then take these beads back! I've had enough of them."

"Believe me, it's not about the beads, it's more about you."

"About me… really? My life has been a living hell. No, thanks, no more. Take these beads from me."

"You can be angry, but you cannot change things."

"What *things*?"

"The fact that you and I are the same"

Trying to digest what she heard, Sarah felt even more lost. Again, nothing made sense. Then she looked at her own body and let out a scream in shock, seeing that it was shining exactly the same way as the one with whom she was talking.

"There is no point in screaming, everything was decided and happened a long time ago. Do you remember the pond in which you once fell? Do you still think it was a nightmare or perhaps you just prefer to believe it was a nightmare?"

"I don't believe you!" Sarah shouted and tried to take off her beads, but they seemed to be connected to her body. "Stop this, let me go!"

Then, as if carried on the wind, she was relocated to another part of the deserted area where on the horizon appeared the outlines of a dilapidated fortress. The one she considered an angel eventually disappeared without a trace

"Look around. This is a sign, a bad sign. This is what will happen to your world. Everything will die, there will not be a single living soul left." came the dreadful words from the same voice who was no longer present.

The girl deliberately walked forward to the fortress, not having the faintest idea what might be there. The voice continued to whisper words to her, most of which it was absolutely impossible to understand. Grayness, sadness and emptiness - these three terrible things surrounded her already for almost an hour. She walked ahead here in this vast land without borders. Soon visibility began to grow dull, and Sarah had to squint her eyes to be able to see anything. It was at this instant that the space shifted again, and now she was standing in front of the ruins of a fortress made of gray stones, with crows ominously cawing from up above. There was a particular smell in the air, like after the rain, and there was an unimaginable calm present that was not characteristic in the real world.

Sarah was fascinated by the ruins which made her give thought to its history and what life in it had been like a long, long time ago. More questions rose in her thinking about those who once lived there and what might have had happened to them. Its mysterious atmosphere evoked thoughts about the eternal, about the meaning of life, and about the path of humanity and where it was headed. On the one hand, it was calm since there was a kind of universal harmony. On the other hand, there was a fear and not at all unfounded. The main fear of anyone, including Sarah, was to find out the truth, to know the future and what could possibly happen in it. To look into the crannies of fate was a risky and dangerous business. She wanted desperately to trust this reality, but she could not be sure.

"You are at the source of the creation of the world," A voice said. "The time when the light and the dark matters collide. This is what brings life, but also death. The question is how to maintain balance and move ahead. Many worlds had perished in their time, leaving only the memory of what once was. The time for your world has come, and these beads are a talisman to protect all of you from the spread of Darkness. Take a good look at these ruins, and you will understand what is in store for your world without them."

All Sarah wanted to do was to find a way to respond to the words of the alien voice.

"But the beads, how can they help?"

"You don't need them, but they need you. They belong to you. You are the keeper of the world order."

"This is all so crazy..." Sarah said vehemently.

The next moment she was at the top of the main tower inside the fortress, where a round hole gaped in its center, revealing a view of the large interior space. Cautiously the girl walked to the edge and looked down. Shuddering from her fear of heights, she realized that she was looking upon something like a throne room. From below, voices were heard. Shadows black as tar with other glowing creatures, blended into battle. It was not exactly clear what was going on, but one thing was clear - this was a fight. Inhuman voices flooded the rose up from the space, shaking the tower like an earthquake. Two faceless silhouettes, one was black and one was white, shot up from below, entwined in battle. Sarah jerked away from the edge in fear, and she could do nothing but observe this violent and strange event.

"This was the very moment when it all started...," The voice whispered.

"Started what?" Sarah didn't understand what the voice was talking about.

She had not yet heard a reply when thunder rumbled across the sky. The black silhouette released unthinkably long claws, and grabbed his rival, sending them both tumbling back down to the throne room and raising a whirlwind behind them. Sarah immediately rushed back to the hole and saw a multicolored beam of light burst out from below. After that, there was a blinding flash, and the space was covered by brilliant white light. The girl coughed and gagged, because it had become impossible to breathe. The air had become unbearably hot and filled with caustic dust, and her body convulsed in response. It felt is she had been thrown into oblivion, where there was nothing: no light, no thoughts, no words, no sounds, only an endless darkness.

Sarah was seized with a very strange feeling. As if floating either in the air or in the water, she moved forward into the unknown until she saw in front something blacker than the darkness itself. It was someone tall and frighteningly scary. As if finding herself face to face with a starving beast, she thought that there was nowhere else to go. She looked at the absolute evil. Out of the eternal darkness there were two red lights that were redder than red, which lit up the scene as if two matches had been struck. Looking at the inevitable, Sarah knew that she had nothing to lose. She exhaled, closed her eyes, ready to accept what was going to happen. She really did not believe that her life would end like this, but she was so tired of all the endless escaping. Her complete trust in God left her feeling completely abandoned. If not, she would surely find herself in a much more satisfying place.

"Sarah, it's time to wake up," came a voice that seemed to be unreal.

The girl slowly opened her eyes and saw that she was sitting in a familiar room with a spiritual board in front. Antoine was on the opposite side of the board and was now sitting silently, looking at her. His eyes were open wide, as if he had seen a ghost, and his hands were squeezing the edge of the table with such force that veins appeared on them. His face changed dramatically, as Sarah retreated from the trance. It began the moment as deadly pale and stoic, now the edge of his mouth was cut by a faint smile. The medium never took his eyes off his patient all this time, and what he saw was one of the most disturbing things in his entire life. The session of half an hour had jostled his nerves. Seeing how Sarah's body had twitched, how she cried and how her nose had bled was jarring to the psychic. Antoine was afraid that something terrible could happen, something for which he would never forgive himself. He even wanted to interrupt the session, but something told him to stop and wait a little longer to see what would happen next. Remembering what the board had done in the last two sessions, he feared that this innocent girl, so young and beautiful whose life had just begun, could suffer a terrible misfortune. Was this evening of such genuine import, seeking answers to the unknown opportunities to preserving life... precious human life? What was the price for someone who was eager to learn about the *beyond*? Of course, there were no solid answers to these questions.

Antoine saw only fragments of Sarah's visions, but it was enough to understand that she was in a great danger. Everything pointed to an relentless evil that was ready to break through at any moment. Something very dark, more terrible than death itself, was intended for her, and this was a shock from which the medium still could not recover. He saw the last minutes, before Sarah returned to her former condition, and he saw her sitting motionless, even relaxed, and her breathing had almost stopped. Antoine had never seen anything like this before.

"Sarah?" He asked, looking deeply into the girl's eyes. "Are you all right?"

She only looked at him in confusion, continuing to be in the trance-like state processing what she had just seen. Her mouth opened slightly, as if she wanted to say something, and then suddenly her body shook and she fell to the floor, where she began to vomit.

"Lord," Shouted the medium and clasped the girl. "Don't be afraid. Everything will be all right, you'll see, you'll feel better very soon."

Sarah writhed on the floor as if she were being torn apart from the inside. Antoine wanted to call an ambulance, but the girl abruptly stopped shivering, and he picked her up in his arms and carried her to the bathroom. With a helpless grip, Sarah put her hands on the young man's shoulders and only breathed heavily, as if she did not have enough oxygen. She was scared. The medium stayed with her in the bathroom for a while until she finally started feeling better. He helped Sarah to get up, which in itself was quite a challenge because she still did not have her strength back yet. The girl felt if she was a child who was just learning to walk. What a terrible feeling it was to truly believe that life was not fair. Not only unfair, but without justice.

"I need a little time," stuttered Sarah. "...Please..."

"Yes, of course," The medium nodded. "Let me know if you need anything, I am right here."

He exited out of the bathroom, leaving the girl all alone. Sarah greedily slurped water from the sink, cupped in her hand. No matter how much she took in, it could not appease her thirst. Her head was a mess and she needed again more time to regain her composure. After hearing the voices in her head, she was still not sure which reality she was experiencing. Wherever she looked, a memory of those terrible blood-red eyes that belonged to something evil, shone before her. It was the first time when the girl knew that an unprecedented danger had approached her, but she did not know how to explain it. There was no longer any feeling of hope. She could not count on anybody – there were no friends, no relatives, and a feeling of no God. She was sure that if someday something happened, no one would be around. It was a simple truth. Sarah found herself thinking that in the most difficult times she was always alone. What could bring so much suffering, and why?

"I still have this picture in my head," She said, walking back out to Antoine; he was sitting in a rocking chair and nervously tapping his fingers on armchair. He was thinking and thinking very much.

"You do not have to tell me everything now," He said, looking at the girl with great sympathy. He wanted to just hug her and say that she has nothing to be afraid of, that everything would be all right for her. But that would be a lie; he had no idea about the future and about where the fate would turn.

"I saw very strange things…"

"You saw what spirits showed you. Sometimes it is a façade."

"I saw terrible things, and I do not know what it was. Some kind of fortress, shadows, eerie monsters, and many multi-colored lights. I still do not understand what all this has to do with me…"

"Try to understand the big picture, you'll see, it will help you," Antoine promised.

"I talked to someone. It was not a person, but a creature. It seemed as if I was possessed by it," Sarah shook from the unpleasant feeling in her whole body, which still felt like it did not completely belong to her. "I do not know how to say this, but I feel like my soul was taken."

"Interesting details," The psychic said thoughtfully, leaning forward a little. "Someday, it will all make sense."

"I am afraid," Sarah said with a great fear in her voice.

"You must rest. Try to free your mind of all thoughts today; don't think about anything in particular or taxing. Such rituals take a lot of energy. A good rest will help reveal a more accurate and complete picture of what you have seen."

"But I feel like I am being *persecuted*," Sarah snapped.

"By what or by whom?" Antoine asked.

"Something evil … I think I remember, yes, yes. My sister, John …."

She suddenly trembled again, have remembering what had happened in Elena Barbella's mansion. By a strange coincidence, she still did not have any memory of the terrible event. Like a knife stabbing her head, something stung her, and she screamed. Antoine, terrified by his patient's scream, immediately approached to her.

"What happened? Tell me…" He exclaimed.

"I have to help them, they are all in big danger," Sarah mumbled, looking at the ceiling with a lost gaze. "No, I should not be here."

"Please Sarah, calm down," The medium begged.

But Sarah did not, or would not, listen to him. Driven by a ghostly voice, she quickly made her way to the exit. Her pupils widened, and her hands shook as if she was in bitter cold. Antoine tried to grab her, but he did not succeed in holding her. The girl quickly twisted out of his grip and ran onto the night street. All around her was smoke, the roar of hundreds of cars and the shouts and screams of strangers. The sidewalks were littered with plastic bags of rubbish, and a stinking steam swirled up from the ditches. At first glance Sarah thought it might be a vision of an post-apocalyptic world. As hard as she tried to make sense of everything, nothing was familiar. She blindly ran down the street toward Eighth Avenue without looking back, and only thinking of her loved ones. Her heart was pounding so hard that it became unbearable to breathe. The area around her was filled with a mixture of confusing sounds that made her head spin further. Staying in a half-trance state, she walked swiftly toward the busy street. With the sounds of road works and car horns blaring, Sarah continued to walk, confident that she knew where she was heading.

"Hey… look where you're going", came a sharp and very rude man's voice.

Someone pushed Sarah very strongly in the back so that she fell down, falling to her knees. A strong pain instantly grabbed her, springing tears from her eyes. Even so, she got up and looked back to see the face of that bastard that she had done this. The only other thing she saw was a crowd people crossing the street back and forth, in front of her. None of the passers-by even stopped to help her. Here again she was in a situation where no one was around to help her.

A familiar alien voice sounded in her head again, which felt like a knife cutting through her brain, causing an unbearable breakdown. The poor girl just wanted to stop - by any means.

"AHHH! Leave me alone!!" she cried. Sarah burst out and ran forward to try to get out of this crazy place as soon as she could, but then saw a tall man through a foggy mist ahead of her. His eyes were exactly the same as from the vision - fiery red, dead and full of eternal darkness. Sarah stopped for just a moment, when suddenly the figure strode toward her, taking with huge steps. The next moment, a strident car horn blasted onto the scene and struck the girl. Her head violently met the pavement and the force knocked her unconscious for a few seconds. Sarah felt a burning sensation in her whole body, but a very odd and indescribable feeling came over her, as if her missing soul, or whatever it was, was back.

CHAPTER 3: CLOUDED CONSCIOUSNESS

The wall-mounted TV noticeably hissed. Suddenly, the crawl on the bottom of the TV screen rolled as the news presenter read: "Terrorist attack at the world's fashion show of the year. A number of victims have been identified. Hotline: 877 616-7778". After that, the screen became noisy again and it was impossible to gather any further details. It was strange to half-wake to this hiss, to hear the most important announcement, and nothing more. It felt as if it were a plan, some kind of psychological teaser.

Sarah struggled to open her eyes from a half-forgotten state. She wanted to turn her head to the right but her neck was wracked with unbearable pain from which she moaned and caused her to immediately give up moving. Looking up, she tried to focus her senses to understand what was going on. To her misfortune, her head buzzed so badly that to concentrate on even the slightest thing was a challenge. The whole situation was a mystery. From somewhere on the left came the sound of a computer, like a whirring sound at first, then becoming a rhythmic, steady beat like some kind of pump. A person with a vivid imagination might well have thought that it was some kind of spaceship; in reality, this was a hospital ward. Sarah realized that when noticing from her right arm a thin tube led up a drop counter.

Her first reaction was a sickening, horrible feeling. She had no idea what she was doing in a hospital, how she got here or why, and it all frightened her. Not understanding what was happening was one of the most unpleasant of all feelings. Sarah gently touched some leads with her left hand, and shuddered as her muscles sharply contracted. The feeling was as if she had been thumped on the knee with a reflex hammer. Completely weakened, she felt that it was a better idea to wait for someone from the staff to come to her, and she would act in accordance with what she could learn. But a half an hour later, which felt like it lasted for an eternity, no one appeared to respond to her pressing of the summons button clipped to her pillow. She noticed the air was filled with a smell of something burnt, which nearly caused a gag reflex. The annoying TV continued its steady, headachy hiss and quickly became the most hated object in the room.

"Hey… is there anybody out there..?" Sarah called weakly.

Still no one appeared. The fear from unknown, strange memories flashed in Sarah's head: terrible shadows, voices and faces of people unfamiliar to her. All this seemed to be too scary as she could not explain what was happening to her. Placing her ever so slightly to the edge of the bed, she lay her head to her side and breathed in deeply the cool air that circulated upward from below. It helped, as because of the stuffiness she had not been at ease, but now it was becoming better. Reaching down to the floor, she propped herself up with both hands, she cautiously slid down, when suddenly one of the leads snapped off. In the agony of wild pain, Sarah yelped and slid helplessly onto her back.

"No, no, no," Her lips whispered, almost without a sound. She was horrified at the thought of how abruptly life changes course. Yesterday she was healthy and full of energy, and now she was lying on the floor almost at death's door. Here it is - confirmation that no matter how you feel today, tomorrow everything could be different. Tomorrow may be better, but it could be worse.

Waiting until the pain had subsided, Sarah pulled off the remaining leads with one movement, and again let out a cry and burst into tears because the pain was excruciating. The poor girl felt half dead - a condition she knew well, especially in recent days. She shuffled over to the window and stopped, finally able to relax, hoping that the pain would go away. It happened, but not as fast as she wanted. Sarah put both of her hands on the seat of the chair that stood nearby and somehow rose from the floor and looked out the window. She did not see anything, only a fog. It was a dark night and oddly quiet for New York.

Sarah stepped back and looked toward her hospital bed. There was a nearby machine pumping a vile liquid across the room and into the dropper. It contained a capsule with a caustic green liquid and was inscribed with "ENTAL". What a horrifying thought it was for her to realize that she was being infused with a certain radioactive substance. The eventual shock was so strong, that Sarah didn't pay attention to the mess around her and was concentrating only on her fears. However her eyes could not lie. At some point she saw what one would have thought was something of such magnitude come into the room. Realizing that something very strange was going on, the girl decided not to stay in this "sinister" clinic for one more second. Rather, she took off her hospital gown, put on her partly-torn dress which was neatly folded on a chair next to her bed, and from underneath it found her shoes. Looking and feeling a bit more put together now, Sarah walked toward the door, but stopped just in front of it.

In her head however, everything still felt so mixed up that even remembering her own name was not so easy. The strangest thing was that she did not know any details - where did she get bruises and cuts all over her body? Why was she here alone? Where had she been before she got here, where was her home, and whether she had family or friends.

"I've lost my memory. I think I've lost my memory," She said in an earnest panic. "No, no, no ..." She felt like a child who was lost in a big city.

Sarah could imagine herself in many dreadful situations, but not now when she had completely forgotten who she was. For her it was the same as being disabled, but in reality the situation was even much worse because here she was all alone. Focusing on these thoughts brought her something like a pain in her stomach which pierced her from the inside. Sarah opened her mouth to scream, but something stopped her. It was such an odd feeling - discovering that her soul was now living its own life, and not in her body, but somewhere else. No matter how ridiculous this sounded, Sarah knew that it was true. If somebody asked her to describe it, she could not find a single word, but could only say, that her soul was gone.

Not wanting to accept the reality, she was making herself nauseous. Part of the thoughts in her head were her own, but the rest were something alien about which she had no idea. Scary that things would only get worse so the girl decided to not waste a second and leave this place as soon as possible. She stretched out her hand to the door, but all at once some invisible force struck her inside. Instead of opening the door gently, as she always used to do, she squeezed its handle with an unexpectedly rising anger. Her eyes had become bloodshot, her nostrils began to expand as if she had not enough air to breath. She tore the handle from the door with such force and flung it across the room.

"My daughter, come to me. Don't let anything in your mind stand in the way of our reunion. Come to me my little child," Said a voice in Sarah's head. This was definitely a voice that she immediately recognized. It was not about her lost memories; it was a part of her, something from the past, something she used to hear every day. It was deeply imprinted in her mind such that it would never been erased no matter what.

"Mom, "Sarah said with faltering voice, almost crying.

Her heart stopped racing and her mind cleared. Yes, certainly it was her mom, but how was it possible to hear her again? That beautiful voice of someone who died many years ago. Sarah became very anxious, thinking that because of that substance, named "ENTAL", she was slowly going mad. All she knew was that she wanted to find the way out and this was what she did with her next steps. Somehow, she managed to open the door with its missing handle, and went out into the corridor. It seemed like it had been hit by a hurricane: everything was turned upside down, wheelchairs were scattered so that they obstructed the passage, on the walls bore many holes and from the cracks extended wisps of smoke, and was startled by the electrical crackle of a lamp.

Sarah glanced ahead to see what looked like a waiting room at the end of the corridor. It was a small botanical garden filled with green plants and many blooming flowers. On the wall there was a big sign: "MAGiC Corporation". Without the slightest hesitation she walked over to an area where nothing looked disturbed, hoping to at least find someone. But to her chagrin, there was no one behind the reception counter, only the quietly whirring computer fan that cycled on and off. Making sure there was no one around, the girl went behind the counter and pressed the "enter" button. The MAGiC logo instantly appeared on the screen, and then the system requested the password.

"Oh please… come on…" Sarah said.

She began to rummage through the papers on the desk, hoping to find a password, but there was not a single clue. She gave up and went back to the corridor and sat down on a small bench, nestled next to which was a man-made waterfall, decorated with plants. It was the only place that seemed at least somewhat alive. Sarah lay her face in her hands, resting her elbows on her knees and concentrating on this strange hospital. At some point, the thought came to her that none of this was real, that she would wake up and she'd be back on the right track. Sarah just needed to push herself to try to remember something that made sense. All that was in her head at first, was the environment - no names, no faces, and even more so. But then out of nowhere there shown eerie, red eyes, the only things more red was human blood. Although it was a vision, the girl felt unease inside.

Coming back to her senses, she rose purposefully and went to the phone which had come into her awareness. Tensely looking at it, she tried to remember someone's number, just one, which could possibly shed light on the strange situation in which she found herself. She whispered the numbers, but was not exactly sure of them, until the one configuration that unexpectedly came to her head. Sarah picked up the phone and dialed the number. Endless rings were heard, and it looked like no one was going to pick up the phone. Sarah was ready to hang up when a recorded message came on: "*Hi, this is John, please leave a message and I'll get back to you as soon as I can.*" … beeeeep….

"John… " Whispered Sarah. "John, it's me, if …" She faltered, not knowing what to say. "I… I'm in a hospital…" Her sight suddenly fell on big image of *MAGiC* Corporation logo, that was next to the desk, and she continued with a more anxious voice, "Or in a *MAGiC* Corporation something or other. I have no idea what it is… everything is turned upside down and there's no one here that I can find. I don't have the slightest idea what I'm doing here or how to get out of here. I hope you're okay…"

She hung up the phone and gave it a long gaze, expecting some kind of miracle. In her head, the name "John" fought for recognition, and she really wanted to remember him. She did not know who exactly it was or how she remembered his phone number. Right now, the only important thing was trying to find a way out. Very close to the waterfall there was an elevator. Relieved, the girl walked to it, but found that it did not work. Truly, this was not any surprise. At this point, everything seemed to be an obstacle and there was nothing to be done about it. A red emergency lamp flashed above the elevator, and a squeaking sound came from the shaft, which perhaps meant it had been blocked somewhere on the lower levels.

It was necessary to find an alternative to the broken elevator. Surely, there must be an emergency exit staircase somewhere. Without wasting any more time, Sarah started her way forward when, for no reason, she felt that terrible chill again. Cautiously she looked into the wards and pushed the wheelchairs away, making her path, when suddenly a clap came from behind, like an explosion of firecrackers. She turned back and saw black smoke, which very quickly began to envelop the corridor, reducing visibility to a minimum. Absolutely not understanding what was happening, her single thought was to get out and not just somehow, but the fastest way possible.

At the end of the corridor, in large red letters, she saw the happiest word she'd seen all day: "EXIT", was lit up. Sarah moved quickly forward when the space in front of her became blurred. She heard a persistent and deafening shriek, everything around shook like a massive earthquake, and where there was an emergency exit door had just belched a giant flame. Streams of soot and dust clouded the air and struck Sarah in the face. She was caught in a fit of coughing since there was little air left in the room. Her head was spinning and she fell to the floor covered with shards and stones. Everything became filled by darkness, and all that could be seen were diabolical flames swirling ahead. Still coughing, the girl moved her hands jaggedly across the floor, hoping to grab at least something to get back on her feet, and then heard a strange noise from behind. It was a sound if someone was approaching, throwing wheelchairs aside and stepping hard on the floor. It felt like another nightmare. It was obvious this person was possessed by superhuman power; he threw heavy objects to the sides as easily as if they were light as a feather.

What it seemed like for Sarah was as if she were in a cage with a starving beast, and the only thing that could protect her would be a weapon. Yes, exactly, a weapon! To her big surprise Sarah remembered that she had the multi-colored beads that at the time played a role of mythological vanguard - a shield between her and evil. She didn't remember in details how to use them, but it was not that important now. She moved her hand to her neck and to her horror realized that the beads had disappeared. They were stolen, taken away – the most precious thing that was ever entrusted to her, now... gone... How it did feel understanding that that something that was supposed to protect not only her, but also others, a sacred artifact, was no longer here? It felt like a stab in the heart. Sarah literally lost all her concentration, replaced by a feeling of emptiness inside. She didn't know or didn't understand why, but those beads were one of the most important things in her life. She was sure they played a special role that now ended.

Sarah started to silently crying when she again felt something inexplicable, like something else was trying to co-exist with her in her body. Again she heard the voice of her mother in her head As a result, all anxiety quickly left her body.

"My sweet Sarah, stay there. I am coming. We'll be together soon! I miss you so much."

Sarah started smiling, but then something strong inside her pushed ahead that made her nauseous. She had heard another voice say:

"No, you will not destroy her!"

As if by magic, the girl could see through the veil of blackness – such an odd thing. Without reason she was able to see what was in front of her, while a minute ago was not capable of even distinguishing her arm. It lasted a couple of seconds, and then the area again was cloaked in darkness. Sarah's heart slowed down and she felt very much alive again. She could not to find any reason for the inexplicable fight inside her which had bothered her very much since she woke up in this hospital which definitely belonged to the *MAGiC* Corporation. Its logos were seen everywhere up and down the corridor, before the black smoke came.

Someone's heavy steps continued to be heard from behind and Sarah knew she had no time to piece together some kind of plan. If she only had an idea where to move. All the area around was choked by fire and it seemed like there was no other option, but in fact there was. Sarah soon found it in the light of the flames ahead, she noticed something like a hole in the floor, which could perfectly play a role of life preserver.

Stretching her hands and palming the floor, Sarah looked back. At this point she could see nothing but the pitch black darkness, where something big and frightening was moving. Being afraid to get up, the girl thought that if she did, she would become too noticeable, so instead crawled forward as quickly as she could. Meanwhile, the flames spread out even more, and approached the punctured hole at a very dangerous proximity. Sarah had no idea what caused this terrible explosion, but one thing she did know for sure was that the only one on whom she could rely in this moment was herself. Approaching the hole, she felt the inexorable heat begin to burn her face, and she felt like her skin was about to ignite.

Down on the lower floor was flashing a light and pieces of concrete were scattered all around. Without thinking, Sarah clung to the hot floor and slid into the hole. It was at this moment, before letting go, that she saw those very red eyes that appeared in the dark. As if the Devil himself was looking at her. She released her grip and jumped down, happily without breaking an arm or leg. She did scratch her right shoulder and wrist, having unfortunately landed on some fragments. After all the smoke that enveloped the upper level, here was an opportunity to again breathe freely. The girl quickly stood up to her feet and looked up being afraid that those eyes would still be there, but they were not; they disappeared. From the break was pouring smoke, and still there were unknown noises.

Sarah moved her sight from the hole in the ceiling to the floor where she was now. The floor was very long, but clean and shiny, not as messy as the upstairs. Here it felt more like a hospital than anywhere else in the building. At least here the way was free with nothing obstructing it.

Not wishing to spend a single second here, Sarah knew she had to go on, but again felt some kind of fight going on inside her body. Wild pain sharply enveloped her and she shut her eyes, let out a loud wince. Bending over, she brought her arms to her knees not able to catch her breath. As if her utterance was an order to stop her anguish, the pain was instantly gone. Sarah opened her tear-filled eyes widely, and what she saw was like a dream. It was as if somebody once again changed reality. She was sure what she was seeing now wasn't true at all.

The previously clean and tidy floor now had pieces of concrete under the gap, the elevator still did not work, and another emergency exit burned with fire. Throughout the perimeter were screeching sirens and the fire sprinklers were in full force. This was the situation in which she had to act immediately. Sarah still couldn't believe how quickly one reality could be replaced by another; but knew she had to act whether this was just a dream or a reality.

The whole situation seemed to be one of real madness; crazy like during wartime. Without even thinking about it, Sarah ran in another direction, trying to convince herself that soon the worst would be over. But as she rounded a turn, a sound like when something very heavy falls to the floor, captured all her attention. Again familiar, eerie steps gradually grew into a run. In an indescribable panic, the girl ran even faster wishing not to let that invisible creature to get her. Garnering all of her forces she eventually managed to reach a window at the end of the corridor, whose frame banged repeatedly against its wall. Hoping to meet the daylight or some kind of understanding of where Sarah was. To her misfortunate, she could see nothing but clouds of fog and she heard a strong wind that was whistling through the dead silence.

"Get out of here. This is a nest of pure evil. I cannot protect you anymore." A voice rang out in Sarah's head, and she had no idea what it was or who it was, she knew only one thing - the voice was right, it was necessary to leave this hospital that was dark and sinister, without a single living soul.

Turning the next corner Sarah finally saw another emergency exit. With all her strength, she flew down the dark staircase, when she noticed the numbering of the floors. She was on the forty-first floor and she could only venture a guess what kind of hospital this was. Sarah was not in a rush, but moved very fast. Quickly she reached the thirty-sixth floor and would have continued to descend, if it had not been for the appearance of a tall, naked man. He was tattooed with strange symbols, similar to Egyptian hieroglyphics, and was standing on the platform between the floors. This man was oddly familiar to her, but she could not place him. There was absolutely no time to find an answer to this question. She abruptly came to a halt, as if she were trying to avoid a rapidly approaching train. Before taking any further radical actions Sarah caught a few more eerie details of the appearance of this... well... it was difficult to call him "a man". His face was deathly pale, his mouth was sewn with thick threads, and his eyes - that was a whole separate conversation. His hollow, bloodshot eyes looked at her with a funereal calm which was much more frightening than if he were full of hatred. The monster - and that's who he was - blocked the way. To think at this inopportune moment was impermissible. Intuitively Sarah emerged onto the floor.

At first she believed she was leaving the horror behind, but she was wrong. What she met face-to-face happened to be even worse, something that could not fit into the poor girl's imagination. "Hell", "a nightmare", "the world of the dead" - this place could be called any of those names. There were bodies everywhere, with bloody marks not just on them but also on the walls and the floor, and their frozen, bulging eyes showed incredible terror. It seemed that they all saw the same thing before their death. Among them were both staff and patients, and Sarah now had to make a choice: either stay paralyzed by shock and waiting for that terrible Egyptian monster, or sloshing through the puddles of blood to advance, not once looking into the faces of death while trying herself to stay alive.

"None of this is real," Sarah said aloud to reassure herself.

The space became flooded with such a bright light that nothing else could be seen. Sarah seemed to be stuck to the floor like a glue and could not budge her feet. At first, she felt that she had simply lost her mind and that all these visions would sooner or later pass. But soon an indistinct voice was heard again. At first, the words seemed foreign. A human-like figure appeared in a distance, but it was not clear if it was a male or female. It was flat and smooth with skin that resembled hard plastic and with glowing white holes instead of eyes. This one approached Sarah so closely that it would have frightened anyone.

"Look what they have done to you. Resist Sarah... you have no other choice," said the figure.

Sarah wanted to answer, but no words came, she could not even open her lips. Feeling that some force was holding her like a captive victim of a sorcerer, she had no idea what might happen next, but didn't have long to wait. From behind her back there was a clap that was strong enough to shake the building. Immediately the light went out, and the girl again found herself in the familiar corridor, but only now there were no corpses in it; they had all mysteriously disappeared. Sarah whipped around and saw the tattooed monster standing there in the doorway. His broad, sewn-on mouth stretched wide into a wicked smile, so that the strained threads might burst at any moment.

"Lord help me!!" burst out Sarah.

She felt a familiar chill in her body and then the Egyptian morphed into a tall, handsome man with broad shoulders, sculpted muscles, and a beautiful smile. Most notably, there was not a single trace of anything alarming. He stretched his arms toward Sarah and whispered:

"Don't be scared, you and I have a special mission together! Come to me."

"Run, now," exclaimed a different, but familiar voice in Sarah's head. It sounded so loud that for a moment it distracted her from the man, who was still staring at her with his dazzling smile. And when she heard those words warning her to run, she no longer saw the beautiful man, but the monster, who really hadn't changed at all.

Sarah was so confused because everything had happened so quickly. Only when the demon rushed toward her did things suddenly become very clear. Sarah instinctively knew what to do. She ran all the way to the very end of the corridor. At the same instant, there was a sound in the air as if someone were snapping tree trunks like sticks and a powerful ray of light hit the Egyptian. The girl was keenly aware that this was a chance to escape that should not be missed. She knew that the elevator did not work and immediately turned to a second emergency exit, when all of a sudden the door literally was torn to pieces by an invisible power. In a split second, Sarah practically plastered herself against the wall, leaning with bloody palms. All around her whizzed metal fragments, aiming to pierce through someone's body. Filled with incredible fear, Sarah turned her head toward the area where the door had just been, and saw that everything there was turned to a nightmarish darkness. There was nowhere else to run, confirmed by the blink of two red eyes. Yes, the very eyes which were having such pleasure from the game of cat and mouse.

Even though she was about to give up, a small flame of desire to live was still burning in her heart. Finally releasing herself from the wall, Sarah ran around the corner and burst into the first office that she came across. Slamming the door behind her, she immediately noticed metal cabinet that was right next to the desk. Maybe this was a ridiculous idea, but there was nowhere else to hide. She climbed inside and shut herself in, fearful but finding the courage to look through the gaps. There was not so much to see: the front door, the window into the corridor with the blinds half shut, and part of the desk right in front of her nose had a MAGiC Co. mug sitting on it. Before there was at least some kind of weak light, but once Sarah locked herself in and closed the door, she had the feeling as if she was sinking into a black hole. The only thing Sarah could do now was to pray. Much to her surprise she remembered what to do to help herself when she needed it. It came to her as if she never lost her memory, and so she went on. Even if the results were often not what she expected or hoped for, she did it anyway. It was something that she did by rote, like touching her beads in a moment of danger, when she had them, or long walks, when she felt anxious about something in her life, or at a loss for words, or even when she was angry. All these details in fact were more a habit than a solution to any problems that Sarah had to face. She understood this, but couldn't help acting in her usual way: believing that some kind of miracle could happen. Sometimes it would, but sometimes it wouldn't.

The corridor outside held something black, dangerous and provocative. Ethereal in nature; whatever it was, it completely filled the space. Again, she heard familiar steps, so heavy that it was not clear how the building had not yet fallen apart. Sarah's heart raced so much so that she was sure it might stop. When the door to the office was opened, she saw a black shadow slip inside and immediately it began to sniff around the corners like a hungry dog, creating a dreadful noise. The strangest thing here perhaps was the fact that there was a presence of something ultimately invisible, but at the same time very large and heavy. Slowing her breathing Sarah stopped moving, but she was not sure how long she could remain in a motionless pose, she already started feeling the effects of her right leg which had fallen asleep.

Meanwhile, a shadow or a demon, ambulating through the office approached the closet, and Sarah could clearly feel it -- either its breathing or energy. Somehow, she was seized by a great cold, like a deep Siberian winter. This creature, was dangerous and unpredictable, and the girl knew only one thing - it was better not to interact with it at all. It was a terrible thing to be in the balance either of death, or a pain, or of eternity, which cannot be described either in words or in sounds. Sarah's concept of eternity was something that was indestructible, always present, and was as present as time itself. But at the same time, it was also something dangerous,

All those teachings that connected the life of Sarah with everything else: God, family, friends, work - were such an integral part of her existence. Without them there was no meaning to life, and without meaning there was no space for eternity. Up till now, the girl had lost so much, but she finally felt that eternity was back within her whole body - she inhaled it, she could touch it, she was a part of it.

Strange. Sarah never thought about her heart and soul so deeply. The danger gave her the motivation that she needed to continue, and the first thing she thought about was a great sense of self-preservation. She knew one of the simplest things, if she gave up, then eternity will certainly pay her a visit, and maybe even devour her, like a hungry beast. What would others do in such a situation? Some people would start praying, some of them would simply leave everything to the mercy of fate, and the others would call an emergency service for help. The most curious thing was that all these actions really had no bearing on the whim of Eternity. What was inevitable-would-happen in any case, regardless of the confluence of cases and circumstances.

It seemed like the end of the world. The end of everything could be right here, right now. Darkness and light were separated only by a breath and a heart which was beating only because it was so necessary, but which could stop in any moment. Much depended on a will of God. Sarah blinked, she was scared and she could not continue to look through the crack. Gritting her teeth, she waited for what would happen next. Hot tears streamed down her cheeks, and she could only silently ask God to forgive her for everything she had ever done wrong. If she could only forgive herself first so that she could accept forgiveness. She sighed deeply, and began counting down the seconds, the next of which became more precious than the previous ones. This was not surprising, because only on the verge of death does someone really understand the value of time and of life and Sarah knew this now. She waited for her fate to arrive, but nothing happened after even five or ten minutes. The cold left the room in the same mysterious way it arrived, and the temperature returned to normal, which was actually quite warm.

Sarah allowed herself to relax, when she smelled that something was burning. She opened her eyes, and saw eerie red eyes staring back at her through the door gap. The girl's adrenaline raced through her veins like rocket fuel. She continued to look to the one in whose hands held her life. The demon did not move, remained silent and just looked straight at her. What purpose of all of this? What did that demon have on his mind? Sarah was paralyzed, having nearly grown together with the wall and could not even move a finger. Looking at this pure form of evil, she wanted to run away, but was too scared to even dare to blink. The shock transformed her into a rigid posture.

A hellish fire flared in the corridor, only partially lighting the darkness. In the glow of the red-orange flame, shadows played, and the cracking sound from the melting constructions only aggravated the already depressing situation. Corpses, monsters and endless darkness - these were horrors in reality, which were the rewards saved for the most irreconcilable sinner. Sarah did not understand how it turned out that she was here once again with only her past experience to encourage her. If she was destined to fall victim to something unthinkable, it would be here in this place. Danger lay in every square foot, like subtle traps, quietly waiting for their victim.

Sarah felt that her body started to burn from the inside out. And then she heard a wild scream in her mother's voice in her head. It was a madness the girl wanted to stop at any price. No longer able to stand it she contemplated leaving the closet, no matter the risk, when she heard another voice:

"Don't do this! Wait! I will get you your beads back and will stay until you get out of this building."

The girl felt empty inside, and then something heavy hung from her neck. These were the beads that were taken away by someone -- and now Sarah knew by whom.

"Dark forces learned they have gotten nothing – a fake artifact that I have replaced when I sent you to the medium's house. Now they will not stop at anything to seize them since they know you have them and you are in their territory."

"But how?" Sarah whispered.

The voice disappeared from her head. She now was face to face with *the evil*, and only a thin door separated them.

Evil looked at her through the gap in the door. With a piercing gaze, it scanned everything around it. Sarah shivered and began to slowly exhale air from her lungs when a powerful force pulled off the door. A scream of horror came from her mouth and she grabbed the beads. The air between her and the invisible demon twisted and caused a powerful clap, which threw Sarah back. The space immediately glowed red, but then something strange happened - the black clouds of smoke occluded the light, and the darkness was again extinguished by the tongues of flame. Sarah groaned with pain, and tried to stand up, putting her hands on the table, but its metal borders were so hot that the bleeding wounds on her palms literally cauterized touching the surface. Screaming wildly the girl somehow recoiled having part of her skin remaining with the table and ran out into the corridor, sharply turning to the right. She hadn't the faintest idea of where she was going, she just kept running away from the demon who surely was somewhere nearby. Its presence hung heavily in the air and Sarah could only rely on luck that the monster would not find her.

There was crackling and whistling everywhere, and the temperature was so high that it was physically impossible to stay here much longer. Sarah fled at full speed, coughing, afraid to be burned by the vicious flames. All she saw was the smoke-framed way forward and the fire that was consuming everything around her. Salvation was not so far away. Up ahead flashed yet another long-awaited red sign of EXIT, and then - a dark staircase. She was rushing down without any concern for her safety. All of Sarah's thoughts went to only one thing - how to escape from here. And again, in her head resounded an uncompromising voice urging her to run even faster. At the twentieth floor, she heard a buzz that she would have ignored, had it not been for the mechanical voice of the computer. Looking into the corridor, she saw a body lying between the doors of the elevator, which opened, then closed, but only half way, and re-opened, and each time there was the same voice message: "The service is temporarily unavailable. Please, call the technical support." Now it was clear why the elevator did not work.

With all the horrors that Sarah had experienced today, she did not dare to approach the corpse. She was at a crossroads when it became necessary to urgently choose her path. One of them could well be the elevator - a simpler one - all she had to do was push the body aside. The other way was back through the same dark staircase where anything could await. Sarah eventually leaned toward the choice of the elevator. With great uncertainty she moved forward through the empty corridor, seeing only her feet in front of her. Along the way she calmed herself down by the fact that it was "just a dead body that would not hurt her". She could not believe she was thinking like that. She continued ahead and approached the body with small steps. The corpse was a man of about thirty-five, dressed in a white coat who was probably a laboratory assistant or medical researcher. He was splashed with blood from head to toe, lying flat on his back with his mouth gaping open in a scream. His skin looked yellow and there were only bloody holes where there were once eyes. Unable to stand what she saw, Sarah sharply turned away, lowering her head as if she could not catch her breath. A few seconds later she could not contain her nausea and vomited all over the floor.

Her body was shaking and tears formed in her eyes which quickly became red. Sarah felt as if she was possessed by something - clearly realizing it but not capable to resist the orders from her head in a voice that sounded like her mother.

"Smash his head, crack it like a nut. Release your power, show me what you have".

Sarah felt great anger at first. She was sure that some supernatural power was forcing her anger to reach a fevered pitch. As a result she clenched her teeth so firmly that she almost cracked them, when she glanced at the body. One of her top front teeth eventually broke and blood started running down into her mouth, altering her appearance into something inhuman. She approached the body and lifted it up, with two hands and started squeezing it, when out of nowhere there was a bright flash of light, that took all her attention. A familiar figure that looked made of plastic appeared again. Sarah looked at it, wishing only one thing – to kill it as quickly as possible. She threw the corpse aside, like an unwanted toy and took three steps toward the glowing figure. Her thinking continued to remain half-human, and her thoughts were not connected to her actions. To the naked eye, it was clear that ENTAL had done its sinister job, putting the human mind under the control of supernatural forces. Death would be the only solution to stop the agony and suffering; Sarah felt like she might already be dead.

"Fight what you feel inside of you. Do not listen to what it is saying! Remember the beads!" The figure said aloud. "I will help you to escape from this place!"

"Help yourself," Sarah growled and spit the blood out of her mouth.

The figure turned into an even brighter light, and passed through Sarah's body and merged with the corpse. The girl screamed in pain as if a searing flame rose inside her, and then her mind came back to her. She was human again, at least this was what she felt. She looked at the stiffened, frightening corpse, without a clue to understand, who, or what, could bring such violence. While she imagined the horror that this poor man experienced in his last seconds of life, he suddenly grunted. All this happened so quickly that when the girl realized what had just happened it was too late to do anything. The corpse jumped to its feet like a puppet suspended from a string, and turned his face toward the girl. His mouth was still open, and the body was swaying from side to side, and his gait was so unsteady that he could easily fall to the ground again. Feeling that she was losing her mind, Sarah began to run away when she heard:

"Wait! I need his body to communicate with you. The more I possess you, the weaker you will become. At some point, you won't be able to continue living separately from me".

Sarah stopped halfway, unwilling to turn around. She was fully confident that this was her biggest mistake. What stopped her was despair; she was afraid that she could not get out of this hell, and she needed help, any help from anyone. She stood sobbing while looking at the exit ahead, not daring to run to it, until she felt a disquieting breath from behind.

"Please," She shouted in panic. "I beg you".

"Calm down… said a voice. "I won't hurt you. You must trust me. Do you understand?"

"Who are you and why are you here?"

"I am here... for *you*."

"Me? Why? Why are you protecting me?" Sarah asked through her tears. "Just take the beads, they are more important than I, aren't they?"

"I could take the beads, but the act would be useless."

Sarah slowly turned back with a great fear looking at the living dead who was standing there. She was more than speechless at his sight.

"I know, you hear me," The dead man continued. "There is only you and me. I couldn't find the others. Together we will do it".

"I... I don't understand anything," Sarah stammered, forcing herself to stop crying, but there were still tears streaming down her cheeks.

"You don't have to understand anything now. For a moment our priority is to get out of *MAGiC*."

"*MAGiC*?" Sarah echoed. "So... it *is* true, I work here. So ironic".

"Unfortunately, evil can masquerade with different names, people, faces. There's no place to hide. It's all about us knowing how to mask ourselves".

"Look at me," Sarah said desperately. "What else I can I possibly do. I have become nothing..." Her hands were a bloody mess and inside she felt nothing. She was quite sure that her soul was gone, forever...

"You're wrong. They brought you here thinking that their experiments would be a big success. Don't doubt yourself; you are stronger than you think. Just follow me. We have so much to do," The dead man warned. "Our way is to head down and then we will have to take another elevator to go back up to the main lobby of the corporation. Unfortunately, that's the only option."

"Are we underground?" Sarah was frightened even more, realizing, that all this time she was not on one of the higher floors of the gigantic building, but below.

"Yes, we are, and we must go now. Darkness is so close..."

The lab assistant turned back and staggered toward the elevator and pressed the call button. A bell rang and the doors opened. Inside, there was a sulfurous odor and a corpse that had begun to decompose. These smells were so disgusting that Sarah wanted to run away. This was not like Sarah to go into an elevator with one of the living dead. Two personalities fought inside her: one insisted on trusting, the other rejected everything and pleaded to escape at any cost. Whatever the case was, as the girl stood motionless, black smoke suddenly burst out from behind the emergency exit door. Just then the familiar ominous figure of the Egyptian appeared in the aperture. His skin was burnt in some places and bloated with huge bloody blisters, and his pupils were covered with a white film. He turned into an even scarier monster, and as always, was silent. He did not need to speak to scary anyone, his presence was already an indescribable horror.

This is what prompted Sarah to scurry into the elevator and hit the first floor button. The doors immediately began to close when she heard ever more rapid footsteps from the outside. A beam of light burst from the dead man's mouth, and when the doors closed an explosion came from the other side. The cab shook so strongly that Sarah thought the cables might break. But there was no further calamity, save for a few jerky jolts, the elevator reached the ground floor.

"Laboratories", The voice of the computer announced. Sarah stepped out of the cab into a corridor with a high ceiling, lined with heavy metal structures, filled with some kind of gas, or fog. Both sides were ominously lit with green lamps whose light gave the impression that everything was radioactive.

"Remember one thing: under no circumstances are you to part with the beads, they are the only thing that still keep your body from changing", the dead man said.

"Changing into what?" Sarah was so confused.

"You, probably haven't noticed anything... They have created a weapon called "ENTAL", which was used on you. It is a poison for which there is no cure. And it turns people into the *unhuman*.

"You're scaring me," Sarah was shocked. "Am I going to die?"

"I don't know... but this thing had already affected your whole body. You have already lost your tooth, and it's just the beginning. If you ever will take the beads off, the dark forces will immediately attack you, and not from the outside, but from the inside. You won't notice when you turn into something evil, like a demon. You don't have a soul any longer and you will become something terrifying, a unwilling warrior of The King of Darkness, who will destroy everything. This is why, YOU MUST NOT TAKE OFF THE BEADS, to prevent the danger that breathes down your back. From my side I will be always around you, trying to give you the maximum protection I can."

"What do you mean I have no soul?" Sarah was nervous but no longer afraid of the sight of the revived corpse. She had to know what the sinister corporation had done to her while she was unconscious, especially since she might not be a human any more. "Tell me what's going on. I need to know."

"Well ... " The dead man began, barely opening his half-rotten mouth when he suddenly stuttered and shouted so loudly, that the echo of his voice swept through all the floors of the building. "Run! Now! Get out of here!!"

A mass of light burst out of the dead body, turned into a swirling ball and flew forward along the corridor, making a lot of noise. There were claps and blows, after which the lab technician's body went limp and fell motionlessly to the floor, Sarah heard the noise of the elevator and the creaking of the tight cables, and then she saw the floor numbers rapidly accelerating on the control panel. Surely someone was going to come down next.

The building was nothing more than a forge of fears. There was so much in this place. The most dark, sinister and secret parts were hidden deep in the bowels of the computer corporation. Under a shiny, successful business were seriously scary things, things that were better not to know. Sarah's mind could not process the fact that such dark things were ultimately the true purpose of a seemingly great company. She had only to pronounce the word *MAGiC* in her mind and macabre memories surfaced in her head, among them, pale faces of mysteriously appearing long-dead people.

Every second was precious, so the girl ran forward, thinking only of salvation. Death itself was still breathing down her neck. What an unpleasant feeling: standing one step away from a bottomless abyss. With the coast clear, she rushed ahead hoping to get to the elevator and get out of the dungeon when she stopped abruptly, finding herself near a huge glass-paned round space. Behind a thick semi-transparent glass, metal robot arms protruded, gripping cryogenic capsules that resembled coffins. Sarah did not expect to see such a contraption and contents. There was a strange swirling fog behind the glass, but it was less dense than in the corridor. Her curiosity would have guided her inside had the situation been different. She wanted to know the true purpose of this machine, but now was not the time. Seeing a sign pointing to the exit only made her move faster. At that moment, somewhere behind, there was an odd cry.

Sarah flinched, but did not stop, realizing that every lost second could cost her life. She heard only her own heart as she moved toward her goal. At some point the fog lifted momentarily to reveal a set of heavy metal doors, damaged but open for escape. Everything was going almost too well, and Sarah caught herself doubting this reality. Right in front on the path appeared an elevator, promising no more nor less, than salvation. In a panic the girl pressed the call button at least ten times, believing it bring the elevator even faster, which was not the case at all. Her fear and her desire to live was everything. She just needed to be a little more patient, which in this situation was nearly impossible to do. Leaning her back against elevator doors Sarah started counting down precious seconds, while staring into the fog from where were heard horrendous approaching footsteps.

Only thirty seconds passed, but Sarah panicked even more. Time for her seemed to be standing still and the elevator was so slow in arriving that she wondered whether it worked at all. Turning her gaze to the control pad, the girl realized there was nothing to do but continue to wait. Biting her lip, she expected that at any moment just about anything could happen. Due to poor visibility it was difficult to understand how far away the demon was. With great fear that he was about to appear soon prevailed over reason, Sarah's heart beat nervously. She was so tense that at some point her body went limp and her legs buckled sending her to the floor. Believing that all her hopes were gone, the poor girl was ready to face the inevitable, but her rush to calamity was unfounded. Very opportunely, the doors behind her opened, smooth and almost soundless, and she literally fell inside and deftly pressed the button to the main hall.

The doors started closing again, ever so slowly as luck would have it, when at the distance of 13 feet, emerged the silhouette of the tattooed Egyptian monster. The demon knew that he had almost no time to act so he puffed out his eyes and opened his mouth in anger so that the threads that bound his lips tore the skin. There was a blood-curdling scream and this was the last thing that Sarah heard, before the doors securely shut. She just slipped down to the floor, unable to move from the numbness that entirely overtook her. The elevator swiftly swept upward toward the light. The nightmare might just be over.

Minutes. Happy minutes. The horrors have evaporated, the dungeon and secret laboratories - all this was now behind. Sarah's mind had difficulty processing everything that happened to her. In her head serious anxieties flared up, driving her thoughts first one way, then to another. She really felt lost. She remembered nothing, all she knew was her name- and the name of a man named "John", and a corporation named *MAGiC*. It was a puzzle that was yet to be solved. So, in this state of suspended thinking, Sarah floated somewhere into the depths of her consciousness, trying to pay attention to everything, but losing track of time. She didn't even notice that the elevator passed the "Main Hall" mark and moved further upward, but when she did, it was too late. By the time she glanced at the control pad, it was already at the fortieth floor.

"Lord, NO!!!," The girl burst out hysterically. She jumped to her feet and tried to stop the elevator, but the buttons did not obey the commands, and she was uncontrollably going higher and higher".

Sarah continued to unsuccessfully press all the buttons in a row until she gave up. The figures stopped spinning on the control pad, and a flashing "M" for "Management" appeared. The elevator slowed down, and soon completely stopped. The computer's voice from the speakers announced: "The Office of Migren Litsiona". The doors slowly opened up, but the girl continued to press the buttons, hoping to go down. She did not want to be in this place, let alone in this building. She had decided if she managed to escape from this hell, she would never return again. Alas, all her efforts to redirect the elevator were in vain and nothing worked.

"A waste of time", a loud and rude voice rang out as if from the speakers; Sarah was dumbfounded. It was no longer a computer, it was a living person - and definitely a female.

The girl gingerly peered out into the corridor, anticipating the next traps and monsters, but all she saw was a hall that looked like a small waiting room with chairs, armchairs and a coffee machine by the counter of the secretary, who for some reason was absent. It was quiet here, so much that it would be easy to fall asleep while walking the area. There was an unobtrusive scent of floral perfume, which was just as much a sleeping pill as was the area itself. There were no windows, only filtered light and burgundy colors. One could only guess what it would be like to work here as a secretary, imprisoned for a whole day in a dimly lit room. Surely that person would be subject to constant depression, except if there were other reasons to work here. Sarah was interested only in one thing: why did the head of this world corporation call her up to her private floor and then keep her here like a prisoner, not allowing her to leave. Well, of course, it was all about the mysterious, powerful beads and nothing else. Sarah was a guinea pig who almost managed to escape. But the guinea pig fell into the hands of the owner, and only he could decide its fate.

There was an open door into the room with a sign on it that read "Migren Litsiona". A cool wind was blowing toward the door, so pleasant that Sarah felt ridiculously cozy. Yes, these were memories from Blackwood, which so suddenly surfaced in her memory. Strange affair. Sarah began to remember things she had not previously remembered as a result of the sensations. She felt now what she felt back in Blackwood. Sarah often loved to lie under the willow near the river in the fine weather and read books, a cool breeze washing calm over her. In those moments life seemed as perfect as possible and Sarah wanted to stretch those minutes as long as possible. The smell of flowers, the coolness and nature all around her created the most beautiful place in the world. But it was time now to return to reality. Sarah glanced ahead and saw that in the doorway to the office of one of the most powerful people in the world stood a dark-haired woman with hair trimmed to her shoulders. She looked completely calm, not in the least bit scary, even beautiful and hospitable. Widely smiling as if she expected her guest.

"We have something to talk about. Come in." Migren Litsiona said and motioned the way forward without waiting for Sarah to decide to move, she went into her office.

Sarah very quickly understood that she was hostage of the situation and there was no other choice. This place probably concealed a danger that could be avoided, it was all just a theory that ran through her mind. The girl had to meet with someone who had deliberately kept her here. She felt something inherently uneasy with each successive minute. Uncertain and afraid, she slowly moved toward the open door. Each next step felt heavier than the previous one, and Sarah had already predicted a verdict to herself in advance. There were no more serenity and harmony around her. Caught in the doorway, she saw in front of her a working table of the head of the corporation, on curved legs, made of African mahogany. At the table in a stiffly upholstered velvet armchair sat Migren herself, and behind her towered gigantic crystal-clear windows from floor to ceiling.

From here you could see a whole city, great and beautiful. The sun was slowly setting down on the horizon. The sunset today was more beautiful than ever. The red rays illuminated the office so much that it was breathtaking. Absolutely everything was bathed in the red color so that you might have thought it was the end of the world, but in spite of the circumstances, such an amazing and soulful experience. The strangest thing was that just for a few moments Sarah caught herself with such a grandiose view of the city, she completely forgot about her anxieties. All her attention was drawn to something more amazingly beautiful. The panes of glass reflected the glare. The December air was filled with incredible warmth, and the color of the sky now shifted into a purple twilight. Whatever it was, it was the most perfect thing that the natural universe could create.

"Beautiful, isn't it?" Said Migren, turning back to the window, also watching the sunset. "This is what I would like to see every day".

These words immediately woke Sarah, and she turned her gaze to the dark-haired woman now sitting motionless at her desk. All the girl saw was a kind of dark essence. Clearly Litsiona was not an ordinary person, something was hidden inside this shell; Sarah knew it for sure. She continued to look at Migren, examining her all the way: the expression on her face, her eyes, her nose, her hands neatly folded together, her rigid posture - all the details told a lot about that person. Not daring to speak or move, Sarah gazed forward with wide-open eyes, her heart predictably beating wildly without realizing it.

"If I wanted to do something with you, I would have done it long ago,"

"You already did that in the labs. Those explosions and monsters. You wanted me dead," Sarah said in a shaky, rapid voice.

"No, no my dear," laughed the woman. "There was no one, but you and your hallucinations. What you saw was not true. If you want I can help you to stop it once and forever".

"Once and forever?" Sarah repeated with a great concern.

"Yes. Those visions... They can be gone..."

"Visions?" Sarah was at a loss that even now after all, when there should not be any more secrets, Migren was taking her for a fool. "That creature - the Egyptian monster, it was not my imagination..."

"Well, would you believe me if I said that it was an effect of "ENTAL"?

"I don't believe it was all about it..."

"Most of it was, believe it or not, and I am not going to try to prove you anything. I pursue only one goal and so we need to discuss what I want and not what you want. Do you understand me?" Migren sounded threatening.

Sarah just nodded, understanding that whatever the truth was, it didn't matter. That lady was not going to tip her hand to anyone, especially to her. The facts would forever remain silent and unknown, here in this office.

"Perfect, so now, "Migren Litsiona said with a grin, and starting to lose her patience. "Maybe you will stop standing there in the doorway and come in and sit down, so we could talk like normal people?"

With her right foot she pushed the chair on wheels away from the table. It instantly slid and turned toward the statue-like Sarah. She wanted to go away, but she could not control herself, and there really was nowhere to go. All she could do was obey. Gathering her spirit, the girl took a step forward, then another step, and noticed how the woman at the table smiled even more, feeling an immeasurable superiority behind it. Sarah sat down in the chair where it had met her and moved no closer to the table.

"If I had known that eventually you would show up here at my Corporation, and even start working here, I would not have made the effort to send my men to your house and make a big deal. Ah, hindsight… Well, it doesn't matter now".

"What men?" Sarah asked in a hoarse voice.

"Oh, yes, of course, you do not remember anything. I see "ENTAL" did its usual great job. So strange that after everything that has happened you still look healthy enough. You walk, you talk, you have even managed to somehow substitute the beads. I knew that you were not an ordinary person. So, tell me girl, what is your secret? Where were you hiding the beads and how have you managed to destroy *Sample 1*?"

Sarah didn't know what to say or how to react. It all seemed to her so unreal, more like a nightmare. She was completely unable to divide fiction from reality. In the end she had no idea what *Sample 1* was or what Migren was talking about. She could not understand what her final purpose was in kidnapping her and putting her into the fake hospital - which was just a cover for labs to experiment on unsuspecting people.

"You don't say much," Migren Litsiona smirked. "Then let's finish our conversation and you can go home and get a good rest, but I need your beads. Right now. They are all I want. Believe me, for you there is no need in them, no interest, but for me!"

"The beads?" Sarah repeated.

"*Yes, the beads*," The woman said coldly and held out a pale hand. "Give them to me".

Sarah had no idea what would happen if she rejected the demand. She looked at Migren and realized that she was not asked, but ordered. She could obey immediately, but what would happen next? The girl remembered that the spirit that had defended her in the bowels of the earth told her, and so it said to keep the beads and not to part with them. It seemed that a simple and uncomplicated request was in fact presented a hard decision. Sarah looked frightened at her interlocutor, and her hand slowly reached her neck. Only a brief moment passed when all around became redder than before, everything sparkled like it was at dawn, and the head of the MAGiC corporation turned into a faceless shadow. The air in the office immediately boiled like water in a teapot. Sarah rose abruptly, staring in horror at what was left of Migren, and then a white light flared between her and the table. The bright rays proved so powerful that the girl immediately shielded her face so as not to go blind. It all lasted a couple of seconds or, maybe, even less, and when everything stopped, Sarah opened her eyes and saw before her a familiar plastic-like, androgynous silhouette.

"I am really sorry," The silhouette said. "There is no other option, but this".

After what happened next, in depths of her consciousness Sarah realized that fate was a thing so unpredictable that if there was something predestined, it remained invisible until the very last moment. Not even a medium could forecast it. Fate is the spontaneity, like a splash of cold water to the face at the most unexpected moment, that you cannot avoid.

Sarah felt the warmth of the dying sun gently warm her whole body. The sky was unusually red, it seemed that life was leaving this place forever, shadows appeared here and there, devouring the light. In the sky, birds floated here at a great height in their last minutes. High above the rare wispy clouds, three stars caught fire. The glare of the dying suns was blindingly reflected off the tall, silver skyscrapers, that stretched up into space itself. The greatness of this outlandish planet was fading away, the emptiness was approaching, and nothing could stop it. Before Sarah's eyes, a whole civilization was dying, and there was nothing to be done about it. Such a sad event caused only tears in her eyes, a bitter, inopportune sadness that came so quickly. Witness to such a terrible event, Sarah suddenly felt something quite strange in her body, as if it was taken over by something and she was no longer the mistress of her being. All she heard and saw turned into a kind of theater; her physical movements, including breathing, ceased to belong to her.

"Do not be afraid of anything," Sarah heard a voice in her mind. "You are no longer Sarah... no longer a preacher's daughter from Blackwood".

Sarah's mind started running pictures, memories that were not her own, and the now fading planet was one of them. In a few seconds she relived her entire life, remembering everything to the smallest details. But there was something else. Her body stood motionless in the light of the rays of the setting sun, and right in front of her there was also a motionless body, a black silhouette of a dark-haired woman who was no longer smiling, but frozen as if time had stopped, and there was nothing else but *time*. This was the moment when the two great forces were facing each other once again, and one of them undoubtedly stronger, but the second had some real advantages.

"Do you think that by creating C.L.O.U.D.S. you could destroy the universe?" Sarah said, but it was not in her voice. "Maybe, you better go back where you came from?"

"Ha-ha-ha," laughed Migren Litsiona. "Too late. We all have become a part of C.L.O.U.D.S., whether you like it or not. It's done, and you, you're just a reminder of the old days. But you will disappear, including the memories and your existence".

Migren glared at Sarah, devouring her with her sinister eyes, feeling her superiority. This was a long-standing confrontation, which was supposed to end right here and right now. The forces of light and darkness again came together just as they had long ago in someplace far away called the Land of the Angels. Becoming part of an inexplicable spirit, Sarah now understood many things that happened to her earlier, and visions that she could not explain. Now everything was falling into its place and had become more clear than ever before. The house of her grandparents was built on the site of an ancient castle, where once a long time ago there was a battle of light and dark spirits. Yes, yes, the very same castle that Sarah was dreamed about at the medium's salon. That's why then, when she fell under the ice, she was immediately chosen. The remnants of the bright side needed an uncomplicated keeper of their energy, and Sarah's body was chosen as the prime candidate. The subsequent many challenges to her faith made her soul stronger, tempered her, which made her very noticeable, like Sirius, but not in the physical world. From the clutches of darkness, a most important artifact that could change the order in the entire universe, was torn away. Multicolored beads were only a cover of what was hidden behind them. Now Sarah knew why these strange beads were so important. The planet Earth was not the only place where life existed. Long before the Earth there were other worlds, and each of them had its own color. But because they had their own imperfections, they were all hidden in energy crystals, and life and time in them stopped. The Earth became the result of a clash of such powerful forces that would not disappear. Those very ancient forces also spawned a new force - spirits of Light and Darkness, in whose memory still existed the memories of the other worlds. There began a fight for control over everything which would allow the establishment of absolute order in the universe. In fact, the Earth was only a small part of something vastly more grandiose.

"I am afraid you will fail in all your plans, whatever they may be," Sarah said ironically.

Because of what was said, at last the beads burst out with bright light and the beams of multicolored energy violently struck Migren with such force that even before she shouted, she flew toward the window and collapsed onto the floor. In the large panes of window glass ran cracks in many directions, like cobwebs, covering every inch. In the sunlight they seemed like flowing lava. But that was not all. From Migren Litsiona, motionlessly lying on the floor started pouring black smoke, as if she was burning from the inside. But as if nothing had happened, she suddenly rose to her feet, with her eyes now flashing red, and through her clenched lips she hissed angrily:

"You know well that this pitiful attempt is useless with me".

In the next instant, multi-colored rays again burst out of Sarah's beads, but this time Migren moved abruptly to the other side of the office, as smoothly as if she were floating in the air. It seemed that she was sucked through a wormhole and thrown into another part of the room. And all would be nothing, but the rays, not having managed to reach the goal, striped like a rainbow in the air, and as soon as the demon woman appeared in the other corner of the office, like a huge gun-machine they burst in her body piercing her through.

"Enough!" Migren bellowed. She was angry and put forward her right hand.

Sarah felt as if she was being torn to pieces. A strong, invisible force tried to drain all the life of her, and she could feel it. It was impossible to resist such a powerful energy. What was called Evil had already managed to destroy all the Spirits of Light, with only one still remaining. Multiple streams of black smoke, like threads, more like the legs of a giant spider, pierced Sarah's body, striking her with terrible pain. The beads again released an array of colorful energy rays, causing the air pressure to fluctuate, and then the room darkened. The red light outside continued to ominously illuminate the building and the glass. This was not the end of the world, but something more terrible. Migren Litsiona's body became enveloped by a black substance that turned her into nothing more than just a shadow of incredible size with eerie, red burning eyes. It was the same shadow that persecuted Sarah in the underground laboratories, the very shadow whose eyes flashed in her mind time to time, plunging her into the depths of her consciousness. True Evil in its purest form.

Sarah was about to rush to the exit, when a giant hand, formed of black smoke, emerged from nowhere and with a simple movement tore off the beads from Sarah's neck. A snap, as if scissors had cut a tightly wound cable, rang in girl's ears with a dangerous sound, impossible to forget. Like peas, the beads fell to the floor and rolled in different directions followed by loud, thunderous claps. Here and there in the darkness flashed lights of different colors: red, green or yellow, and it seemed that it was not a real world, but some fantasy scene.

"No-o-o!!" Sarah cried out, reaching through the web of darkness, and grabbing a bright blue bead.

She found strength in herself purely by instinct, like a mother does to protect her child. Turning sharply, she ran with all her might to the elevator. Her legs carried her with uncharacteristic speed. The claps continued from behind, but it didn't matter. It was necessary to escape at any cost, saving herself and the last bead, which remained the final hope for the balance of power in this world. Pressing the button for the main lobby, Sarah saw that the shadow of the Migren Litsiona dividing into several parts as if the Devil himself decided to visit the Earth. If the Spirit of Light possessed her body, Sarah would never have managed to start the elevator, but now everything was different because she was not just a human any more.

No longer on the necklace and joined together, the other worlds were on the loose, which did not bode well for anyone or anything. The time that had stopped in them again began to tick and they ceased to be invulnerable against external forces. The loose beads and worlds had become like time bombs carrying danger on an unprecedented scale. Sarah knew this. She could see something terrible approaching at great speed. The planet Earth was only a tiny grain in a giant sea of forces that opposed each other. If the equilibrium of our galaxy shifted, then in a parallel galaxy its equilibrium stopped existing. Something terrible had been awakened. Something that was able to erase everything in its path. Tears streamed from Sarah's eyes, because she knew how much pain and suffering this world would experience.

The elevator was going down very fast, only seconds remained in reserve to calculate a further course of action. What Sarah faced here would not leave her alone and certainly would not let her escape with the last part of the artifact. The doors only had to open, as she found herself in a place where a regular life was frenetic There was a fuss, but it was sham. No one would have believed that behind such a huge corporation was something that would paralyze anyone in horror. Sarah darted out of the elevator when suddenly she bumped in a tall dark-haired man.

"Sarah... oh my God, it's you!" John Wishep said joyfully and rushed to Sarah with stretched arms, but the girl stepped back. "I checked most of hospitals and morgues before I received your voice message saying you were here.

"You're alive... John," That was all Sarah could say at the moment. She was not expecting to meet her dear John here and now, especially when it was not a good moment at all; the danger of the MAGiC building still palpable.

"Yes," he said painfully as he revisited the horrible memories of the fashion show where only by the grace of God, he miraculously survived. John saw the look of his friend: her bruises, the soot and scratches on her face, blood stains and missing a few teeth - her face looked strangely scary. "Lord Jesus, Sarah, I hardly recognize you. Let me call Julia, we will go to the hospital..."

"NO!" The girl said abruptly. "No more hospitals!! I know you have a lot of questions, but we must get out of this damn place RIGHT NOW!"

"What's going on?" John frowned and tried to touch Sarah, when an internal force pushed him aside so that he almost fell to the floor, only miraculously managing to keep his balance.

"Do you understand that we must leave *MAGiC* right now John?" Sarah said nervously.

"What the hell are you talking about?" The guy shouted as the blood in his veins pulsed with urgency.

"We can't waste any more time, I will explain everything to you later. I need your car".

"Don't even think about it" John started, but Sarah was already running to the exit making her way through the crowds of lost workers and visitors.

People heard angry voices and looked around trying to understand what was happening. Needless to say, they were quite shocked by what they saw and heard. Even the guards stunned by the perplexity, not expecting to see a fragile-looking girl acting like a strong man who just come out of the boxer's ring. John had no choice but to run after his friend. He could not leave Sarah alone in such a state. For him it was just some kind of insanity, which he had to indulge now and figure out later. The one whom he had known for so many years was strangely no longer the same person since he last saw her at the show.

Sarah did not even have to ask which car belonged to John as she ran out of the building. She already knew everything ahead of time. This knowledge was a kind of adventure for her. It was both shocking and pleasurable. Directly in front of her stood a yellow Ferrari 448 Spider, whose 660 hp engine was now more than welcome. Mentally, she was very grateful to John only for the fact that street racing was his hobby, and that he arrived today at the office in one of his favorites. This joy was not unreasonable, the girl knew in advance what would happen next, and therefore did not lose a second. Without even using a key, she just opened a door, jumped onto the passenger seat and eagerly yelled at John, urging him to hurry.

"How the hell did you open the fucking door?" John couldn't believe his eyes. "Either you explain what's going on to me, or you won't get the keys, I mean it," he threatened, realizing there was no communicating with his crazy friend in language that made sense to her.

"Just let's go, please," Sarah begged.

"I told you… I need an explanation," The guy insisted.

"Well …" Sarah began to say, and at the same moment from her body separated either a silhouette, or a light, or something supernatural. In any case, it was something bright, like a flash after a sharp solar activity event. John could not understand anything he was seeing or experiencing when he felt that some kind of inexplicable energy force him into the driver's seat, and the motor started itself.

"GO!" Sarah ordered.

John obediently pressed the pedal to the floor, not daring to utter a word, still in a state of shock and not yet able to digest what had just happened to him. They drove at great speed away from the sinister corporation and John had no idea why. His head was clouded by a strange feelings that he could only describe as "asleep in reality", and all around him had to be a dream. But after he almost crashed with the truck on the next turn, it became abundantly clear that everything was real. His heart was about to pound out of his chest. Not for Sarah. She sat motionless next to him like a stone. She focused forward, and did not comment on what was happening.

"I don't know what it was," The guy finally found words. "Just explain everything to me. If not now, then you must when we get home".

"You said *at home?*" Sarah suddenly turned her head to the guy as if she were a robot. "No. Brooklyn is a bad option. Go to Pennsylvania ... Pennsylvania," Her last words turned into a barely discernible whisper, which seemed as if she were talking to herself.

"No, no, no. This is not how this is going to work," John said angrily. "Sarah, either you tell me what's going on, or..."

"Or do you want a repeat of what happened at Lena Barbella's fashion show?" Sarah said, but it was clearly not her voice. "You survived that nightmare, because you left the show room, fortunately, right before the massacre started. And I'm glad that Julia you are both fine".

"How do you know about all this?"

"Believe me John, but it's impossible to put into words. I know things you can't even imagine. To me, everything is painfully so obvious. Things that you experienced are just the beginning. If you don't do what I tell you it will be a big mistake. You do not understand much right now John. Perhaps you never will. If you don't trust me, then all of us will be in unimaginable trouble".

"This is all crazy nonsense," John shouted as he sped along the road at a blistering pace. "At first you completely disappear into nothing from the fashion show, and then I get a call from a special line that belongs only to *MAGiC* laboratories, and now we're going to the devil knows where ..."

"So, you know about laboratories and what's going on there?" Sarah's eyes bulged and she grabbed John's wrist.

The first thing the guy felt was burning, stronger than he ever felt in his life. It was not a usual burning sensation, like from a fire, it was something else that could not be explained. Then he cried out and looked with horror at his friend, who now seemed completely different to him. It was not Sarah, but someone else hiding behind her face who frightened him in the truest sense of the word. He now felt more like a prisoner than a free man, not capable of making his own decisions. Grabbing the burned place on his wrist, he looked at his friend with fear, and then again looked at the wrist, which now showed red fingerprints. Not understanding anything, John wanted to stop by the side of the road, not mentioning his intentions, when Sarah shouted angrily:

"Don't!" she barked, "Keep going!!"

"And if I disobey, then what?"

"Not again, John… Please don't make another mistake".

"What are you talking about?"

"About the fact that you don't know anything about the place where you've worked for so many years. And even if you did know … It's not too late. There's time to quit this damned corporation".

"Sarah, what's going on? What happened? And why are you implicating me in whatever-the-hell you're talking about?"

"John, you've already made quite a few mistakes, but you still can fix things. Your work at *MAGiC* will kill both you and your loved ones if you do not leave it. It is evil incarnate. What this corporation has done to me… if you only knew. The experiences they have put me through will never be forgotten and do not fit with your conscious ideas about them".

"What?!?" The guy was horrified. In his shock he pressed down the accelerator so hard that the tires squealed on the asphalt, and the car almost flipped over as they went into a turn. "I don't believe you".

"While I was unconscious, I was injected with a drug, developed by *MAGiC*. It's called "ENTAL". I don't know if it is familiar to you, but this thing is dangerous. It turns people into monsters".

"God, Sarah… it all sounds just crazy. Why would *MAGiC* perform experiments on people, and even more so, turn them into monsters? Yes, I've heard about this drug, but it was at the development testing stage to cure mental disorders. It would help to bring many lives back to normal. Sarah, I really don't understand anything you're talking about now".

"That's why you need to get out of there. When you do you will finally understand everything, before it's too late. This drug very quickly mutates all organic compounds inside humans, and turns the body into something terrible. That clown - he was one of the guinea pigs, and so your friend Indigo. Be very cautious of him".

"Indigo? That makes absolutely no sense. Well if you were given this drug, why are you still a human?" John asked this question in such a way that he did not really expect to hear the answer, because he was keenly aware of Sarah's changed features that did not belong to the one whom he always knew.

"Because I have this," Sarah showed the brightly glowing blue bead that she held tightly in her left hand.

"It's from your beads!" John said.

"Yes, and this is the only one that can protect my body from changing," After these words Sarah gagged and began to cough loudly and wheeze, as if she could not draw in enough air.

"Sarah," John cried out. "What's wrong?" He suddenly became so scared for his friend that he pulled off on the side of the road when the girl firmly ordered:

"NO John, don't stop, keep going! I am... I am all right".

John looked at Sarah with a fright in his eyes and then at the road, and had no idea how he really should act. The story just told by his friend sounded insane, but looking at her sick state, he was quite sure that there really was something evil in the corporation, something unforgivable. He had to make decisive steps.

"Listen, I need to know all the details of what happened to you," The guy said. "Look at yourself, the way you look. This is not normal. We must go to the police, and you need a medical help. You can't ignore the violence that experienced there".

"No," Sarah disagreed. "If the police get into the details, we'll all be dead in no time."

"If you ignore it, then I won't. You're acting out of your mind right now," John said plainly. He was completely sure now that he should not indulge Sarah, who was obviously not in a proper state of mind. "You don't look well at all, I cannot take you anywhere in such a state. I'm calling the police and we're doing things the way I want to." John applied the brakes sharply near the gas station and firmly placed a hand on the seat behind Sarah's neck.

"That's not right," The girl shook her head, feeling the growing desperation inside herself.

"You act as if you broke the law," The guy said. "Believe me, I want you to be safe".

John wanted to leave the car when some kind of invisible power would not let him move out from his place. He felt if he were glued to the seat. He tried again and again, but his whole body wouldn't obey. Then he looked at Sarah who was piercing him with her gaze, continued to keep her stone facial expression without any emotion.

"You cannot keep me here forever," He said through his teeth. "Release me, let me go, whatever you are! Leave my Sarah alone. Let us go!".

"Hush, please," The girl put forward her hands and closed her eyes as if something was bothering her, and it was not by John.

For no apparent reason there was a strange buzzing in her head and she felt a sudden anger in her whole body. Her hands trembled, and somehow forgetting about what was happening inside her, she turned her attention to the horizon, from where thunderclouds began to build in the dark evening sky. Being a decent distance from Manhattan, Sarah could still see the tower of the *MAGiC* Corporation and also feel that some dark forces were revived. Something was happening there, and it was not just something alarming, but fully frightful, piercing to the bone. At some point the wind had stopped blowing, and it became unbearably stuffy.

John suddenly felt that an invisible force released him and he was again able to move. Finally breathing freely, he looked at Sarah with fear and slammed the car door, blaming himself for not being able to help his dear Sarah exorcise whatever demon possessed her. Wiping the sweat from his forehead and looking mistrustful at his friend, he walked away from the car and took out his phone. After a couple of minutes, he returned to the car.

"You'll need to tell the cops all the details, okay?" He asked with a scowl.

"As you wish," Sarah resentfully replied and stepped out of the car.

She only touched the ground with her right foot when a bright light lit up the sky, as if an atomic explosion had occurred. The brilliance lasted two seconds, no more, and then it became dark again. John only opened his mouth, not believing his eyes, and trying to realize what he had just seen. Sarah sternly stood, giving all her attention to monstrous tower, with the ominous black front and a flashing red antenna. This event happened for a reason, it was a turning point, when new worlds were born again, full of their secrets and mysteries, and yet that was the moment when Migren Litsiona noticed the loss of the blue bead, without which her plans could not come to fruition. Shuddering, Sarah looked at John, and tears formed in her eyes, mixed with horror, incomparable to anything of this world.

"I think I need to find a restroom," she said in a lost voice.

"You better make it quick. I don't like what's going on here and I think a big storm is coming".

"Don't worry, I'll be back in just a few minutes," Sarah assured her friend.

At a quick pace that resembled a run, she soon arrived to the restroom. Sarah walked over to the sink and stared at her reflection. Inside her everything was burning, and she clearly knew that something was wrong. Like in an intoxicated state, she paid no attention to anything, not even the hot water pouring from the open tap. Her head was at a tug-of-war with strange thoughts. In one moment her memory was intact, then suddenly absent, leaving nothing but emptiness before mysteriously returning once again. Sarah's muscles contracted in spasm. In addition, she felt something else but could not understand exactly what it was. The air was saturated with an odd kind of death - not the death of someone specific, but the death of everything.

Strength was quickly leaving Sarah's body, she consumed too much energy as the superhuman she had become. The only thing that she was able to do for now was to save the last particle of the artifact, and to do everything possible, so that John would be in no danger. It was so important to find some way to protect her loved ones. Long moments went by when everything seemed lost, but in reality it was not. Awakening from her reverie, Sarah sighed and turned off the water. She again looked at her reflection when her gaze picked up a shadow behind her. Before, she would have been paralyzed by fear, but not now. It was an unimaginable feeling, when consciousness ceased to feel fear of formerly overwhelming things! Sharply she turned back and locked her gaze with familiar, eerie yellow eyes that belonged to someone she had met before: the clown-killer, whom she now knew to be a by-product of *MAGiC's* experimentation.

"They did the same to you, as to me," He croaked. His mouth gaped and from whose corners down to his chin slowly trickled scarlet blood.

Once the clown-killer spoke there were sharp zings of blades as they sharpened themselves on each other. The shadow, in the wafts of steam, had grown considerably in size. Sarah immediately backed away and in her movement stumbled into the sink. The steam began to evaporate at a rapid pace and with it the clown began to melt, like snow in the sun. From outside there were heard sirens, and then the door to the restroom flung open and John appeared in the doorway. He looked more than flustered.

"Are you okay?" He asked. "It's already been fifteen minutes."

"Fifteen minutes?..." Sarah repeated, making her eyes big and looking through John.

"The police have just arrived. You have to tell them everything".

"John," The girl said with deadly calm voice. "I need to talk to you".

"Uh… okay" He didn't like her tone.

They walked out and stopped right in front of the supermarket. Nearby, there were blinking lights atop two police cars and in the distance peals of thunder rang out. Sarah intuitively knew exactly what was going to happen. Having a clairvoyant vision, she saw that far away from here along a half-empty road approached a car with three passengers. She also knew that it would take exactly fifteen minutes to arrive where she stood. It was urgent to make an immediate plan.

"John, you must forgive me for what happened," Sarah said.

"What do you mean?" Again, the guy sounded confused.

"You know what I mean. Some things have happened that are hard to explain which have serious consequences. If I could travel back into the past, I would make different decisions," The girl sounded almost disappointed, "But I can't undo what has been done."

"Sarah you have nothing to be sorry about. Forget everything. The most important thing now is to keep you safe. It makes better sense if you speak to the police. You can't stay silent about what happened, or just walk away. It is not the way to solve problems".

"You are incredibly kind," Sarah smiled. "I know, even after everything that has happened, you still fight yourself *not* to believe in anything supernatural. Well, you have every right not to believe. Soon you will learn things that will change your mind and your life. It's unavoidable."

"Well, maybe you're right" John said. "But right now, we gotta go".

"Wait," Sarah said loudly and grabbed his hands in hers. "I am so sorry John, it's necessary".

Immediately John felt as if he'd been hit by a bolt of lightning. Everything before his eyes turned white, and nothing could be seen, and his ears were filled a strange noise that carried him somewhere to the unknown. As if enchanted, with an empty gaze he stared at the girl, with an opened mouth, breathing evenly, but not moving. Sarah gently released him. He swayed, but did not fall, continuing to remain immobile. The girl knew that when she would leave her friend, she would have a minute, perhaps two, after which the police would quickly learn what the matter was. Sarah sighed and gently kissed John on the lips, after which she whispered with trepidation in her heart.

"...I love you John... Goodbye...."

Her red hair began to wave in the wind right before John's eyes, which had sadly lost their vision. Sarah was deeply upset that she had made another, and probably bad, choice. But it was her choice. She knew that her beloved friend, was no longer just a friend, and that he knew about her feelings. She could see it only now, being possessed by a spirit of light. But the most important thing that allowed her to stay calm in this pivotal moment, was that she could feel the heart of someone she had always loved. Sarah had great confidence that he would reciprocate if circumstances had developed differently. Turning around, she looked toward the horizon covered by the storm clouds, and hurried to the sleek Ferrari.

"Miss?" Questioned the voice of a policeman.

"Give me a second, uhhhh… I am trying to find my driver's license," Sarah gave a quick retort.

Suddenly John again swayed, but this time falling to the ground in front of the policemen's eyes. Immediately there was a roar from the 600 horsepower-engine.

"Miss… get out of the car with your hands up!" There was a loud order, but Sarah pressed the pedal with all her might.

First, the echoes of the portable radio were heard, and then the sirens howled. The girl never imagined that she would have to escape from the police. Just a couple of days ago, none of this would have made any sense. She immediately caught herself thinking about the uneven path of faith her life had taken. How did she end up here? Pursuit from the police to some extent even became comical. If it were some guy in the place of Sarah, he would have turned up the music to the max, and really take off -- especially in a rocket like this Ferrari! No wonder John loved street racing so much, it charged him with adrenaline and made his life an incredible adventure. Speed, expensive cars, and crazy ventures into the unknown. The motor roared like a Serengeti lion, but then Sarah heard another sound, and another. But these sounds were not from the here and now; they came from another dimension, from another time and another place.

"What is it?" Sarah whispered aloud, trying to understand what she heard.

They were only signs, sounds and shadows of uncertainty. She could not see anything, not the slightest detail, but could only hear the sound of many engines like an irreconcilable diabolical race. And... and there was John. She suddenly flinched, as if she had been pierced with a spear. Her whole body was covered with goosebumps which brought her back to reality, back to the chase which still continued. The police had not yet realized what kind of danger to which they exposed themselves. Sarah narrowed her eyes and clenched her teeth when she felt that in the area something was changed. The sirens died down without any apparent reason, and a powerful explosion came from behind. A bright red flame shot up into the black storm sky, which did not bode well for anyone or anything. All that was left for Sarah to do was to drive on as fast as possible.

Her pursuers still remained behind, but not as far as Sarah would like. They were no longer police officers. As for the real officers, there was only a hope that they managed to survive, the probability of which was as great as the possibility to escape unscathed from demonic forces. The demonic creatures were born in a void they knew what they were hunting for and were ready to snatch it at any cost. Every now and then Sarah turned around, afraid that an ominous car was about to appear on the horizon, but all she could see was the blackness. Having turned on a two-lane road, she accelerated at full speed through the countryside. What irony, *deja vu* – something similar had happened to Sarah in Pennsylvania. All that she dreamed of was to confuse her pursuers and disappear from their sight.

Lightning flashed in the dark, after which powerful thunder rolled through the sky, followed by the rain which finally started to fall. The storm had most certainly arrived. The trees on the roadside rustled so furiously that they could be heard over the sounds of purring engine. The increasingly heavy, steady rain made every turn more dangerous, and Sarah eventually had to slow down. Nervously looking ahead, she thought first of all about where she should go to protect the Blue World, held tightly in the blue bead. There were not so many options nor was possible to hide forever.

Sarah heard new voices of ghosts which emerged from nowhere, that had slept for a long time and who remained hidden for centuries. Eventually they found the one who was marked as the keeper of balance in the whole universe. As the last of the survivors in the great battle, Sarah had the trump card in her hands. Hope, however, had always been an option, but it became more a question of faith and about how strong it was. The preponderance of good over evil was neither definite nor decided. But now as never before it became a question.

It was very hard to see the road through the sudden torrent of rain. The windshield wipers were already working at peak performance but simply not coping with the downpour. Turns started to show up more often on this road, which seemed very strange. One could have thought that it was not a countryside, but the hairpin turns of a mountain pass. Sarah regretted having left the main road. Her sweaty palms were firmly planted on the steering wheel as she intensely watched the road up ahead. Her anxiety was short-lived when a flash of light occurred from behind, which was not from the lightning. Sarah paid little attention, just wanting to get back on track, but the unfortunate road endlessly stretched somewhere forward. A couple of minutes passed before the girl finally realized that the end of the pursuit was near and that the villains had almost overtaken her. She was nearly redlining the engine, but increased the speed, hoping for a speed miracle. Without reason her head filled with a rush of voices. The clearest of these repeating only one thing over and over: "John, hurry, you still can do it! Do you hear me, John?"

Sarah became very nervous, she felt, that her dear John had taken action and started to search for her, and she didn't want that to happen at all. She was frightened for the life of the one she loved so much, having no idea what to do to protect him. Through a flash of inexplicable visions, she saw the darkness approaching John through many sports cars with demon-drivers attacking him, thirsting for his blood. It all made Sarah quake with fear, but then her emotions abruptly disappeared and she stopped feeling anything. If earlier she felt like stopping, now she felt like using every one of those horses. The voices in her head were gone, except one that sounded like a wild scream from her loving mother:

"You will kill us all. Stop my child, don't run away, there is nothing of which you should be afraid. Come home... come home".

"Mother..." Sarah whispered. The ENTAL brought an uncontrollable anger to rise inside her.

Again, the thunder rumbled, and then the car was picked up by some powerful force and knocked to the side. Sarah didn't understand what was happening, when suddenly everything turned upside down. With an unimaginable din, and a rain of car parts, the Ferrari flipped over a couple of times. The girl was battered from all sides, shrapnel scratched her face, arms, legs, and the airbag was not particularly useful, even if there had been three of them. Unfortunately in a crash of this magnitude, no matter the protection, nothing would have been able to soften the blows or damage which would have been enough to drag any living thing to the world of the dead.

As if newly born, Sarah opened her mouth and began by wheezing in a single breath. She felt the oxygen-rich blood flowing through her veins, breathing life into her. Her face was doused with water and her skin was burning. With difficulty turning her head to the left, she found to her horror that the car was on fire; she needed to get out before it was too late. Wondering why and how she still had so much strength, the girl escaped through the half-smashed windshield, and glanced into the distance on the road. There seemed to only be Sarah, Darkness and Fire. The girl cringed at the thought that the predators would not wait and would run to the fire for the feast, and in her superhuman state, she ran away from the road to the black forest ahead through a muddy field. Now she had only one choice: to get lost in the woods, find shelter, any place where the henchmen of Migren Litsiona could not find her. Sarah felt dead cold. She didn't give up and ran ahead without looking back until she heard an explosion. One could only imagine how much attention it attracted to itself. Dark forces were close, and it was necessary to disappear as quickly as possible.

Sarah ran faster than a desperate antelope being chased by a ravenous lion. For her time didn't exist anymore, the only thing was speed, and not a human pace, but more powerful and *un*human. It helped her to very quickly reach a distant hill covered by many trees. Climbing the hill as far as possible, at some point Sarah stopped under a giant oak, finally daring to look around. Only now could relax a little; the girl found it hard to breathe because something was stuck in her throat. She grabbed her neck and then her face horrified by discovering deeply bleeding, mutilating wounds all over. If she had a mirror, the person she would see in the reflection would not even be close to the face she knew her entire life. At first there was fear of what would happen next; death or maybe even something even worse?

But then in her mind rang out words imploring her to continue running regardless of anything else, just to save the last of the worlds. She was about to lunge from her spot, when in her head she heard an innocent and clear new voice that Sarah had never heard before. The sound was magnificent and nothing she could have ever imagined. It sounded inspiring, caring, calm, loving, kind and hopeful. Was it an angel? Unsure, but Sarah simply couldn't recognize it. There now was only one thought about all this: He came to take care of her, to protect her from the Evil. Sarah gently lowered her hands that were completely riddled with cuts. She narrowed her eyes, gazed into the distance, and her innermost thoughts began gratefully thank God. He didn't let her die in that terrible car crash. He saved her life for a very important mission to save this world. Her time spent in gratitude was meaningful, but short. Was it enough? Certainly not. Even if she had hours and hours it still wouldn't reach satisfaction. However Sarah was glad she heard Him, and that in itself was the most meaningful; the rest was the rest. She wore a short-lived smile and then noticed three figures moving through the field, directly approaching her. They were too fast, uncharacteristically quick, like bloodhounds who knew where they were going, and what they had to do. With all her strength she ran, having no idea where she was going. Wet branches scraped her face, but no matter. She was not worried about herself, but about the future. Knowing perfectly well what would happen, she was willing to survive the great efforts it took to take possession of the blue bead - whatever the cost. Seeing nothing ahead, except the impenetrable night and endless bushes, Sarah swiftly entered into the forest, rising even higher up the hill. It seemed that the scene was animated, and the demons set off into a mad dance, spreading chaos. The trees swayed like during a hurricane, and the weather was not going to calm down, but was in great variance.

The path became more difficult: everywhere there was mud, depressions and sometimes even precipices. Much to her relief, Sarah miraculously ended up on a narrow trail, which greatly facilitated the journey. It was only necessary to decide whether to go down or up. The first option seemed to be more dangerous, only because the demons could easily intersect her path, so she chose the second one. She began in a rush, but not for a long. After a short time, she abruptly stopped, as if there were a wall in front of her. She scanned the area, trying to understand where she was. Everything for her was new, and she felt that it was only a bad dream, a strange nightmare. Shivering from the cold, she looked at her hands marked with blood and mud. Sarah tried to calm her body down, but could not, and she cried out from the sudden pain that swept over her. She grabbed the trunk of the nearest tree for stability and let out a quiet moan. All she could feel was the growing, insurmountable fear inside her. Everything was clouded in front of her eyes, her head buzzed, and she had the feeling as if her muscles had turned to Jell-o. Slowly sliding down the trunk to the ground, she cried helplessly, uttering only one word: "John."

"John, I am sorry, I am so sorry," She whispered through tears, when her consciousness interrupted an angry voice.

At first Sarah could not understand anything, but soon the words became clearer:

"die… Die… DIE!!".

"Stop it!" Sarah shouted in anger, and then her mind cleared again.

All her emotions instantly disappeared and she stood up as if she remembered something very important. She truly needed to keep her mission in mind. Demonic forces never sleep; they were chasing her and they were very close. The best thing for Sarah to do was to return to running. And yes she could run, but her weak, damaged body made troubles for her. The girl looked around one more time, making sure there was no one else in the area, and quickly started walking up the hill. It was very hard to see anything ahead with the downpour streaming into her face. Unfortunately, there was no possibility of changing the weather, and Sarah just hoped that in the end the storm would keep her invisible and help her escape from the evil forces. Sarah didn't notice how she eventually arrived at a small meadow on the top of the hill. There was the sound of a waterfall in the distance, and the rain didn't seem to be as bad as in the chaotic forest. At first Sarah looked back, fearing to see what might be there, but there was nothing. Instead, she put all her attention to a tiny trail going down to the other side of the hill, right in direction of the waterfall.

"I can do it," The girl whispered to herself as she was about to descend, but unexpectedly her way became blocked by two tall figures. Yes, they were the same two thugs who broke into Sarah's house causing her to flee Blackwood, and to ask John for help. How ironic it was that when their paths crossed again, it was no place other than Pennsylvania. It was useless to hope for rescue; from this trap there was no way out. Sarah backed away at first, but after five steps she realized that she was surrounded. From behind her the terrible demon came out of the forest, the one tattooed with Egyptian symbols and torn, bleeding lips.

"This is it," The Egyptian said coldly. "There is no place to which you can escape. You better give it to me".

"It?" Sarah said with indignation. "You really think that after all I will just give it to you??"

All the descendants of Hell appeared and only now she understood the inevitability of the situation.

"I know You have always been here with me, otherwise I would have been dead a long time ago. My Heavenly Father, I am ready. Please, please help me".

Even through the pain and the purpose of His plan, Sarah knew in her heart that He existed. Yes, in anger or desperation she could think many things: that life was unfair, that she was abandoned, or that she would spend the rest of her life in darkness. Sarah always sought the light because she never doubted God's existence. It was He, and only He, who had always saved her life. No matter the situation she had remained alive and that was what was important. He had chosen her for His special mission, and if that meant life would be hard or unfair, she would do it to save humanity for God. She had to remind herself that what was happening now was another big step of what she must to do. From this point forward, Sarah did not think about results anymore, she believed that whatever would happen was part of His plan and all would turn out for the better.

She was surrounded by pure evil – three demons who were longing to get the last bead. Like hungry beasts they lay low in darkness, with only their sinister red eyes remaining. They were waiting patiently, knowing their glory moment was near. Sarah didn't even notice her own fear. In her head she counted down: five, four, three, two, one… then she touched the still deeply bleeding cut on her right palm, and screamed from the pain. Her eyes widened and points of white light immediately lit up in them.

"It won't be easy," Sarah said aloud. "But I will do all necessary so that you will go back to Hell forever!!!".

The Egyptian grinned, and moved toward Sarah. The girl was ready for this, since he appeared only as a shadow hanging over her, and she exposed the bleeding palm before her. From it, a blue ray of light struck the Egyptian. His two henchmen recoiled in terror. Sarah opened her mouth, let out a mad scream and, continued emitting the powerful blue light from her palm as the monster quickly approached. Seeing that the coveted blue bead was sitting deep in the cut, the demon held out his long arms to try to grab her, but the intensity of the light was so strong that he felt like he was being torn apart from the inside, but he was not going to retreat. His eyes were burning with fury and he did not see anything, only the desired bead, and therefore he, like Sarah, was ready for anything. Baring his bloodied mouth, the monster growled, and his henchmen suddenly shook and began to dissolve. It took only a couple of seconds before puffs of black smoke was all that remained of them. Sarah felt empowered and was ready to resume her attack on the now weakened Egyptian just as he unexpectedly became enveloped by the smoke of his henchmen.

Sarah and demon fell to the ground and began to fight. The blue ray was continuously firing into the black cloud, but nothing helped. Roaring like a wild beast, the Egyptian once again took on his former appearance and dug his long fingernails into the shoulders of the girl. Sarah cried, feeling her energy start to quickly run out, and then the demon inexplicably seemed to grow in strength, deftly twisting her wrists so that the beam struck upward into the empty sky. Wracked with pain, the girl tried to escape from his grasp, but it was all in vain; she realized that she had lost. The tattoos covering the whole body of the Egyptian for some unknown reason lit up red, and he was heard to laugh wildly.

"Too bad. You continue fighting not just with me, but with yourself. I am surprised you have not yet become a servant of our common goal" Dripping blood onto Sarah's face, the Egyptian said. "Well, at least the Madam tried. You were her precious choice, who eventually disappointed her. She put so much work into you… For nothing. Your time has come to the end".

"I would rather die than serve any of you," Sarah shouted while crying.

"Of course you would, because all your beliefs are only a sham," The demon said with a grin and pressed the girl's hands with his. "Somehow you managed to stay silent, hidden but that didn't help you and you will die anyway".

"Then I will die because I have nothing left to lose," Sarah said. "These beads are a part of a much bigger picture. These worlds will not help you to win. You know well, that there is a weapon waiting that can kill you all. Again, it doesn't matter if I am dead or alive, because the truth will still be there".

"As you wish," The Egyptian said in the seminal language and smiled.

The girl smiled back, already stopped crying and gathered all her strength and hit him in the chest. The impact was like the concussion of an explosion, flinging the demon to the side. Sarah jumped to her feet and again pointed her bloody palm, with the blue bead still in the cut, in his direction. The ray of blue light burst out of the bead again and hit the monster directly in the face. The Egyptian screamed out in the madness and then as a last option, Sarah slammed his forehead so hard with her palm that the blue bead pierced into him. With an incredible whistling sound the bead flashed with a blue flame and burned the demon's face skin. The light of his eyes immediately extinguished after which no further life remained. The monster froze, fell to the ground, and remained motionless. Sarah stood over him and gazed at his disgusting body. Filled with contempt and hate, she was watching the hieroglyphs disappear on his body one by one, gradually dragging him into eternal darkness. The rain poured without stopping, raising a lot of mist in the air, and this only spoke about one thing - it was time to go far away.

"Heavenly Father, thank You, thank You, thank You," Sarah whispered through the tears of happiness that formed in her eyes. "I always knew You would protect me!"

But her peace lasted only a moment; she turned around when suddenly she was grabbed by strong male hands and thrown against a side of a fallen tree. The girl saw then that this was the familiar face of the one who pursued her then in the mansion of Elena Barbella. The demon, in the guise of Indigo, came to visit her with a nefarious reason. *MAGiC*

Corporation had clearly thrown all of its forces into the pursuit.

"A little bird told me that you've stolen something," he taunted.

One moment later a giant shadow emerged from his body, reminiscent of a canine creature. It was as if an evil hell-dog had broken free from its chain. With an eerie bark, he threw himself on the confused Sarah and tore out of her a chunk of white light. For a second the area shone with a kind of radiance, and then plunged back into darkness. Sarah felt the great pain of the missing piece of her being. The beast returned back to Indigo's body, and who did not even glance at Sarah, lying helplessly. He had more important things to which he had to attend. Most urgently he walked over to the immobile body of the Egyptian and pulled from his forehead the bead, already faded, almost discolored. Rolling it in his fingers he frowned and looked at the demon that lay before his feet. Again a giant canine jumped out of him and tore out more chunks of luminous matter from body of the Egyptian.

"*Sample Zero*, the primary, failed," Indigo said with annoyance, and began to fill the bead with the glowing matter of Sarah and the Egyptian, that was still flickering in the air. It took only a couple of minutes and the bead again flashed radiant blue.

Sarah's energy was completely spent. She remained on the ground, observing everything that was going on around her without saying a single word. For a short period of time she still could see the blue bead, but in short order it disappeared with a loud clap. The girl did not even have time to guess what happened when suddenly a vortex appeared and transformed itself into a huge glowing ball of a blue energy, nearly the size of an elephant.

Absorbing everything in its path, the ball was growing and becoming bigger and bigger. At first it seemed that there was a fire but no, it was just a light, a blue light. Sarah's consciousness seemed to float away, and she understood little of what was going on until something awakened her. Through the whirlwind flows of supernatural energy, she to all her unwillingness she saw a scene as if she were looking out through a watery surface. She could see a huge snow-covered field with dark mountains on the horizon. There on the other side was a real blizzard, and the girl could very clearly feel the cold of the place that was trying to get into this world. With difficulty she lifted her head and simply could not believe her eyes. She saw Indigo. He went to her and bent down.

"There is nothing else to take from you," He said ominously.

For a while he watched Sarah as she unsuccessfully tried to open her mouth to say something, but could not. Her physical suffering brought Indigo a lot of pleasure. With greedy eyes, he stared at her, and smiled when she stopped moving and turned over on her left side, absorbing the view over the cliff with her half-closed eyes, he straightened up and rested his foot on her body. Seeing that Sarah did not even try to resist, he left her alone and disappeared into the night. The vortex of blue energy, meanwhile, continued to emit buzzing sounds, and began to slowly fade. From it, like from a snow blower, white flakes burst out with a cold wind, and it lasted about fifteen minutes, until night fell on the terrain. The whirlwind disappeared, and Sarah remained lying motionless on the edge of the cliff, almost in total silence, broken only by an occasional, distant clap of thunder. The storm calmed down, the pouring rain became very light and the air became noticeably warmer.

The girl had difficulty breathing and had trouble focusing her thoughts. The energy was leaving her so rapidly that she needed a little more time to fully have her life back. Time was fleeting, and trying to catch it was useless. Sarah and the area where she lay became enveloped in a warm mist once the rain stopped. She lay motionless, not knowing for how long, or imagining any further happening.

Soon the dawn loomed on the horizon, the sky gradually changed colors, sending away the darkness and opening the way for warmth. Unusual for winter time, it was unseasonably warm. If not as warm as summer, then at least like spring. Sarah fell asleep, or so she thought, and was unafraid. She just wanted to remember who she was. At some point she heard a voice in her head that was not her own, as if someone in her mind was sitting down with her and having a conversation.

"You did everything you could, and there was no fault of yours," The voice said. "Don't blame yourself. Don't be sorry."

"If I could change things…"

"You can. Because if you did something wrong, you would not have been chosen for this. What you did was right, I know it because I was always around you. If somebody must be sorry now, it would be me. I am sorry I cannot stay with you any longer. My energy has dwindled and I will soon meet the others. We were all together in the same body, and I needed to save you. All is not lost".

"I saw the future, and there was nothing good," Sarah said weakly, in and out of the conversation. She was slowly moving her lips.

"No one can see the future. The philosophy of Eternity is simple: there is no end, but everything is a beginning. It was you who laid this new beginning".

"How?... Where?"

"With John. There at the gas station, remember? You asked him for forgiveness, and it was a right thing to do".

"John…" Sarah whispered ethereally.

To her eyes opened an indescribably beautiful valley with a warm glow on the horizon. Sarah heard the melodic singing of birds, and she also thought of Eternity, which now seemed closer than ever. Earlier she witnessed the phenomenon of the Blue World, she clearly saw the passage into it. No, this was definitely not a dream.

"Sarah! Oh my God!!," She heard a wild shout in the distance.

"John… John… how is this possible? How did you find me?" She repeated, while remaining motionless.

"Don't move, I will help you," She heard the guy say the same words over and over. He took his phone into his quivering hand and called 911.

His large, warm hands held her cold, fragile, broken body. She moaned, hearing John's sobs and seeing his hot tears run down his cheeks. John could not believe his eyes when he saw his dear Sarah covered in blood.

"I'll help you, I *will* help you," He could not stop saying, lost in his actions. He was overwhelmed with emotion when the operator finally came on the line, he begged them to send an ambulance as quickly as possible.

"Please hurry," He repeated over and over, holding Sarah's hand. "I told you, she is in a very critical state, please, please, we need help now!".

Sarah felt like she was the main character in a tragic film. John, dear John, who was so precious to her, was now worried about things that could not be changed. He shouted in anger and despair, but nothing could alter the situation. Sarah just wanted to be with him. It was such a moment of pathos: him hanging on the phone but still holding her as she felt such intolerable pain. The accident caused serious injuries which her body simply could not physically stand.

"They're on their way," The guy said but still couldn't stop the flow of tears.

"I love you John" Sarah could barely whisper through her tears. "I do".

"I love you too," John replied. "Please, just don't give up. You will see, you will be alright... I need you. You hear me? Your sister and father need you too".

"If something happens to me..." The girl started.

"Nothing will happen to you," John interrupted with a shaky voice. "No, Sarah, don't even say that."

"Please John..." Sarah was unable to pronounce more words; she almost lost what little breath she had. "Be careful of *MAGiC*. Indigo... he was here".

"Indigo?" John caught the horror in the girl's eyes. "Indigo was here??"

"There's nothing human left of him, and I don't want anything to happen to you or Julia." After these words, Sarah shivered like a maple leaf, swallowing saliva with blood.

"Shhh... you can tell me everything, when you get better, okay?" John spoke with great hope that this might happen. He bravely forced a counterfeit smile.

"*MAGiC*, Migren, Indigo, Igor, …everyone and everything is too dangerous," Sarah muttered and her eyes began to roll back into her head, no longer feeling capable of remaining conscious.

"Sarah…SARAH," John started to shake the girl, desperately trying to keep her awake, and not let her pass out. "Stay with me, help is coming".

"John… my John", Sarah said as if she was just awakening and didn't understand what was going on. When she saw John's face, she weakly stretched her right hand to him. "I am so sorry I couldn't do things differently… I just wanted to save you and Julia".

Through wild pain that was tearing at her from inside, Sarah wanted only to touch the one she had loved all her life at least one more time before she could touch him no longer. She wanted to cry, but she couldn't anymore, there was no tears left. Her attempt to speak any further words became impossible as she realized that she was forgetting her own language. All she was capable of producing at this moment was a mournful moan. The girl touched John's cheek. Her lips quivered and she, filled by mixture of emotions and pain, wanted to tell him her true feelings from the very beginning, when they first met. However, she knew it would be another mistake to make such a wonderful man suffer in guilt, thinking he had done something wrong when he never had. No, he didn't deserve suffering; there was a bright future between him and Julia, and Sarah was not willing to ruin this relationship just because she had so much to say.

"John, I don't want to die", she said instead, realizing that death was all around her. Everything smelled of death. It was a terrible feeling knowing all the horrors of her impending, unavoidable date with destiny, which was approaching in giant steps.

"No, you are not going anywhere," John said with all his seriousness. "Stop talking about these unthinkable actions, do you hear me?"

"Ahhh," Sarah suddenly screamed as her body twisted in pain. "It hurts me, please… John, please help me".

In that moment the guy began to panic; all he could do was gently cradle her head in both his hands. For him it was more than a horror to see someone who he deeply cared about to be tormented in pain, and realize that he actually was not able to help anyhow in such indescribable suffering.

"Sarah, I beg you, tell me something I can do to make you feel better?" The guy asked with painful pangs in his heart, and tears in his eyes.

"Nothing John. Sometimes we can do nothing", Sarah managed to verbalize through her moans and stifled screams. "Just please stay with me. I don't want anything more than that".

"I am not going anywhere", the guy promised and lay next to Sarah, hoping it would bring her a little bit of relief.

"Thank you…" The girl exhaled. "You know that I love you and have loved you all my life, right?" Sarah asked when the pain finally went away. "I truly mean it John. You were the one who held me in this world and made my days happier when I thought of you even though you were far away. I think without you I would go crazy, I would not survive that life if you were not a part of it. It's so silly that I was always afraid to talk to you about it, and now… don't worry John, I will stay with you. I won't go, I promise". Her voice suddenly trailed off into silence.

Sarah opened her eyes and saw nothing but white light, brighter than the angel that used to come to her from time to time. She just stretched upward a little, as if to get up, when she realized that she was already standing on two feet. She gazed downward seeing herself lying in John's arms, no longer breathing, but finally complete and free from her mission.

John kept holding the body of Sarah, his face softly caressing hers, forcing himself to keep the rest of his tears to himself. He could just not accept the sad fact that she was gone forever and that nothing could bring her back. If only there *were* true magic, he could turn back time, guide all the events in a different direction, and Sarah would still be alive. He would allow nothing to bring such sorrow as this. But despite all the mystical events John had witnessed, there was nothing more left now than the harsh realities of what fate had brought. The world was not a fairytale, there were no wizards, no fairies, and definitely no magic.

"There is only one horrible and evil *MAGiC*," John whispered through tears, boiling from inside with despair and anger. "Damn them ALL to Hell!" He screamed in a voice louder and more powerful than he had ever used before.

Printed in Poland
by Amazon Fulfillment
Poland Sp. z o.o., Wrocław